Serendipity's Footsteps

Serendipity's Footsteps

SUZANNE NELSON

Alfred A. Knopf
New York

THIS IS A BORZOI BOOK PUBLISHED BY ALFRED A. KNOPF

Visit us on the Web! randomhouseteens.com

Educators and librarians, for a variety of teaching tools, visit us at RHTeachersLibrarians. com

Library of Congress Cataloging-in-Publication Data
Nelson, Suzanne.
Serendipity's footsteps / Suzanne Nelson. — First edition.
p. cm.
Summary: "One special pair of shoes, crafted in Germany just before the Nazis came to power, makes its way through time and around the world to connect a string of owners."—Provided by publisher. Includes historical notes about Nazi Germany, Down Syndrome, and shoes.
ISBN 978-0-385-39212-9 (trade) — ISBN 978-0-385-39213-6 (lib. bdg.) — ISBN 978-0-385-39214-3 (ebook)
1. Shoes—Fiction. 2. Interpersonal relations—Fiction. 3. Runaways—Fiction. 4. Down syndrome—Fiction. 5. People with mental disabilities—Fiction. 6. Orphans—Fiction. 7. Jews—Germany—History—1933–1945—Fiction. 8. Concentration camps—Fiction. 9. Germany—History—1933–1945—Fiction. 10. New York (N.Y.)—Fiction.
I. Title.
PZ7.N43765 Ser 2015
[Fic]—dc23
2014032551

The text of this book is set in 11.5-point Bembo.

Printed in the United States of America
November 2015
10 9 8 7 6 5 4 3 2 1

First Edition

For Christy—
truth-teller, touchstone, best friend, sister

• • •

For there is no friend like a sister
In calm or stormy weather;
To cheer one on the tedious way,
To fetch one if one goes astray,
To lift one if one totters down,
To strengthen whilst one stands.
—Christina Rossetti, "Goblin Market"

PROLOGUE

Shoes are the keepers of secrets. They hold pieces of history captive in their soles. A single sliver of glass from a night of terror long ago, buried in the worn heel of an oxford. A grain of sand from Coney Island beach, trapped under the insole of a silver stiletto, an accidental souvenir from an enchanted moonlit tryst. Bits of Houston Black soil beaten into the trenches of a pink sneaker from a frantic run for survival. A priceless heirloom locked away in the hollow heel of a delicate dress shoe, marking a quiet act of bravery one chilly November night.

A tattered shoe that's been well worn and loved is a much happier sight than the unworn, forgotten shoes swallowed up in the black throat of a closet. That shoe has been places, has been tickled by someone's wiggling toes and warmed by their skin. But what about the shoes left in the street? The sneakers hanging dejected from a telephone wire in the sluicing rain, the red peep-toes lying topsy-turvy on the shoulder of the

Palisades Parkway. Do they have a story to tell? A story as complex as the people who, however briefly, owned them?

If you stopped and took the time to look closely, a shoe might give up its secrets. It might tell you how it made one young girl feel beautiful on a lonely night, or how it gave another an extra inch of height for her breathtaking first kiss. If Cinderella's slippers could change her from peasant to princess, and Dorothy's could transport her home, surely ordinary shoes can have power, too. The magic is there, deep within the sole. A pair of shoes can enchant an onlooker, transform a wearer, cradle tiny toes, or sustain an aching arch for one last mile. Yes, a shoe can even save a life. And sometimes, when fate and magic mingle, an extraordinary shoe can walk into many lives and change them all.

PART I

And I'm not a cobbler who writes, thank heaven,
But a poet who makes shoes.

—Mani Leyb

DALYA

"It's time."

In a hushed tone, gentle but panicked, those were the words her mother spoke as the first tinkling of shattered glass came in the distance. She'd been looking out the window of their upstairs apartment, keeping watch, as she'd done each night for weeks now. Most nights, nothing of much importance happened. But today, Dalya had been sent home from school early. There were whispered rumors of something awful coming, though no one knew exactly what or when. As Dalya biked home that afternoon, dread crept through the streets of the West End, forcing her schoolmates inside long before dusk.

Now her mother turned from the window, her face waxen.

"They're coming," she said. "I'll stay with your brother and sister. You go get your father from the shop." She grabbed

Dalya's coat, mittens, and scarf from the coatrack. Quickly, she tucked several rolls of bread and a hunk of cheese into a hole she'd made days before in the lining of Dalya's coat.

Dalya slid on the coat, the lumps of bread pressing awkwardly against her side. She nearly argued that it was a ridiculous precaution. The Gestapo had made their searches for weapons and contraband a dozen times before. Yes, they'd arrested Herr Rozen, the neighborhood butcher, after he was caught selling kosher meat. But after they closed his shop, they released him. What was so different about tonight? Still, the fear in her mother's eyes kept her silent.

Her mother slipped her rings from her hand, then set them in Dalya's palm. "Remember what we talked about."

"But I'm sure it's nothing—"

Her mother raised a finger to Dalya's lips, stopping her. "They set fire to the Schellers' shop!" she whispered, making sure only Dalya would hear. "They're destroying everything!"

"What?" Terror flared inside her. This was different from the boycotting of their store, from the ugly vandalism happening more and more often. It had never been like this.

"Tonight, *liebchen,* everything begins." Her mother hugged her fiercely. *"Beeil dich!"* she whispered. "Hurry now! There isn't much time."

Dalya glanced at David and Inge, who were sitting at the table eating their *abendbrot.* Her mother was ushering them into their coats between mouthfuls, filling their pockets and liners with rolls, too.

"Where are we going?" David protested, shoveling in one last bite. "I'm not finished yet!"

Dalya swallowed thickly, her blood humming in her ears. Poor Inge and David. At five and seven, the most frightening thing they'd known so far was the prospect of losing their suppers.

"And Dalya promised me and Dolly a story," Inge said, pouting as she hugged her doll. With chubby cheeks and tiny features, she still looked babyish, and she was doted on because of it. Her mother coddled Inge more than she ever had Dalya, letting her throw tantrums without punishment and escape household chores. Nearly every night, while her mother helped her father clean the store after closing, Dalya put Inge to bed with a story. At times, she resented being pulled away from the store, especially when Inge was difficult. To ease her own impatience, she wove shoes into every story she told so they'd never be far from her thoughts. When Inge's eyes finally fluttered closed, though, Dalya loved the sweetness of that small hand resting in hers.

David was Inge's playmate, but also her nemesis, and now he smiled mischievously at her. "I'm going to give your dolly a trim," he said, making his fingers look like scissors. Inge shrieked and leapt behind their mother, cuddling her doll protectively.

"I'm sure we'll be right back," Dalya said. "And then, Inge," she added, grinning, "maybe we'll give David a trim of his own."

David's eyes widened as Dalya lunged to tickle them both, but then her mother snapped, "This is no time for teasing."

Dalya straightened at her harsh tone. "I was trying to help," she said, but her mother hustled her to the door with a stern *"Go."*

With Inge and David looking after her in surprise, she ran downstairs and into the back of their shop. As soon as she stepped through the door, the musky scent of leather engulfed her. It was the smell that had encompassed her whole existence as a young child, when she'd sat behind the shop counter eating potato knishes and watching her mother and father work. It was the scent of the familiar, of the loved—a scent she hoped would be with her for life. Because just as her mother and father made shoes, so, she hoped, would she. Someday, she and her husband would run this store together, like her parents did now.

Her father sat on his stool, his lapstone perched across his thighs, hammering a sole. He glanced up absently with a half smile, an expression that he wore when he was thoroughly absorbed in his task.

"Vati," she croaked. "Vati, they're coming. Muti says they're burning shops."

His smile collapsed, his ruddy cheeks sallowing. He stood, and the sole he'd been holding fluttered to the floor. Peering out the large front window, he gasped. "But this . . . this is madness. . . . They can't!" Sharp cracks split the air, making them both jump. "Gunshots," he whispered. He rushed to the cash drawer and emptied it.

She ran to her father's side, and together, they pushed the wooden display shelf across the floor, exposing an almost imperceptible panel cut out of the wallpaper. Her father slid a pocketknife into the seam and lifted the panel out from the wall, revealing a safe.

"I'll take care of this," he said. "You do as your mother wanted."

8

Dalya nodded, then grabbed the tin box from its place at the back of the supply closet. She raised the lid, and there inside, exactly as she'd left them last night, were the shoes . . . *her* shoes. Even with her growing panic, she thrilled to look at them. The first pair of shoes her mother had let her make on her own, start to finish. She'd sketched them out in her notebook last spring. Normally, she hoarded her drawings, guarding them from her mother. Her mother doled out more criticism than compliments, constantly correcting Dalya's handiwork, making her redo the stitching on an outsole or reconstruct a vamp that wasn't absolutely perfect.

"The shoe," her mother always said, "must be a second skin. It's a resting ground for the foot, something that beautifies *and* cushions. A person must never feel they're wearing the shoe. If it rubs, scrapes, or pinches the toes, then it is not well made."

But when Dalya had first pictured these shoes in her mind, she'd sensed the inspiration was rare and should be put down on paper before it flittered away. She'd felt such intense affection for these shoes that she hadn't wanted her mother niggling over them, picking them apart. One day, though, she'd left her notebook open at the kitchen table, and she'd come home from school to find her mother bent over the sketch of the shoes, studying it intently.

Dalya waited, holding her breath.

"This shoe . . ." Her mother traced the silhouette with a finger. "This shoe is fine. You may make this one."

Her father made a new last for the shoe, one carved from oak and shaped from Dalya's own foot. Dalya chose a champagne satin with a rosy sheen for the upper and spent hours embroidering it with a delicate floral design. Her mother rarely consented to such extravagance, but surprisingly, she had let Dalya choose the finest fabrics and materials for her shoes. A Louis heel paired with a rounded toe box gave the shoe a soft femininity, and a border of tiny pearl beading embellished its throat. Finally, the satin laces added above the vamp tied across the slight arch at the top of the foot like a silken bridge. Once, Frau Kaufmann had stopped by and seen Dalya working on the shoes. She'd wanted to buy them on the spot. Dalya had blushed with pride, but her mother said simply, "These shoes are for my Dalya. Someday, she will be married in them."

Just like that, the fate of Dalya's shoes was decided. Her mother had made the statement as if it were fact, and Dalya hadn't even minded. As soon as she heard the words, Dalya knew they were true. She had no prospects for a husband and, at fifteen, no wish for one for years to come. Still, she knew that someday, when she found a young man worthy of the shoes, she would wear them for him on their wedding day.

Now, with the sound of shouts and shattering glass from the street outside growing louder, more insistent, Dalya lifted the right shoe from the metal box. She turned it over, then carefully tilted the heel back from the outer sole. A hidden hinge her mother had designed allowed the seat of the heel to pull away from the sole to reveal the tiny compartment hollowed out of its top.

The hiding place had been her mother's idea.

"A place the Nazis will never look," her mother had said. "We hope for the best but must plan for the worst."

Dalya took her mother's rings from her pocket. The wedding band was a muted gold, and the engagement ring had a center stone with six smaller diamonds surrounding it. The diamonds often threw rainbows around the shop while her mother worked. Dalya had never seen her take off her rings before, and she shuddered to think what would let her mother bear being separated from them. She tucked the rings carefully into the heel next to the thin piece of paper she'd slipped inside weeks ago, then sealed the heel with glue.

The shouts in the street had become deafening, and Dalya's father was hurrying through the store toward her.

"You *must* finish!" His voice was stiff with urgency. "They're next door already."

She laid the shoes back in the tin box. Her quivering fingers struggled to latch the lid. When it was fastened, she bent over the floorboards behind the counter, scrambling for the right one. She edged her fingernail into a crease and eased the board up, then tucked the box underneath. The second the floorboard slapped back into its slot, her father was there with his hammer, nailing it into place. It was on this very board, over the shoes she'd lovingly handcrafted, that Dalya stood when the two soldiers burst into the store.

The first thing she noticed was the red band with its black swastika on their gray uniforms. The sight of it withered her insides. The second was their boots. Polished to a glossy black, they were meant to impress, or intimidate. When Dalya looked at them, she saw a garish, skeletonized reflection of her face in the gleaming toes. And she suddenly hated the boots—hated them for bringing terror into this place she loved.

"We are looking for Herr Amschel," the taller soldier said.

Her father nodded. "You've found him."

The soldier stepped forward. "You are charged with being an enemy of the state. You and your family must come with us."

"An enemy of the state?" Dalya locked eyes with the soldier, her heart striking against her ribs. "That is ridiculous." His mouth thinned into a line. "My father has done nothing—"

"Shhhhh." Her father gave her arm a squeeze.

She waited for him to protest, to plead his innocence. But her father, who had never broken eye contact with any man in his life, bowed his head to stare at the floor.

"Of course we will come with you," he said in a polite, supplicating tone foreign to Dalya. "Please, I need a few moments to collect my wife and children."

"Three minutes," the tall soldier snapped.

"Thank you." Her father bowed his head appeasingly, then pulled Dalya up the back stairs, clutching her hand so firmly that it ached.

"They can't arrest you," Dalya whispered. "What have you done?"

Her father stopped on the top stair, his face pained. "We are *Juden*. That alone is a crime to them."

Opening the door to their small apartment, they found her mother, brother, and sister waiting. Gone were David's playful teasing and Inge's melodrama. Their eyes were wide and scared.

"We must go with them, but we will be back." Her father kissed her mother on her forehead. "This will pass soon enough."

Together, they walked downstairs to the shop, where the soldiers waited. The tall one stood near the counter, inspecting her father's shoemaking tools, his lips curled in distaste. And then Dalya saw it—the pot of glue she'd been using earlier, perched on the counter, within perfect range. As she moved past the soldier, she pretended to stumble. She grabbed the counter to catch herself, deftly knocking the pot off the edge.

It overturned, pouring thick yellow glue all over the soldier's boot.

"Schwerfällig!" the soldier growled. "Clumsy!"

Dalya covered her mouth, feigning horror. "I am so sorry," she said. "I slipped."

Her mother yanked her out of the soldier's way. "Forgive her," she said quickly. "She is just a young, absentminded girl."

The soldier's eyes burned, and he raised his hand, ready to strike. But a wail broke from Inge's throat, surprising him. The hand dropped.

"Take them outside," he said through clenched teeth. "Now."

Dalya was hurried out, her mother risking one scolding glance in her direction that said she knew the glue wasn't clumsiness. But Dalya didn't care. She was glad she'd done it. Even if his hand *had* come down on her, she'd still have been glad. There was a hidden smile inside her as she watched the soldier trying in vain to wipe the glue from his boot. Finally, he gave up and joined them outside, his face a blister of rage.

"Get in line." He nodded toward the other side of the street, where their neighbors stood in one trembling huddle. There were the Buttenheims, the Felsbergs, the Rozens. There was Aaron Scheller, one of her classmates, with his mother, father, and little sister. Chava Scheller was her mother's best friend, and their families often got together for Shabbos dinner. Dalya had known Aaron since the two of them were toddlers. As a child, he'd often followed her from room to room like a parched animal following a cloud. She'd never tried to hide her annoyance with his devotion. She remembered putting on countless puppet shows and dance performances, laughing and twirling around him as he sat watching somberly on the floor. Though part of her appreciated the attention, there was always too much adoration in his penetrating gaze. It vexed her that he granted it so easily when she felt she hadn't earned it. Now here he was, watching her again with those same inquisitive chestnut eyes.

Dalya stepped into the street, glass crackling under her shoes. Shopwindows up and down Kurfürstendamm sat gaping, their glass shattered. The street was one of the busiest in the Charlottenburg district, usually bustling with shoppers, but tonight it was desolate and broken. Whimpers and sobs from neighbors she'd known most of her life, people she'd never seen cry, were an undercurrent to screams and gunshots echoing from the surrounding streets.

She glanced back at their shop and saw her father, still at the door, hesitating.

"One more moment, please," he said to the soldiers. As he turned off the shop lights and locked the front door, a smirk streaked across the tall soldier's face.

Her father joined them in line beside her mother and the Schellers.

Smoke drifted in the air, burning her lungs. A strange yellow haze glowed in the sky over Fasanenstrasse, a few streets over.

"What is that?" Dalya whispered.

A cry escaped her mother's lips. "The synagogue. They're burning it."

Dalya's stomach churned. Their beautiful synagogue, with its glorious domed roof, on fire. For what? She couldn't understand. She doubted she ever would.

Inge's sobs grew into frenzied howling, and the tall soldier lifted the butt of his gun. "Someone shut her up, or I will."

Dalya reached Inge first, sweeping her up because her mother already had David in her own arms. Her mother shushed Inge desperately, but it didn't work, and soon David's lip trembled, too. Dalya had to do something.

"Should we tell a story now?" she whispered to them. She turned her back on the soldier, pressing Inge's little head into her shoulder so she couldn't see.

Inge shook her head, sniffling. "But . . . it's not bedtime," she choked.

"It doesn't have to be." Dalya held her tighter while her father and Herr Scheller planted themselves between the gun and their families. "There once lived a lovely shoemaker's daughter," she began, trying to focus on the words rather than the gun at her back. She spoke quietly as Inge's hummingbird heart thrummed against her chest, her voice the only calm part of her. Aaron moved to stand protectively beside them, and that, along with the story, worked to quiet Inge enough for the soldier to lower his gun. After a few minutes, Dalya was able to hand Inge to her father.

"They're destroying everything," Aaron whispered once Inge was out of earshot. "If they could, I bet they'd shoot every one of us right now."

"Aaron!" She stared at him. "What are you saying? They have no right . . ."

"They'll take the right." His fists clenched at his sides. "They won't stop after this. They'll *never* stop."

Her father appeared next to them, his eyes grave. "Listen to me, both of you," he whispered. "There's a man here in Berlin. Leonard Goodman, a friend of mine. He's an American, a Quaker. He has many influential friends. He's been working these last few weeks to secure visas for us. He said he would help if . . . anything like this ever happened." He took their hands in his. "Once this is over and they release you, go to him."

Aaron nodded, but Dalya added firmly, "We'll all go together, Vati."

"God willing." Her father pressed his hand to her cheek, then moved to rejoin her mother.

Aaron leaned toward her, his mouth nearly brushing her ear and sending an involuntary and unwanted heat through her. "Dalya, I made a promise to your father that I would look after you. If they take us out of the city, if they separate us, find a way back here. Find Herr Goodman, and I'll find you."

Dalya gave a short laugh. "That will never happen. Why would my father have asked *you* to look after me, when I'm perfectly capable of looking after myself?"

She fixed her eyes on him, waiting for his answer, but he dropped his own in embarrassment. Suddenly, she guessed her father's intentions. He must have been hoping that something else—more than friendship—would grow between her and Aaron. That Aaron would be her protector, her caretaker. She bristled. As if her mind could be molded that easily. Why should her future be discussed and planned for in the third person, giving her no part in it? And worse, why should Aaron be privy to the plans when she was not?

"If there *is* some sort of trouble, which I doubt," she said resentfully, "I will find my own way."

Aaron's eyebrows lifted in surprise, and the hint of a smile played around his mouth without ever settling onto it. "I wish . . . I wish you liked me better." There was a woundedness in his voice, but Dalya convinced herself she hadn't heard it.

She opened her mouth, but didn't know how to say it wasn't true without lying, so she shut it again. Maybe she *could've* liked him better if he didn't always beg for her approval. But of course, she couldn't say that out loud.

Just as the silence between them was becoming awkward, the soldiers positioned themselves around their group and told them to start walking.

"Where are they taking us all?" Frau Scheller asked, a quietly contained hysteria tingeing her voice.

Dalya's mother took her hand. "I don't know, Chava. But we're together. And that is a blessing."

Dalya glanced at Aaron, and an understanding passed between them. She positioned herself on one side of Inge, David, and Aaron's sister, Hila. Aaron took up his post on the other. Together, they formed a protective barrier around the children, holding their hands through the street. Inge was still crying, but silently, her earlier outburst having drained her to exhaustion. After she stumbled a third time, Dalya swung her onto her back so she could keep up.

Aaron offered her a small nod of encouragement. If he was angry with her, he showed no sign of it. His eyes were bright, unwavering, the darkness giving his face a sharpness that was more man than boy.

"Do what they tell you to," he whispered. "It will be easier that way. But remember what I said. Even if . . ." He paused. "Even if you don't want me to, I'll find you. I made that promise, and I can't break it." His eyes held hers. "No matter what happens to you, what they do to you, hide the best of yourself away where they can't find it. Until this is over."

No matter what they do to you. She shuddered, then nodded, instinctively feeling a division going on inside her. The Dalya of Before tucking herself into the recesses of her heart for safekeeping. The Dalya of After emerging like a fortress ready for attack.

The moon was a bright orb in the indigo sky, and the loveliness of the night seemed that much stranger when steeped in the bitter fear wafting off the people around her. As they walked, glass shattered a hundred times louder than before. Dalya turned to see the windows of Amschel's Shoe Store smashed, an open wound in the dark.

She thought, *How silly of Father to lock the door.*

Every step took her farther away from the pale pink shoes buried under the floorboards. She prayed they'd stay there, undiscovered. Then she lifted her chin high, turned her back on her home, and walked into the night.

CHOPINE MILLER'S BEGINNING

He was standing on the corner of Wall Street and Broadway when he took off his shoes. The oxfords still gleamed from the coat of polish he'd brushed on at dawn. They were the most expensive pair of shoes he'd ever bought himself. He'd bought them, along with his custom suit, on the day he'd been offered the job of floor broker for Jefferies. His father, of course, had offered to pay for everything he needed, but this time, for the first time, Kent refused to let him. He'd thought of the shoes as a good-luck charm, and maybe even a step toward independence, hoping that if he looked the part, success would follow.

He hadn't factored in the panic he felt at the sound of the opening bell each day. Adrenaline was normal, his friends in the industry told him. Adrenaline gave you an edge, kept you hyped up on the trading floor. But Kent could taste the bile in his throat before he even got out of bed.

This was supposed to be his calling. That's what his dad had always told him. It was supposed to be instinctual, not excruciating. In the end, though, it was all money. Nothing more. Money that didn't even exist in hard cash, but spun around the world as a concept, making and breaking corporations, countries, and men.

On the day Kent abandoned his shoes, he lost two mil on the floor. By the time the closing bell sounded, his toes were numb. Crushing tiredness overwhelmed him, and he staggered off the trading floor, wanting fresh air. But New York City summers are unforgiving, and this one had saved a last hurrah for October, spilling over into fall. Heat smothered him as soon as he stepped outside. He dragged his feet, his shoes tightening with every step. How was it possible for the feet of a twenty-three-year-old to feel so old, so beaten down?

He sat on the steps in front of the stock exchange, his lungs straining for air. His feet throbbed inside his shoes, and suddenly, he was tearing at the laces, yanking on the tongues. His feet pulled free with a soft sucking sound. His socks were next. He slid them down his calves and off his feet. He sighed and wiggled his pasty toes, laughing. Then he stood up and walked away.

Linnea Chantal had just cracked open her two-dollar dinner, a can of soda and a Heath bar, when she saw him. He was wandering through the litter-strewn grass of Battery Park, his suit jacket stained with the mustardy remnants of a hot dog, his tie scruffily undone. His suit screamed money, but he seemed way too young for it, with peach fuzz and a lost look that was adorable. Every few seconds, he gave his shirt collar a tug as if he were battling to keep it from choking him.

Partly because she was new enough to the city that she understood how lonely it could make a person, and partly because she was bursting for someone to share her news with, she offered him a smile.

"Hey," she called, "no killjoys at the party!"

His head snapped up, and he blinked a few times like he was trying to bring her into better focus. "Sorry," he muttered. "Um . . . what party?"

"Mine!" She spread her arms, twirling. "You are looking at the best Éponine that Broadway will ever see!"

"You're in *Les Miz*?" he asked doubtfully.

"Not yet, but I will be!" she cried. "I nailed my audition today, and now I'm celebrating!" She held her soda and candy out to him and, in her best British accent, asked, "Would you care for some champagne and caviar, sir? I only buy the best."

"Thanks, but I'm not hungry." He gave a hollow laugh. "Just tired. So tired."

"Yeah, I know that kind of tired," she said. "The kind that makes you want to sink right into the ground and never get up again. I used to get that way sometimes, too. But that was before I came here." She thought of the unaccountable sadness that sometimes swallowed her whole, without warning, for weeks at a time, until she pulled herself up from its depths, wasted from tears. It frightened her. It had frightened her parents and teachers, too. But it would never be able to find her here . . . among thousands of people. She swept her arms across the great expanse of buildings, ignited in the dark like earthbound stars, and felt the thrill of the city's promise coursing through her. "*This* is where I belonged all along."

"I thought I knew where I belonged," he whispered, pacing the grass. "Until today." He stepped on a bottle cap, then cursed, yanking his foot from the ground.

"Hey, there's a way better place to go barefoot," she said. "*If you're brave enough to follow a stranger.*" It was a teasing challenge and, she recognized, possibly a reckless one. But nights as brilliant and perfect as these were made for recklessness, and anyway, she was feeling invincible.

He hesitated, glancing at her ripped jeans and oversized sweatshirt, and she guessed he'd probably never talked to a girl who wasn't decked out in pearls and cashmere thanks to Daddy's pocketbook. She wondered if he'd ever done anything for the sheer fun of it, and decided, with certainty, that he hadn't. She thought he might walk away. But then he surprised her.

"You have the most beautiful feet I've ever seen," he blurted, then shrank with embarrassment.

She laughed, her blond hair springing. "They're only beautiful when I'm wearing my lucky shoes. My Marilyn Monroe shoes. She was born normal-nobody Norma Jeane, but she became somebody." She swiveled her ankle so her silver rhinestone stilettos glittered. "That's what's going to happen to me, too. I gave myself a glamorous new name worthy of the stage, and my shoes will do the rest. I wear them to every audition."

He leaned forward and, before she understood what he was doing, gingerly brushed a finger over her ankle strap. Her breath caught. "'Your ladyship is nearer to heaven than when

I saw you last, by the altitude of a chopine.'" He smiled, then shrugged. "It's Shakespeare."

She stared at him, her heart pirouetting. No one had ever spoken to her like that. It didn't matter that they weren't his words. His saying them meant he understood something about her no one else ever had, and she determined, in that instant, to rescue him. She lifted her hand to the base of his chin and, with a flick of her fingers, unbuttoned his shirt collar.

He sucked in a long, deep breath, drinking in the air.

She cocked her head toward the South Ferry subway station. "So, *Shakespeare,* are you coming with me or not?"

His eyes rested on hers, the lost look in them gone. "Let's go."

She led him across the street to the subway, and they disappeared over the city's gilded rim, hand in hand.

It was a night dipped in magic. Years later, he would still remember the muted sounds of the music and laughter that drifted down the beach from the Coney Island boardwalk, the warmth of her hand in his. His aching bare feet sank into the sand, wicking up its coolness.

She whipped her hair out of her eyes and faced him, placing one hand over his heart. "Listen to the waves," she whispered, brushing her lips against his ears. "It's the rhythm of the world. . . ." She spun away from him. "Doesn't it make you want to dance?"

He shook his head at her cartwheels, wishing he could bottle up some of her abandon. It was seductive, and so was she.

But there was something feverish about her joy, like it was too excessive not to also be dangerous.

"I'm guessing you haven't lived in the city long," he said.

"Two weeks," she announced proudly. "Why? Do I look like a rookie?"

"No one stays that happy in this city," he said. "It isn't possible. Not without money." As soon as the words left his mouth, he hated himself for saying them. They belonged to his father, and here he was, regurgitating them because he was too scared to believe anything different.

Her glare was a mishmash of anger and playfulness. "Who needs money? I have a place to sleep already. On Avenue A . . . rent-free."

"You're squatting?" He raised an eyebrow. He'd heard about the runaways and dropouts taking over abandoned tenement buildings in Alphabet City, struggling artists or actors who built whole gypsy villages behind boarded-up windows. He envied their daring, but not their poverty.

"Squatting . . . for now. And then . . . we'll see. I'll eat air. Bathe in the Hudson. I'll *make* it possible." She lit a cigarette, took a long drag, then passed it to him. "Don't tell me you're a dream killer. I hate dream killers."

"So . . . you know some personally," he said.

She shrugged. "Only everyone I knew before I came here." She dug the toe of her shoe into the sand. "They said I was too young. That theater wouldn't be good for me. They wanted me to stay at home, where I'd be safe." She threw her head back and yelled, "I'm bored to death by safety!"

He laughed, then sobered. "Maybe safety's my problem."

He stared out at the water, where the boardwalk lights winked on the waves. "I'm stuck in a net of it. I can't do anything except what I'm supposed to do. My father made the mold for me before I was even born. It's my fate." He pulled an old-time pocket watch from his jacket and flipped it open, holding the inscription up to her face. "'Time wasted is money lost.' So said my grandfather and now my father."

She scoffed. "Screw fate! People fall into things and call it fate. Fate is a lame excuse for choices we're not happy with." She stretched her arms toward the stars. "And time . . ." She smiled at him. "Well, time is only wasted when it's spent worrying over fate."

Looking into her radiant face, he wanted to slide down the slippery slope of dreaming with her, to ignore the pounding of his father's plans being hammered into his brain. For the first time in his life, but not the last, he let himself go.

She pulled him into the waves, kicking up seafoam and laughing. For a moment, the moonlight flickered across her stilettos in the water, and they became the glittering scales of a tail, and she became the mermaid with the irresistible song.

They splashed and swam until, exhilarated and dripping, they tumbled breathless onto the beach in each other's arms. She made a pillow of his jacket and laid his head on it, fashioning a bed for him in the sand.

The shushing of the waves lulled him. The trail of stars quieted the numbers racing through his head. And as she kissed him, the dollar signs finally blinked out.

When he left her sleeping in the moonlight, he was smiling. And he was still smiling when he showed up at his parents' brownstone on East Seventy-Third to tell them he was going back to school to study art.

She woke to waves lapping her toes. She sat up, blinking into a tangerine sunrise. The tide had come in, and the sand sparkled, clean and new. She'd heard his whispered "Thank you" in the wee small hours, felt his kiss on her hair, but she let him believe she was sleeping. It was better to avoid a morning of awkwardness. This way, if he had regrets, she wouldn't see them. Besides, she felt like a bona fide New Yorker now. She'd made a random connection, and after a brief blaze of glory, she was moving on.

She reached for her lucky shoes and found his pocket watch beside them, tucked together like they were sleeping in the sand. She picked them all up and danced up the beach toward the subway, a tiny universe of chromosomes already starting to spin inside her, happy to have a home.

On Wall Street at dawn, a hobo stepped out of the filthy dish towels wrapped around his feet and slipped into a pair of abandoned oxfords, polished and brand-new. They fit him perfectly. He walked away without a limp.

On July 10, 1991, Sara "Linnea Chantal" Miller gave birth to a beautiful baby girl with almond eyes and one extra chromosome, and despite skeptical looks from the nurses in the maternity ward, promptly named her after a shoe.

DALYA

It was on the day Inge's rasping cough began that Dalya found a white rock the size of a robin's egg. She was standing in the "exercise yard" for roll call, shivering. The coats they'd come with had been torn from them as they'd stepped off the train, and the clothes and shoes the camp officers had given them were already threadbare. Even her long brown hair, stripped from her like everything else, had been shorn off to keep away the lice. Her fingers and toes were constantly numb, and sometimes she thought it might be better to stay in her bunk than to face the cold. But people who didn't get up were taken away and never came back, so her mother made her get up, always.

Now her mother stood next to her with an arm firmly around Inge. Dalya hoped the guards would think her mother's arm was a gesture of affection, or protection. But she knew otherwise. Inge couldn't stand alone. Her eyes were half closed, her cheeks flushed with fever, but their mother had to make sure she seemed as healthy as possible. Otherwise, the guards would take her to the infirmary. So far, no one who'd gone to the infirmary had returned.

"Look, Inge," Dalya whispered. "I think we can use this rock for drawing." She smiled at her sister, but her chapped lips split, and blood slicked her mouth. So much the better, she thought, wincing through the pain. Her lips would have a healthy, rosy shine for the guards' inspection.

Dalya crouched in front of Inge with the rock. But Inge's eyes didn't blink, or even flicker with recognition. Dalya sighed, tucking the rock into one of her wooden inmate clogs, where it wouldn't be seen by the guards. She had the urge to shake her sister until some sign of life spilled out of her. Gone was the impulsive sprite with all her changeable moods, and Dalya ached to have her back, regretting every moment she'd ever lost patience with her.

When they'd first arrived, Inge had cried all the time. Cried for David and their father, who had been separated from them as soon as they'd stepped off the train. Cried for the dolly ripped out of her arms that night so many months ago. Cried as their mother tried to explain to the SS officers that this was a mistake, that none of them were supposed to be here. But that was before hunger and exhaustion used up her tears. Now, when she wasn't forced to stand for roll call, Inge was curled into a motionless ball on the bunk in their barracks. Now Dalya wished Inge's tears would start again, because it was too frightening to see her sister, who had always been a whirlwind of energy, be so still, so quiet.

"Stand up straight now," her mother whispered as the guards moved down the line of inmates toward them. "Perhaps today, Inge, they'll send us home."

Dalya cringed at the lilt in her mother's voice. She'd heard it every day since they'd arrived, and each time she knew it was a lie. Still, it was a necessary one. It was the only way to make Inge get out of the bunk, eat, stand in this line. So Dalya lied, too.

"Maybe we'll see Vati and David later," she said.

For a brief second, Inge's eyes flickered to the second yard, on the other side of the barbed-wire fence, the yard where, just once, they'd seen the men and boys lined up for roll call, on their first day here. There were many more men than women and children in this place. Hundreds of men, in fact, but only a dozen or so women and children. It seemed strange, and her mother kept saying their being here was a horrible misunder-standing. Still, the guards made no move to release them, even though it caused problems for them, too. At that first roll call, within seconds of husbands, wives, and children spotting each other, the wailing had begun. There had been a mad rush to the fence, fingers reaching through the wires to touch loved ones' faces and hands. The guards yelled, pushing everyone back with the butts of their guns. After that, the roll calls for men and women were never at the same time.

Now Dalya pulled her shoulders back and her body upright as the guards faced them.

"The little one looks sickly." The broader guard gripped Inge under her chin. "Let her stand on her own."

Dalya's mother slid her arm from around Inge, and Dalya held her breath as Inge swayed unsteadily for a few seconds. But Inge remained standing, and finally, the guard moved on. Her mother hugged Inge as the roll call ended, and when the women and children drifted apart, she nudged Dalya.

"It's Aaron," she whispered, nodding toward the fence. "Go now."

Dalya glanced up to see Aaron pushing a wheelbarrow of bricks through the yard on the other side of the barbed wire. He kept his eyes focused on the bricks, but he moved slowly along the fence, and she knew he was waiting for her. This was the system of communication they'd developed, and a way for their fathers to pass on food rations to their wives and daughters when they could. Dalya and Aaron, because they were younger, were at less risk for punishment than their parents for breaking camp rules. And so far, neither of them had gotten anything more severe than scoldings from the guards. Still, Dalya had to be quick and careful.

She edged closer, and when she was within reach, Aaron tripped, spilling bricks onto the ground.

As he bent to pick them up, he whispered, "David's sick but alive."

"So is Inge," Dalya said. "The rest of us are all right."

"We're fine for now, too. Tell my mother . . . this is everything I had." Aaron nodded toward the ground, where a brick was split open, revealing a small portion of bread in its hollow.

She had only seconds, so she doubled over into a coughing fit, making it so violent that she had to put a hand out to steady herself. In one swift movement, that hand reached through the fence, scooped up the bread, and hid it in her mouth.

She backed away just as a guard strode toward Aaron, the butt of his rifle raised and ready. "Pick those up, stupid!" he yelled, and Aaron instantly bowed his head, falling to his knees.

"Of course. I'm so sorry."

But when he stood with an armful of the bricks, half of them slipped from his grasp. The guard grabbed him by the collar, lifting him off his feet.

"Are you a clown as well as an imbecile?" the guard screamed in his face.

"Please forgive me," Aaron said.

His cowering posture made Dalya turn away. How could he degrade himself like that? Why didn't he look the guard in the eye to show he wasn't afraid? She detested this game of subservience she saw Aaron, and many other inmates, playing. Where did it get them in the end? Not one brick less to carry, not one more morsel of food to eat.

She hurried into the barracks, where she slid the bread out of her mouth and under a slat in her bunk to share with Inge and Chava and Hila Scheller later. (She knew her own mother would refuse her portion, as she always did.)

She was back outside before the guards noticed anything, and as she went to rejoin her mother and Inge, she glanced toward Aaron. He was moving away with his load. For the first time, she noticed the sharp angles of his bones poking out from under his clothes, the deepening pits of his cheeks. A thought struck her. He'd said the bread was everything *he* had. Maybe it wasn't their fathers' food at all, but his. If that was the case, it didn't look like he could afford to give it up.

● ● ●

She waited until darkness fell, then retrieved her pearly white rock from her shoe and wedged it between the wooden beams of her bunk. She could barely sleep for thinking about it. She longed to sketch, if only to stay warm. When at least one part of her body was in motion, the stabbing chill ebbed enough for her to keep breathing. There were no blankets in the barracks, and her mother wouldn't let them cover themselves with straw from the floor. It was foul from the people who fell sick and couldn't make it to the latrines in time. There were rats nesting in it, too. Every night, their red eyes glinted in the dark. Dalya didn't really want the straw, but tonight, in the unforgiving air, she was tempted. She resisted, though, just as she resisted the pull of her white rock as each eternal minute passed.

When the first streaks of daylight shone through the slats in the walls, she retrieved the rock from its hiding place and put her frozen hands to work. She nearly laughed when the rock chiseled a fine white line along the bunk wall. But any laughter she'd had was left far behind on Kurfürstendamm in Berlin. Instead, she made another line, and another, until the graceful arch of a shoe grew from the wall.

By the time Inge woke coughing, Dalya had finished the first shoe.

"Look, Inge," she whispered, pulling her sister close to show her the wall. "Can I tell you the story of this shoe? Like we used to?"

Inge nodded, and Dalya wove a tale of thieves, princesses, and an ancient curse. As the tale unfolded, Inge's dull eyes grew brighter, and Dalya felt a surge of hope. So she began in earnest.

Over the next few days, she sketched shoes in her bunk until the wall was filled. All she had to do was look at a sketch, and the shoe burst forth fully formed in her mind. Just imagining molding the leather in her hands warmed her fingers. For Inge, every shoe held a fairy tale of magic and mystery, and Dalya was sure she could see her improving with each shoe she drew.

But then came the morning when Inge wouldn't get up, when she lay listless, her face ashen, her eyes a bottomless obsidian.

Dalya glanced at her mother and saw the same thing reflected in her eyes that she felt in her heart: fear of the sly, creeping fingers of death. She knew then what her mother had been too kind to say: Inge was too small to be kept alive by imaginary shoes.

The bullhorn blared, announcing roll call, but Dalya and her mother didn't move. They locked arms around Inge and waited. In those precious few minutes, her mother cradled Inge, singing to her and brushing her hair back from her forehead, and Dalya held Inge's wispy, thin hand in her own.

All too soon, boots thudded across the hay-strewn floor, and a guard was shining a torchlight into their faces.

"Get up!" she ordered.

Dalya tightened her grip on Inge's hand.

"I said . . . *up!*" The guard wrenched Dalya out of the bunk to reveal Inge, huddled against her mother.

A single glance at Inge's face and the guard barked, "This one goes to the infirmary."

As the guard reached for Inge, panic rose in her mother's eyes.

"No," her mother whispered. "Leave her here to die with me. Please."

The guard's frown deepened into abhorrence. She wrestled Dalya's mother away and pulled Inge out of the bunk, only to have her collapse into a heap on the floor. Dalya's heart splintered, and she clenched her fists until her nails bit into her palms. It was the only way she could keep from using her nails on the guard's face. Inge whimpered, and her mother tore at her breast, her eyes wild with grief.

An inferno blazed under Dalya's skin, fueling her with daring.

While the guard bent to lift Inge, Dalya jabbed her finger down her throat until her stomach splattered its meager contents on the floor. She fell to her knees, retching again.

"What, you too?" The disgusted guard yanked her to her feet while Inge flopped unnaturally in her arms. "Come on, then." She chuckled over the moans of Dalya's mother. "Death is waiting."

Death only came for one of them.

Dalya guessed that the doctors and nurses in the infirmary knew that, aside from hunger, there was nothing wrong with her. Whether they took pity on the two of them or simply found the morbid drama entertaining, they let Dalya stay. She shared a cot with Inge in a stark gray room surrounded by other sick inmates. She supposed she should've been frightened by the stench of disease and the rasping of the dying, but she wasn't. Instead, she resolved to shield Inge from it, to find a way to pull her back from the precipice.

The first day, she sang to her, prayer songs in Hebrew. A

doctor scolded her once, but when he realized the other patients had stopped their moaning and wailing to listen, he didn't complain again. Maybe he thought that even Jewish songs were easier on the ears than the pleas of those caught in death struggles. So she sang until her voice grew hoarse, until Frau Scheller came in with a tray of food.

Dalya opened her mouth to greet her, but Chava Scheller put a finger to her lips.

"They don't like it when we're friendly with each other," she whispered. "Best to stay quiet, and I'll talk when I can." She set the tray down, and then, bending to place a rag on Inge's forehead, she slid a piece of bread into Dalya's hand. "Your mother's giving me her rations for you. They won't allow her to visit." She lifted a bowl of watery potato soup off the tray. "Come, Inge. Try to eat. Even a few spoonfuls . . . that's something."

Inge shook her head feebly.

"Give it to me. I'll feed her." Dalya propped Inge up against her and dribbled some soup between her lips.

"That's it," Frau Scheller said. "Slowly now." She glanced over her shoulder at a hovering nurse.

"What a waste," the nurse mumbled over her clipboard, shaking her head. "Like pouring soup into the grave."

Dalya held Inge tighter, offering the soup up to the nurse. "Here. You eat it, then."

The nurse's eyes blazed, and as she turned away in distaste, Dalya muttered, "Coward."

"Careful," Frau Scheller whispered, but there was a glint of pride in her eyes as she straightened. "I can't stay, but I know you'll watch over her." She squeezed Dalya's hand. "Aaron told me once that you are like a porcupine who doesn't know where to aim her quills." She smiled ruefully. "He suffered their sting a time or two, even though I'm sure you never noticed."

Heat bloomed across Dalya's cheeks, and she felt a rush of resentment toward Aaron, that he'd spoken of her so bluntly, with such an unflattering description. She'd been brusque with him before, when his watchful hovering had grown too annoying. But it shamed her that he thought she was so lacking in softness.

"Don't worry," Frau Scheller said. "Aaron has always been overeager with affection, but he's durable. And perhaps, now that we're in this horrid place, you can find some other target worthier of pricking?"

Dalya nodded, thinking of the Gestapo that kept them here, living like animals in filth and squalor. But because she didn't know how to answer Frau Scheller's comments about Aaron, she said instead, "Tell Muti I'll keep Inge safe, as best I can." She vowed she would, for as long as possible.

But on the third day in the infirmary, Inge stopped eating. The soup ran down her chin, pooling in the hollow of her neck. Even Frau Scheller was at a loss for encouraging words.

On the sixth day, Dalya woke with a shudder, alone. She blinked against the icy glare of the windows and knew, when she pressed her hand against the cold, rough fibers of the cot, that she'd been sleeping alone for hours.

A nurse standing nearby peered over her chart at her. "It's back to the barracks for you," she said flatly. "The doctor says you're well, and strong enough to work alongside the other women. The guards will give you your orders." She jerked her head toward the door at the other end of the infirmary, and Dalya stood, the question that she dared not ask singeing her tongue.

She walked haltingly, not wanting to leave without knowing for certain. But then she caught sight of Frau Scheller tending to another patient along the wall. Their eyes met for a brief moment, and Frau Scheller nodded, her face barely masking her sadness. Dalya's eyes filled, but she would not let a single tear fall, not in front of the guards and doctors, who looked on with interest, as if she were some experiment in grief.

She found her mother in the barracks, huddled against the wall of their bunk, waiting to hear what her heart already knew was true. Her mother glanced at her, standing alone before her, and the question was answered. A howl ripped the air, piercing Dalya's heart, freezing it in that moment.

After that, winter settled in her bones, and there was no warming them. But still, she sketched her shoes. Now she didn't sketch them to stay warm. She sketched them to stay alive.

RAY LANGSTON'S BEGINNING

The mother crawled away from the heap of twisted metal. Her vision was coming and going in waves, but she'd made out the call box across the street, and she needed to get there.

The strained crying of her daughter rose in the air, and she welcomed it. The crying was strong, healthy. So much better for the baby to be crying when silence would only mean one thing. When she'd looked over at her husband in the front seat, right after the tire of the semi came through the windshield, she'd seen silence etched on his face. She'd known it was no use calling out to him. He was gone even before the car stopped spinning on the road.

That's it, sweetie, she urged Ray as she dragged herself across the icy street. *Keep up that hollering. Let the world know we're here.*

Before she'd climbed out of the smashed window, she'd

checked the backseat and nearly laughed with relief at her rosy-cheeked Ray sitting untouched in her car seat, her sage-green eyes quizzical and calm. But the heavy pain in her chest had stopped her short.

Daylight was dimming as she reached the call box, and with her last bit of strength, she dialed 911, then collapsed into the brittle grass. Soon, joining with her daughter's cries, the wail of sirens sang out. She smiled and gathered all her love, sending it out toward the shattered car and her daughter, hoping it would find its way to her on the wind.

You're going to be fine, Ray, she thought. *Just keep making noise.*

It was then that she saw the running shoes. Her husband's— silver with neon-orange laces and treads. They were strewn across the yellow center line in the asphalt, a good twenty feet from the wreck. One shoe had landed upright, the other lay on its side.

How funny, she thought. *They look lonely.*

Then a curtain lowered over her eyes, and the perfect world that held her daughter slowly ebbed away.

DALYA

Dalya didn't know what she was building, but she didn't care. The sleet that had been falling all morning had stopped, and an alabaster sun was breaking through the clouds, warming her chapped, blistered hands. She pushed her wheelbarrow of broken slate along the crackling, frozen ground, then dumped its contents onto the curved track along the perimeter of the roll-call yard. The track was made up of different sections—sand in one, rocks in another, gravel in another. She'd been building it for weeks, alongside the other able women in the camp. It didn't make any sense, but then, nothing in the camp did. She didn't expect it to anymore.

She heard a small cry and glanced over her shoulder to see her mother stagger behind her brimming wheelbarrow. She tripped and fell to one knee, and Dalya took a step toward her, then stopped when her mother waved her away.

"Don't," her mother scolded, hoisting herself up again. "You know they're watching. I'm fine."

Her mother was right. The guards were always watching, waiting for prisoners to falter so that they could dispose of them. And her mother had been coughing for weeks, just like Inge had before the end. Dalya sometimes wondered if her mother had given up when Inge died. Her eyes were dull and void, unbearable to look at. For now, though, her mother was still standing, still working. That was what kept her safe.

Dalya tilted her head toward the blue sky, soaking in the sun's rays. She could almost smell the earthy sweetness of grass twining up from the dirt, of honeyed blossoms opening on waking tree limbs. Beyond the camp's barbed wire, somewhere, life was in bloom.

One week later, she saw her father walking on the track she and her mother had made. A steady rain fell as she finished roll call, and her head was clouded with visions of the shoe she'd been drawing on the barrack wall earlier. Her mother gripped her arm hard enough for her to flinch, and that was when she looked up to see him. Her father was with a group of thirty or so men and older boys, all wearing heavy combat-style boots. Aaron was beside him, but there was no sign of David or Herr Scheller anywhere. It had been months since Dalya had seen either of them, and as she watched the men now, Aaron caught her eye.

The shake of his head was almost imperceptible, and she wanted to believe she hadn't seen it. But the sorrow in his face was undeniable.

She longed to cry, but found that her eyes were too weary for tears. Instead, she held on to her mother, watching the men and boys form military-straight lines on the track.

"What are they doing?" she asked.

Her mother stared for a long time. "Shoe testing," she said quietly. "I heard the guards talking last week. The boots come from shoe factories. The men in the Schuhläuferkommando are meant to test the quality."

Soon, Dalya saw what "testing" meant. A guard blew a whistle, and the men began marching around the track, through the slate and sand and rocks Dalya had helped lay down.

The marching itself might not have been so awful, but even from a few hundred feet away, Dalya could tell by the men's posture that there was something wrong with the boots. The men were stooped, their legs bent oddly, their feet anchored too far apart or too close together. Dalya had learned how to tell when a shoe was ill-fitting. Her father had always told her that a well-made shoe makes a man walk taller, chest angled toward the sky. These shoes, she decided, were much too small for the men.

Dalya winced as Aaron's face beaded with sweat and her father's tightened with pain. They marched all through the morning until, suddenly, a man toward the front of the line collapsed.

Almost before the man hit the ground, the shots rang out. The guards dragged him away, leaving behind a pool of blood, seeping into the gravel.

Her father and Aaron were not shot. They kept walking.

At noon, they were each given a large sack to carry. Dalya

knew it must be heavy, because one elderly man buckled to his knees as soon as it was placed in his arms. Her father and Aaron did not collapse. They stood, unwavering, the sacks in their arms.

Then they ran. Holding these enormous sacks, they ran without stopping for food, water, or rest. At some point, Dalya's mother left, unable to bear it. But Dalya stayed. She couldn't look away. And then it happened.

Her father lost his footing and started to fall. Dalya's heart shrieked as a guard aimed his rifle at her father. Her mouth couldn't utter a sound. But Aaron, with lightning speed, shifted his sack to one arm and reached for her father's elbow with the other. Barely the brush of a touch, it was enough to brace her father, to straighten him up. It was enough for the guard to lower his rifle, and for Dalya to catch her breath.

She could hear some of the men crying as they ran. Aaron didn't cry. Neither did her father. Her father, whose life had been shoes, whose goal had been to make shoes comfortable for every person, bore the burden of these boots of torture silently. Her father, whose daughter had made the track on which he shredded his feet, surely now bleeding inside the boots, ran on the track until the sky dimmed into dusk. Until, at last, he was taken off the track and led away.

The pebbles raining down on the barracks' roof were a message meant for her. She'd never left her bunk after dark before. It was forbidden, and she shuddered to think of the punishment if she were caught. She waited a few minutes, through another storm of pebbles, and then her body made up its mind for her, and her feet slid out of the bunk of their own accord, walking to the door.

The night air stung her cheeks as she stepped outside, but it was the glittering veil of stars draped across the sky that took her breath away. She was so entranced that she nearly forgot where she was until she heard a low owl call. She checked for guards but didn't see any. She eased nearer to the fence. A shadow, the right size and shape for Aaron, pressed up against the wall of the men's barracks.

He stepped toward her, his eyes glinting with starlight, and she noticed his awkward limp, even in the darkness.

"How bad are your feet?" she asked.

"Not as bad as the others'. They'll heal." He edged closer. "We only have a few minutes. The guards are playing cards, but it won't last long." He glanced up at the sky. "Isn't it amazing? So much beauty up there, and so much ugliness down here."

Dalya nodded. "It doesn't seem fair that somewhere, someone else is watching the same sky. But they're free."

"I know."

They stood silent for a few moments, the clouds from their breaths floating upward until she imagined them mingling with the stars.

Then Aaron asked, "Do you ever wonder what you would be like if you'd been born to belong on the other side of these walls? If you had a different God and different choices to make?"

"You mean if we weren't Jewish?" Dalya whispered.

Aaron nodded. "Do you think the hatred would come naturally, or would you question it?"

Dalya's stomach tightened, and she stared at his face, wondering what she'd see in it if it weren't masked in shadow. "I don't know. I never thought about it that way. I suppose if that's all they taught me, if that was the truth I knew, I might believe it." She flinched, repulsed by the idea of being so corruptible. "Would you?"

"I hope not," he said. "I used to think that truth and right were the same. Not anymore."

He whipped his head around, and Dalya heard faint voices in the distance.

"They're coming," he said. "You better go." She nodded and began to back away, but then he motioned for her to wait.

"Dalya, I need to tell you something. . . ." His voice was heavy, and the weight of it made her feel the consuming pain of what was coming. "I'm sorry, but you won't ever see your father again."

"I know," she whispered, hugging her arms to her chest. It was like Aaron had said. Nothing about that horrible truth was right. But she'd have to carry its certainty with her forever.

RAY

After the horrible thing happened, Ray knew she would run, like she had so many other times. She'd already been running for the last fifteen minutes since she left the school gym. Sweat seeped through the bodice of her dress and coursed down her cheeks, mixing with her tears as her feet staccatoed the pavement. Still, she kept running.

Her feet should have been hurting. They always did, even with feathery, tiptoe steps. But they didn't right now, or if they did, she couldn't feel it. She only felt one thing: the need to run. This time, though, she would run so far no one would ever find her. She'd run to a place where she could get lost forever, where she could fade into the sidewalks and alleyways without anyone noticing the girl with the limp and the charred-black hair.

In the moonlight, she could see that her cherry-red dress was sweat-stained and gray with dirt. It had been so beautiful when she'd first glimpsed it on the rack, but now she hated the sight of it. She couldn't believe she'd ever thought it would make a difference, that it could make Carter think of her as anything other than what she was—a complete waste.

The dim outline of the Smokebush buildings appeared against the darkness, and Ray stopped in the shadows of the Spanish oak. It was only a temporary stop. She'd get in and out before anyone saw her, especially Mrs. Danvers. She yanked at her dress violently until the satin fabric gave way, freeing her. Grabbing her pocketknife from the hollowed-out knot in the tree where she kept it, she slashed the dress into stringy threads. She hurled it into the creek. It landed softly, raising the reedy pitch of the water by a half step, billowing like a spidery flower. Then the current sucked it under, and it was gone.

Ray slipped the pale pink shoes off next, and cocked her arm back, ready to launch them into the water, too. But they glowed ethereally in the moonlight, and Ray hesitated, feeling their mysterious pull just as she had the first day she'd seen them in the Pennypinch. No . . . she should let them drown. Everything that had happened tonight was because of them. It was their fault, and she hated them for it. Still, though, if it was possible for shoes to look pleading, these did. As if they were straining toward survival, as if they'd been built that way.

She closed her eyes, tensing every muscle, but her fingers wouldn't let go of the shoes.

She swore, then ran to the Dumpster beside the main building and tossed them on top of the garbage.

An instant pity and longing for the shoes struck her, but she ignored it, climbing up the oak and into the open window of her second-story bedroom. She slunk past her sleeping roommate, Nancy, thankful she snored so loudly, put on her jeans and holey Carole King shirt, and shoved a few clothes from their shared dresser into her duffel. She pulled on her sneakers, wincing. She kept hoping she'd get used to it, or the nerves in the scar tissue would deaden. But it always felt the same, like a thousand hot needles piercing her skin.

She gritted her teeth against it, grabbed her guitar from the corner, and made her way down the hallway toward Mrs. Danvers's office. The door was locked, as usual, but Ray used the spare key (the one that Mrs. Danvers had "lost" years ago). The office was as cluttered as ever, the desk crammed with paperwork, but Ray knew exactly where the petty-cash envelope was. She'd never taken the entire thing before, only skimmed off the top. Tonight, though, she folded all of the crisp bills into her pocket.

"Sorry, Mrs. D.," she whispered into the darkness.

She turned around, then gasped as she slammed into a thick wall of softness blocking her way, and a sudden flash of red patent leather peeked out from the shadows.

"Pinny!" Ray hissed. "What are you doing in here?"

"Spying on you," Chopine whispered matter-of-factly.

Ray yanked Pinny into the office and shut the door so no one would hear them. "When did you get back from the dance?" Ray asked, wondering if Pinny had seen her there tonight and if she was about to get hit with a dozen questions about what had happened. The look of staunch determination on Pinny's face made Ray nervous. She'd seen that look in

Pinny's eyes before, mostly when Pinny was hogging the TV in one of her *Wizard of Oz* marathons. She'd watched the movie a hundred and thirty-two times (she kept a running tally). One time, Nancy dared turn it off mid-Munchkins, and Pinny had rewarded her by stalking her, singing "Follow the Yellow Brick Road." It only took an hour for Nancy to beg for mercy. No one ever came between Pinny and Dorothy's ruby-reds again.

Now Pinny shrugged. "I've been back awhile." There was a rattling, followed by the sound of chewing and the smell of licorice, and Ray knew Pinny must be eating one of her endless bags of black jelly beans. "You're running away." Her voice was gummy with the candy. "I'm coming with you."

Ray smirked. She had to admit, Chopine always surprised her. Everything from her name to the glitter-laden purple Keds she wore every day was a contradiction.

"I'm not going anywhere," Ray lied. "And neither are you. I don't want to get stuck with bathroom detail . . . again. You don't either."

Chopine tilted her head, studying Ray. "When you lie, your eyes go weaselly."

Ray groaned as panic clamored through her. She did *not* need this holdup. She had to be on a bus out of town before Mrs. Danvers realized she was gone. Otherwise, someone would come to drag her back to Smokebush. With her luck, it'd be Sheriff Wane. Oh, the pleasure he'd have on his greasy, pockmarked face when he found her. He'd had it in for her for years. Last week, when he'd caught her tagging the wall outside the Wiggly Pig grocery for the hundredth time, he'd said as much.

He'd surveyed the trail of notes she'd sprayed so far, a

curving slur of arpeggios in G—the beginnings of a new song she was writing. Then he spit a stream of chew at its base. "If you're going to end up in juvie," he said, "at least make it for something better than this trash."

Well, she wasn't about to give him the satisfaction of nailing her tonight.

"Pinny, just . . . go to bed!" Ray hissed.

"No!" Pinny folded her arms. "You're going to New York City, and you're taking me."

Ray sighed in irritation. "How do you know I'm going to New York?"

"Because you ordered that book from the Julie School there." Pinny spoke in a fuzzy legato, her teeth never quite grabbing the words. "You did it from the computer in the common room. And you hid the book. In that hole in the tree outside. I saw you put it there." She smiled triumphantly. "I'm a good detective."

Ray thought about denying it, but there was no point. She did have a Juilliard catalog. She liked to take it with her when she went down to the lake to play her guitar. Of course, it was a joke, her going to Juilliard. She probably wouldn't even graduate with the rest of the senior class next week. (Her grades were dismal, and she was pretty sure she was flat-out failing English. Mr. Jarvis hated her so much, there was no chance of that grade changing.) Still, it wasn't so bad to have something like Juilliard to cling to when the rest of life was a crapfest. It was a hallucination, sure, but she'd take it over reality any day. Besides, Juilliard might be impossible, but New York wasn't. It was the perfect hiding place . . . the perfect place for someone to get lost forever. And after what had happened tonight, she needed that.

"What do you care about New York, anyway?" Ray said.

"I need to get Mama's shoes back." Chopine pulled a newspaper clipping from her pocket. Ray snatched it impatiently, flipped on Mrs. Danvers's desk light, and stared at the picture of a huge tree with hundreds of shoes hanging from its branches. "Tree of Lost Soles," the headline to the article read.

Pinny stabbed a finger at the page, making the red patent-leather Mary Janes strung around her neck swing wildly. Faded and tattered, one missing a heel, they were a sorry looking pair. But for the eight years Ray and Chopine had lived together at Smokebush Children's Home, Ray had never seen Pinny without her red-shoe necklace, bulky and awkward as it was. Mrs. Danvers had tried to convince Pinny to take it off for school, at least, but Pinny wouldn't budge.

Ray looked at the page, where Pinny had drawn a circle in red crayon around a pair of silver stilettos. "*Those* were Mama's," Pinny said. "She needs them back."

"Pinny, your mom is . . ." "Gone" was the kinder version. "Dead" was probably the real one, although Ray didn't know for sure. Once, when she'd been rifling through Mrs. Danvers's office, she'd come across Pinny's records and the "whereabouts unknown" line beside her mother's name. Not even Mrs. Danvers had the heart to tell Pinny the truth about the odds of her mom still being out there. What was the point?

"My mama needs her shoes," Pinny said with finality.

"Well, you're not coming with me to find them." Ray stepped toward the door, but Pinny moved to block her.

Sweat beaded on Ray's neck, her heart tapping manic sixteenth notes. She didn't want to do it, but she had to, for Pinny's own good. She shoved Pinny out of the way and lunged for the door, yanking it open and slamming it shut in one fluid motion. Then, pulling hard on the knob to keep the door shut, she used her other hand to slip the key into the lock.

She let go just as Pinny began jiggling the knob from the inside.

"No fair!" Pinny cried. "You can't lock me in!"

"Bye, Pinny," Ray whispered, laying the key on the floor in the middle of the hallway. "Somebody will come for you soon. I'll send you a postcard, okay?"

"Don't! I won't be here to get it." There was banging from behind the door, probably from her kicking it. "You'll change your mind. You need me. You'll see."

But Ray was already running down the hallway and out the front door. She made one quick stop at the garden shed to grab the old pup tent and sleeping bag Mrs. Danvers kept from her "wanderer phase," as she put it. Ray didn't know how far she could get on the petty cash, so she figured the camping gear might come in handy, especially if she had to stay below the radar. She tied everything haphazardly to her duffel, then jumped the creek and headed for the tree line. Even with only moonlight as her guide, she wove through the bald cypress and pine trees as easily as if it were day. Her body had a built-in compass that had always pointed her toward safety, those hiding places where she could fade to invisible before anyone had even started looking for her.

As she ran, the piercing pain in her feet brought her back

in time. Back eight years, to a time before Smokebush, to a time when she was bounced from one foster family to another. Back to when she discovered that this strange, elusive "family" was something that would only ever belong to other kids, never to her. Back to when she'd first learned to run. Back to when her feet had been bullets firing through the grass, to when she felt the exhilaration of her feet pounding the earth. Back to a time before the pain began . . .

She'd always been a "runner." That's what her caseworker had called her in the conversations with foster parents that Ray wasn't supposed to hear. Ray listened, though, her ear pressed against the door, the wall, or the window. She found ways. Her ears were buckets, collecting the words the caseworker dropped so carelessly. "Challenging," "aggressive," and "intelligent" were the words she used the most. And "runner." That one was Ray's favorite; it was the one that made the couples go pasty. It pleased her that she had that effect on grown-ups, that she could scare the polite smiles right off their faces. She ran from the moment she could walk—year after year, family after family. She ran, because that was the one thing she was good at, the one thing people could count on her for, and if there was one thing people *did* love about her, it was her ability to know when she wasn't wanted anymore.

That wasn't the only way she scared them, either. All those wannabe mothers who thought that she'd be different for them, that she'd fall in love with them and transform into the daughter of their dreams. What they didn't know was that Ray could vanish clear into thin air. When she put on her pink Converse sneakers, her feet grew wings. Sure, the shoes were ninety-nine-cent Goodwill specials, but it didn't matter. They were magic, and they never let her down. In the time it took those mothers to reach for a box of cereal in the grocery aisle, or pull out their sunglasses from their purse at the park, Ray would be gone.

Her shoes didn't make a whisper when she moved. She could sit for hours tucked comfortably under a rack of clothes in Sears, or hidden behind the packs of paper towels on a shelf in aisle 9. Oh, they always found her eventually, the cops or the caseworker. But the mothers' smiles were gone when Ray resurfaced. Instead, there was a tight-lipped resentment, as if Ray had ruined their picture of a perfect little girl.

The last time Ray had run, she'd been nine and it wasn't for fun. It was for survival. When Ray looked back on that day now, she could see how it had happened. Bearded Bridgette had wanted to teach her a lesson. It might have been because Ray made Bridgette look like she couldn't do her job. Caseworkers were supposed to find suitable homes for foster kids, and so far every one had ended in disaster. Or it might have been because Ray nicknamed her Bearded Bridgette because of the dark fringe of hair stubbling her chin. Whatever the reason, Bridgette had grown tired of Ray's disappearing act. That was when she gave Ray to Sal and Hugh.

They seemed nice enough at the start. Sal, in her cardigan and glossy lipstick, had oozed cuddles and enthusiasm in her first meeting with Ray. Hugh had smiled broadly, too, and even brought her a used guitar, saying that he'd heard she loved music.

But then they took Ray home, and Sal's cardigan, along with the woman she was while wearing it, disappeared. Hugh worked on an oil rig in the Gulf, so he was gone for months at a time. On the good days, Sal spent her time on the couch watching TV. When Ray walked in from school, Sal glanced up, surprised, as if she'd completely forgotten about her. But there was usually some sort of microwavable meal in the freezer, or at least a can of Chef Boyardee, and Ray was glad for that. Because then there were the bad days, right after the stipend check came in the mail and Sal got her hands on the meth.

Those were the days when Ray ran. She waited for the signs. Sal snapping at her for scrounging in the kitchen for food scraps, or yanking her hair for spilling a cup of water. When Sal got dangerous, Ray hid. She slept with her sneakers on so she'd be ready. Then, when Sal came for her, eyes wild, Ray would skim past her and out the screen door, running through the cornfield out back. Running, running, running in those pink Converse sneakers until she got to the cemetery.

It was her favorite place in the whole world. It was filled with overgrown graves where bluebonnets flowered by the hundreds. A small chapel rose from the center of the graveyard, the color of a ripe apricot in sunshine. Ray didn't put much credence in God, but she figured if he *were* around, he sure would appreciate that color. It was like a beacon to heaven, if there was a heaven. And if there was a heaven, then it would stand to reason that her parents might be in it. Maybe if they looked down, they'd see her huddled up next to that apricot church. It was so bright it'd be hard to miss, even from way up there.

Some people would've been skittish about spending night

after night among tombstones. Not her. Dead people weren't nearly as scary as live ones.

Ray usually got her timing perfect. She would wait it out in the cemetery for a day or so, then she'd ease back toward the house. She'd walk in and find Sal worried and tearful. Sal would scoop her into a hug, apologizing over and over again.

But the one day that started all the pain, her timing was off. She came back to the house to find Sal crazed and screaming. She tried to run, but Sal slammed her against the wall. It seemed like her head split right down the center, and then everything went black.

When she woke up, the room was dark except for the flames leaping from the kitchen sink. She struggled to stand, but her legs collapsed under her. That was when she realized she was barefoot.

She crawled toward the kitchen sink and saw them crackling with fire. Her pink Converse sneakers crumbling to ash before her eyes.

On her hands and knees, Ray scrambled out the front door as the flames spread to the curtains and cabinets. Through blurred vision, she saw Sal sprawled on the porch, passed out probably, but Ray still steered clear of her. She stood, but the world spun wildly and she lost her balance, toppling the trash cans full of beer bottles off the porch and onto the gravel road. When she leapt off the porch, a thousand shards of glass sliced into her bare skin. But Ray didn't stop. She didn't even slow. Not for a second. Her feet were slick and shredded, but she pushed on through the cornfield, forcing them to move against their will.

When Bridgette and the police found her the next morning, she was sleeping on a rotting pew inside the apricot chapel, surrounded by a trail of bloody footprints. Bridgette didn't take her back to Sal and Hugh's this time. There was no lecture about being cooperative. Instead, Bridgette climbed into the back of the ambulance.

On the ride to the hospital, Bridgette laid something on the gurney beside her. "Here," she said stiffly. "I got this out of the house for you." Ray opened her eyes long enough to see the guitar that Hugh had given her. Ray figured it was Bridgette's way of apologizing, but she didn't say thank you. She wrapped her fingers around the guitar's neck, and every time she thought she'd scream from the pain, she squeezed her guitar instead.

It took weeks for her feet to heal. When they did, the scars stayed behind as jagged, puffed flesh crisscrossing her soles. The pain stayed, too. Not as bad, but still there, pounding out its ruthless pulse every second of every day.

When Bridgette dropped Ray and her tender bare feet off at Smokebush Children's Home, Mrs. Danvers frowned.

"She hasn't worn shoes since the incident," Bridgette explained to Mrs. Danvers's chipmunk-cheeked face.

"That won't do." Mrs. Danvers shook her head until the skin under her chin wagged back and forth. "You'll need shoes for school."

Ray nearly laughed at the mention of school, knowing she'd skip every chance she got. But she figured she better play along, at least for now. After all, Bridgette had already told her that Smokebush was her last option.

Mrs. Danvers led her down the hallways of threadbare carpet and puce walls to a box of hand-me-downs.

"These look about your size." She offered her a pair of faded gray Reeboks.

Ray was gingerly shifting her weight from one foot to the other, a habit she'd gotten into, trying to make the needles shooting up her soles retreat. She thought about the only pretty thing she'd ever had besides her guitar, the only pair of shoes she'd ever loved. It wasn't natural for her to ask anyone for anything, to let anyone see her want. Wanting led to hoping, hoping led to trusting, trusting to loving . . . it was all too dangerous. But she missed her running wings.

So she took a chance and asked, "Do you have any pink shoes?"

"I'm sorry, darlin'. This is all we have." Mrs. Danvers held out the ugly sneakers, gently cupping her hand under Ray's chin.

Ray snatched the shoes and jerked away, biting her quivering lip. No one was ever going to see Ray Langston cry.

She waited for Mrs. Danvers to go pasty like those foster moms, but she didn't. She straightened, saying, "I bet Pinny could work wonders with those shoes. It's a special talent of hers, giving shoes makeovers." She turned down the hallway. "I'll take you to her."

Ray knew better than to have expectations about the girl called Pinny. There wasn't much point holding people to expectations when everyone failed them from the get-go. But even without expectations, the round teenage girl that Mrs. Danvers brought Ray to in the rec room surprised her. She sat at a folding table hunched over a mound of glitter, her fingers fluttering above the pile. Her lime-green glasses teetered on the tip of her nose, threatening to drop.

"Pinny," Mrs. Danvers said. The girl popped her head up like an astonished prairie dog. "This is our new friend, Ray. She'll be living with us from now on, and she needs some help with her shoes."

Pinny pushed her glasses up to her almond-shaped eyes, but they immediately slid down again. "Hi, Ray." She smiled wide. "Have a seat. Show me your shoes."

Ray tilted her head. Pinny looked about thirteen or fourteen, but the awkward way she fumbled with the glue and sequins in her hands made her seem younger, much younger. Ray stared, trying to unpuzzle Pinny's odd look, until Pinny did it for her.

"Stop staring," Pinny said in a thick, slow voice. "It's Down syndrome. Not the plague." Ray had never heard of either. But if this Down syndrome didn't bother Pinny, it was sure as heck none of Ray's business to be bothered *for* her. Pinny glanced down at Ray's bare feet, her white-blond hair a drifting dandelion fluff about her face. "You look kinda funny yourself."

Mrs. Danvers laughed, then looked at Ray and shrugged. "That's our Pinny, the truth-teller. Everyone needs a truth-teller in life." She motioned for Ray to sit down. "You work on those shoes, and they'll turn into something to love."

Ray thought about running, but her feet were too tired and too sore. There was no apricot chapel here to run to anyway. So she sat down.

Pinny offered her several jars of glitter. "I like mine with sparkles. See?" She held up the remains of a canvas sneaker dripping with glue and globs of glitter. "You try."

Ray examined the other odds and ends on the table: sequins, feathers, puffy paints. Her eyes stopped on a container of safety pins. Ignoring Pinny's attempts to chat, Ray set to work. An hour later, she'd covered every inch of her gray sneakers with safety pins, until the outside of her shoes looked the way the inside of her feet felt.

The second she was finished, a flash popped in her face, and she squinted up to see a photo spitting out of a beat-up Polaroid camera.

"I don't have any like that in my collection," Pinny said from behind the camera. She waved the photo in the air until the picture developed, then added it to a rubber-banded stack. Ray peeked at the stack. They were photos of shoes, dozens of them.

Pinny eyed Ray's shoes intently. "Why do you want to wear hurt like that?" she asked quietly.

"It's all I have," Ray replied. But she only wore the shoes when she had to. The rest of the time, in the middle of class, in the hallways at Smokebush, she went barefoot.

She never liked shoes much after that . . . until the day she saw the pale pink ones in the Pennypinch. But it was all because of those shoes that the horrible thing had happened.

Shoes, Ray thought now as she ran through the night under the wide Texas sky, were just another thing she hated.

DALYA

Memory is a fickle muse. A young girl might recall a random stranger on the street—a woman's striking olive eyes, or a man's shock of carrot-colored curls. But when one person grows to a multitude, memory opens at the seams.

Dalya watched typhus weave its hand of death through the camp, emptying the barracks. Hollowed bodies passed before her in wheelbarrows so frequently that she barely glanced at them anymore. Until a face came before her she would never forget, a face that lay inches from her own one night, gasping for breath. Her mother's.

She'd watched this face exchange its roundness for jagged angles, trade its hope for resignation. Now she watched it contort painfully as the cough choked her mother, time and time again.

Dalya felt the twisting of her own bowels and the fever in her throbbing head, but she ignored them, cradling her mother through another violent spasm.

"It is time to tell you," her mother whispered. "You will live. I will not." She clung to Dalya's hands. "You are all that is left."

"No," Dalya started, tears in her eyes. Her father, her brother, her sister, and now her mother. Lost. Part of her wished to follow them, while another part railed against it, wanting and hoping to live. It angered her, this hope, because it felt so selfish, so greedy. But it stayed, obstinately, all the same.

Her mother raised a finger to her lips. "Find Leonard Goodman, the man your father told you about. He can help you." She told Dalya his address again and made her repeat it until she had it memorized. "Promise you will find him. Promise."

"Yes," Dalya said.

Her mother sighed, and her face smoothed, a peace spreading over it that Dalya hadn't seen since they'd left their shop a lifetime ago. Dalya nestled beside her in the bunk, tucking her head under her mother's chin to listen to her faint heart. The metronome of her mother's life beat on, and soon Dalya was soothed to sleep as she gave in to her own fever, letting it swathe her in heaviness and hazy dreams. Sometime in the night, the metronome stilled, and silence became the loneliest sound of Dalya's life.

Time turned watery, slipping by her in ripples of sadness and delirium, and the night hours passed in a fog. The hope that lay sealed inside her heart shriveled and bruised, but it didn't die.

When the guards found her the next morning, Dalya lay unmoving, her arms clasped around her mother. Somewhere, in the murkiness of her mind, she was vaguely aware of them standing over her, of the hum of their voices. Her body, though, seemed to be made of stone; not even her eyelids could flutter. But she was still breathing. In and out, in and out. That was what she had become. All breath. That was the only thing she could think about. If she stopped thinking about the breathing, the breathing would stop.

For all the effort she put into it, though, the guards didn't see. They couldn't have. She felt herself being carried, then tossed through the air, along with her mother, landing in a pile of bodies. Others were thrown on top of her, burying her, and then they began to bump along the ground. She guessed that she was in a wheelbarrow, like the ones she'd seen ferrying the others over the past few weeks. She forced her eyes open and reached through the forest of skin on bone to find her mother, to touch her one last time.

Suddenly, a firm, warm hand gripped hers, and Aaron's stunned face appeared.

"Dalya!" he breathed, his eyes wide. "How did you ...?" He scanned the exercise yard, making sure no one was watching. "Don't move," he whispered. "They think you're dead. The dead are the only ones who ever leave, so this is your chance."

She struggled to make sense of what he was saying. It didn't seem possible he could be here right now. But then she remembered that the guards had put him to work moving the dead. He was still stronger than most others, even thin as he was, and she'd watched him coming and going with the wheelbarrows, wondering how he could stand it.

He leaned closer, holding his arm over his nose, as if to ward off the smell. "The guards think I'm simple. They think I don't understand, so they talk while I work." He pushed the wheelbarrow faster. "I heard them say they're building a crematorium here. But for now, the bodies get taken to one in Berlin, the Krematorium Berlin-Baumschulenweg. . . ." Hope lit his eyes. "Do you understand? Don't make a sound. Let them take you with the rest. And when you get to Berlin, find a way out."

Dalya tried to shake her head, tried to tell him no, but it was impossible. Her body refused to give her away, refused to accept defeat.

The wheelbarrow stopped, and Aaron lifted bodies off her one by one, tossing them into the truck waiting by the entrance gates. Soon, she was at the top of the pile. He lifted her gently, and she felt the bony sharpness of his forearms under her waist. He brought his cheek to hers for the briefest second.

"Remember what I told you," he whispered. "If I can, I'll find you."

He laid her with the others, making sure she was partially covered, then stepped back as the truck's engine rumbled to life. There were no guards in the back of the truck, and the tarp draped over it gave her decent coverage. She kept her eyes open as the truck pulled away, watching Aaron's resolute face grow smaller in the distance. It became etched in her memory, along with her mother's sunken cheeks and eyes, her father's pounding feet on the track, her sister's final gurgling cough.

But he was not the last memory she took with her.

That was of the mountain she passed on the way out of camp.

The mountain of crumpled shoes waiting for owners who would never return. Those shoes, she knew, had memories, too. They would not forget what had happened here. They might always be waiting for the people they belonged to. There was the imprint left behind by a child's toes on the insole of a boot. A bulge on a loafer where a bunion had once pushed against the leather. The wearers of the shoes were gone. And the shoes lay huddled, abandoned and sorrowful, collecting rainwater and mud.

Once the truck passed through the gates of the camp, an ember smoldered inside her, forcing her mind into alertness. Her fever racked her with tremors, but she fought to stay focused on the truck's movements. Peering through gaps in the tarp as houses and streets rumbled past, she looked for familiar landmarks. There were none. Since she'd left it on that night so long ago, Berlin had become blanketed in black.

The truck made more turns, then slowed to a stop, and Dalya held her breath. Her heart pounded an alarm, and it seemed impossible that the guards chatting on the other side of the tarp couldn't hear it. But they went about their business, greeting a man that she guessed worked at the crematorium.

"Here's another load," one of the guards said.

The tarp was whipped off the truck, and Dalya clenched her eyes shut, making herself as still as possible.

A man clucked his tongue. "So many," he mumbled. "It will take days."

"It better not," another growled. "We'll have more by then. Be quick about getting them off the truck."

Bodies shifted around her as two men unloaded them into a wheelbarrow to be taken inside. Closer and closer their hands came, and Dalya willed herself to be invisible, willed her lungs to wait for breath.

A hand gripped her calf and forearm, sliding her forward in the truck bed.

"This one must be fresh." The man tossed her into the wheelbarrow. "Still a bit warm."

Wheels rolled underneath her, and soon she was out of the damp night and inside a warmer building. The wheelbarrow turned down what seemed like some hallways. Then it tipped forward suddenly, and Dalya tumbled out onto the base of a pile of bodies. Her forehead slammed into another person's head, making lights burst before her eyes, but she didn't flinch. The men's footsteps died away. Minutes of silence passed before Dalya dared open her eyes.

She was in a stark room with a large brick oven a few feet in front of her. An awful, bitter scent hung in the air, and Dalya nearly gagged, but she wouldn't allow herself. She worried another load was coming, and sure enough, minutes later the men returned to add to the pile.

After the fifth trip, the wheelbarrow didn't come back. But one man did, a small, weary-looking man with spectacles, a man who surveyed the piles and gave a heavy, heartbroken sigh. It was that sigh that made Dalya form the words she could barely speak through her fear, that made her take a chance.

"Please," she whispered hoarsely, "can you help me?"

The man gasped, staggering back. She twisted her limbs until she'd unburied herself, but she didn't have the strength to stand. The man's face was white with horror, his mouth open wide.

"No," Dalya said firmly. "If you scream, you kill me."

She waited for the man to make his choice. If he screamed, guards would come running. They'd shoot her on the spot. If he didn't scream, then maybe . . .

He scrambled toward her, scooping her up more swiftly than seemed possible for his size.

"What can I do with you?" he whispered. "How can I help you?"

"Take me to Leonard Goodman at the International Quaker Center." She rattled off the address her mother had made her memorize. "He'll know what to do."

The man weighed the options gravely, then nodded. "You must not move a muscle," he said. "To everyone here, you're dead, understand?"

Dalya nodded. He hurried her to a coffin on a gurney and laid her inside. "I'll prop the lid open when I'm able, but take shallow breaths or you'll run out of air. I'll go as quickly as I can."

Dalya saw his frantic eyes one last time before he closed the lid, leaving her in darkness. The heat from her breath warmed the small space, and she felt the sudden panic of the world pressing down on her. She wanted to scream and beat against the lid, only inches from her face. But instead, she clenched her eyes shut and listened to the squealing wheels of the gurney as it began to move.

Minutes passed, and at one point the gurney stopped and she heard the man explain to someone, "I have a pickup to make. It won't take long."

The coffin was jostled, and then, just as the air inside grew stagnant, the lid creaked open an inch, and Dalya saw she was riding in the back of a hearse.

She didn't know how long the silent ride took, and it didn't matter. The only thing that mattered was that with each passing minute she moved farther away from that oven and its unbearable stench. She drifted between sleep and wakefulness as the coffin swayed through the night. Then, suddenly, the lid swung open, a blinding light flooded the coffin, and Dalya squinted into a pair of eyes full of compassion.

"It's all right, child," a voice said. "You've found sanctuary."

Those were the last words she heard before the exhaustion and fever she'd fought for hours claimed her, sweeping her away into blessed forgetfulness.

PART II

I should be still,
my tongue is like meat,
but the truth, shoes,
where are your feet?
> —Abraham Sutzkever, "A Load of Shoes"

ROBBIE

Robbie Turner was filling a wheelbarrow with rubble when he saw the shoes. He'd been watching a dozen other men from his unit playing a makeshift game of baseball amid mountains of debris. Using a broken pipe for a bat and hunks of brick and stone for balls, Tom, Bill, and the others were making a go of it. Their laughter echoed through the sunken streets, sounding misplaced and foreign. Tom had tried to pull Robbie into the game, razzing him for being such a wet blanket. But he hadn't had the stomach for it. Not here, in this place where the world had come to an end. Not when widowed women were spending their days breaking their backs cleaning up debris from the streets.

The Allied bombs had cratered everything. Nothing was left of most buildings but charred shells. It would take years, decades even, for Germany to rebuild Berlin and all the other cities gutted by the air raids.

He knew he should be relieved the war here in Europe was over. Hitler was dead, and although fighting in the Pacific raged on, Robbie would be going back to the States soon. But it was hard to feel relief when he stared into the faces of the homeless and heartbroken every day.

His unit was clearing rubble to set up a refugee camp for the concentration-camp survivors who were slowly finding their way to Berlin, wrecked by what had happened to them. Some were looking for lost family members and friends; some were trying to find the homes they'd left years ago, not realizing many were nothing but dust. Robbie was so weary of the suffering.

Evelyn kept writing letters from back home, telling him about the beautiful springtime in Ohio and the funny things her first-grade students did every day. Beyond the graveyard that was Europe, life was moving on.

He tossed an armful of crumbling bricks into the debris truck, smiling as he thought of Evie.

Before he'd gotten drafted, he'd been tentative about marriage. He was young, and he wasn't sure he was ready. But the war had made him tired, and he felt older than his years. He loved Evie; it was purely his own obstinacy standing in the way of a proposal. That was done with now. He wanted to bring some new life into this world after seeing so much of it destroyed.

He was just setting his mind on a proposal when he saw something pale pink and shiny peeking out from under a mound of rubble. He dug through the pile and unearthed a tin box, cracked open on one side. Inside was a pair of shoes with tiny flowers embroidered along the toes. Except for a small black smudge on the back of one heel, amazingly, the shoes were untouched. They looked like they could have been someone's wedding shoes.

Robbie glanced around, wondering if there was any way he could track down who the shoes belonged to. He'd overheard his captain say that this was a Jewish neighborhood. Before his unit had come to Berlin, Robbie had seen the nightmare of what had happened to the Jews. They'd passed through Bergen-Belsen; they'd seen the death, and the suffering of those who'd survived. News had been trickling in from other units of similar horrors all over Germany and Poland.

If anyone from this neighborhood was still alive, would they come back? Even if they did, by then Robbie and his unit would be long gone, and so would any opportunity to find the shoes' owner. No, the shoes had obviously been lovingly made, and if he left them here, they'd be destroyed and lost forever. He'd come too late to rescue so many, but these shoes could be rescued, and treasured, as they deserved to be. He tucked the shoes, so dainty and delicate, carefully into his satchel, and as his fingers trailed across their heels, he was struck with the strangest notion. That the shoes longed to be worn, that it was their destiny (if shoes could have such a thing) to make someone feel extraordinary.

It was crazy, he knew, but somehow, he was confident that Evie would believe him when he told her the story. That she, with all the tenderness and reverence a person should feel in the presence of magic, would give the shoes a life worthy of their rarity. He'd make sure that every day he took a breath, Evie would be surrounded by beauty. Better than that, he'd make sure their love together was beautiful so he could forget the ugliness of this goddamned war forever.

PINNY

Chopine stood at the window, watching Ray run until she was a gray smudge on the glass. She couldn't figure her out. Tonight, she'd thrown away the prettiest pair of pale pink shoes Pinny had ever seen! It was the worst kind of wasteful. Good thing Pinny had fished them out of the Dumpster after Ray tossed them and ran. Ray never quit looking over her shoulder, like she was afraid her shadow was out to get her. Pinny herself liked her own shadow, 'cause wherever she went, it was there, keeping her company. A shadow was a fine way to fight a case of the Lonelies. When she saw Ray next, she was gonna make sure to tell her that. But right now, she needed to hurry.

She heaved the stubborn window up until there was space, then punched through the screen. She sucked in her bottom lip, shaking her head at the tear she'd made. Her backpack got stuck on the first try, but she finally squeezed through the hole, landing smack-dab on Mrs. Danvers's favorite magnolia bush.

"Sorry," she whispered, trying to lift its snapped branches back into place. They fell down again. She glared at the branches. "Well, I can't help you much if *you* don't make some effort." That was what Ms. Terp, her crabby special-ed teacher, always said to her, and she figured the bush might need to hear it, too. For encouragement. Course, the words had never worked much for her, and they didn't for the bush either.

She left it flattened under the window, then checked her backpack to make sure everything inside was all right. Sure enough, Mama's story, the pocket watch, the newspaper clipping, and the pretty pale pink shoes were just peachy. So were her camera and her stack of photos. So were her jelly beans. She popped a few into her mouth, sucking their sugar coating off while she walked toward the woods. Once they were smooth and slippery on her tongue, she bit into their gummy insides. She tried to enjoy them, but it was tough when she was worrying over Mrs. Danvers and her magnolia bush.

Oh, Mrs. Danvers's face would radish up when she saw it in the morning! And when she found out Pinny was gone ... oooh boy! She was likely to mumble that word that Pinny could never quite make out but sounded a little like "fudge." Pinny was already sorry for it. She didn't want Mrs. Danvers sore at her, or at Ray, for what they'd done. Course, Mrs. Danvers might understand if she knew why. It wasn't only about Mama's shoes. The itch in her head had been stuck there longer than a while. Since the fall, since Careena and dance-team tryouts. It got way itchier every time she had her Life Plan meetings. In the meetings, everyone else talked. Mrs. Danvers, Ms. Terp, Mr. Sands. But not her. When she tried, Mr. Sands said, "What? What? What?" Like he couldn't hear a word. Funny. He never said "What?" to Mrs. Danvers or Ms. Terp. Mrs. Danvers was nice, though. Maybe, someday, Pinny would be able to tell her about the itch. But not now. Not when she had someplace to be.

She walked faster, glad for the moon lighting her way, and while she walked, her red Mary Janes slapped against her chest. She smiled at the sound, like a heartbeat on the outside of her body, and stroked the cool, glossy toes of the shoes. Touching them made her remember the day she got them. She was eight years old, and the very first day she wore them was the very last day she saw her mama.

It was on that day her mama got lost at Grand Central Station while Pinny was wearing her new pair of shoes.

"Pick whichever ones you want," her mama said when they walked into the Payless on Thirty-Ninth and Second Avenue. "Every girl needs at least one pair of shoes that makes her feel like a princess. So go to it, girl."

Pinny smiled, pushed her glasses, which were forever sliding down her nose, up higher, and walked down the aisle of children's shoes. There were shoes in every color of the rainbow. Some had funny holes for her toes to peek through. Others had shiny buckles and sparkly bows. Some even had heels.

"None of them are as pretty as yours, Mama," she said, sitting down in the aisle to run her hand along the shiny straps of her mama's stilettos. Audition days like today were Pinny's favorites because that's when Mama wore her silver shoes.

"Thanks, sweetness." She kissed Pinny's forehead. "But I can't part with my lucky shoes. I need their magic. Remember the story?"

"I remember. They used to belong to the invisible princess. Then you found them." She loved the story because Mama liked to tell it when she was Sunny-Side Up. Like those eggs she served at the diner. When Mama was Sunny-Side Up, her smile never quit, and she had lightbulb laughs that lit her face from the inside out. Even when Pinny's brain muddied trying to figure out other things, she never forgot Mama's story.

"Exactly," Mama said. "I found them, so these are *my* signature shoes." She bent forward and whispered, "If I ever lost them, you know what would happen."

Pinny gulped. It was the one part of the story that scared her. "You'd disappear."

"Right. Taking them off before my audition would bring the worst kind of bad luck. And today my luck is changing for the better. I can feel it."

The corners of Mama's smile shook, like they did sometimes right before she started crying. Pinny hoped she wouldn't cry. When Mama cried, she couldn't stop.

Mama knelt in front of her. "I know I've had a lot of the Glooms lately. They make you worry, don't they?"

"Yes," Pinny whispered. She hated the Glooms. When Mama was Sunny-Side Up, she got out of bed. She went to her job at the diner. She made peanut butter and jelly sandwiches that they ate with their legs dangling over the roof of their building while they watched the sunset. But when the Glooms came, Mama stayed in bed for days, drowning in tears. She forgot about her job. She forgot about food. She forgot about Pinny. The only thing Pinny could do during the Glooms was wait. She waited, and peeled paint in curly strips from the walls of the room they shared with Hodge and Viv. She waited, and watched Viv cook her baked beans on the thing they called a hot plate. She waited, and helped Viv wash Mama in the bathtub that spit out orange water like Fanta soda.

"Today, I'm going to fix the Glooms for good," Mama said. "So you won't have to worry anymore."

Pinny smiled. "Then you'll be happy?"

"Forever," she whispered in a trembly voice. She looked past Pinny to the rows of the shoes. "Now, what you need are shoes that make a declaration. That announce who you are when you walk into a room."

"I know who I am already." She giggled. "I'm Chopine."

Mama rolled her eyes. "Not your name, silly. The essence of *you*."

Pinny didn't know what that meant, but she didn't say so. Mama didn't like explaining things over and over again. Pinny tried her hardest to understand. But some words knocked around in her head without a meaning ever sticking to them. The best she could figure at the time, "essence" meant some sort of color. She wondered, *Can people be a color inside themselves? Is there a color for who I am?*

Suddenly, she saw the shoes—shiny red shoes with little silver buckles at their sides—and the answer came to her. Her color was red. The color of the Crimson Nights nail polish that

Mama had painted on both their fingers and toes so they would match. The color of the 24/7 PIZZA! sign outside their smudgy brown window that sent flashing light across the ripped couch she slept on every night. The color of the cherry Kool-Aid her mama gave her on summer Sunny-Side Up nights when they sat on the fire escape. The Kool-Aid she sipped through her swirly straw while Mama recited lines for her auditions.

"Those." Pinny grabbed the shoes from the shelf.

"Red patent-leather Mary Janes." Mama smiled. "Perfect for you. Give them a try."

Pinny pulled off her holey sneakers, but her fingers tripped over the buckles of the red shoes. Her mama slid them onto her feet, then snapped her fingers up over her head.

"They're the ones," she said. "No question about it."

Pinny laughed, rocking on her feet under the store lights so the shoes gleamed. She'd never had anything so pretty before.

Mama glanced at the wrinkly man behind the sales counter. "I'm going to have that nice man help me try on some shoes. When he walks back here to me, you go see how those beautiful ruby-reds look outside. I'll be right behind you."

"Okay," Pinny said.

She stepped into the sunshine of the humming city, shuffling her shoes along the sidewalk. They made a bright clicking sound, like popcorn popping. She loved it.

A minute later, Mama came out of the store. "We have to hurry," she said, pulling her so fast down the sidewalk that Pinny had to run to keep up.

"Hey, bring those shoes back!" a man hollered. Pinny looked back to see the salesman from the shoe store chasing them. Then he bent over, cheeks ballooning. "I'll call the cops!" But he sounded too tired to mean it.

Mama finally let her slow down when they rounded the corner of Forty-First.

"Did you forget your money again?" Pinny asked quietly. Lately, Mama'd been forgetting it all the time, and Pinny sure didn't like getting yelled at in stores.

"Don't you worry." She lit a cigarette and streamed smoke in a line toward the sky. "I'll remember it next time and we'll pay him double." She winked at Pinny, squeezing her hand. "Now let's go somewhere you can show off your shoes."

"Home?" Pinny said hopefully. It had been days since they'd been home. It had been fun at first, sleeping under the trees in Central Park. Mama called it camping. But Pinny was starting to miss her couch. It was a lot softer than dirt.

Mama sighed. "No, baby, we can't. The police won't let us into the building, remember?"

" 'Cause we're condemned," she said, remembering the word Mama had used.

"Not us." Mama's voice was pancake flat. "The building."

"Maybe it needs a doctor," Pinny said. "A doctor could make it better."

Mama grinned. "There's an idea! I'll call one right after my audition."

"Good," Pinny said. That would fix everything, and Mama would be happy. And when Mama was happy, Pinny was happy. They walked a few more blocks, and Pinny smiled, listening to her shoes poppity-popping. Then they stepped through glass doors and into Grand Central.

As they walked through the train station, her heart went wibbly. There were so many people walking so fast. Some even ran. None of them stopped, not even for a second. She wanted to go where they were going. Because wherever it was, she was sure it was special. Why else would they be in such a hurry to get there?

"Let's sit." Mama led her to a wide stairway in the large, open room, the only place there was to sit. "I'll leave for my audition in a few minutes. But you're going to stay right here. Nice and comfy?"

Pinny nodded and scooted herself onto a stair, then smiled down at her shoes. They hugged her feet and made them itch to move. It was a yum feeling.

Mama slipped an arm around her, and Pinny tucked her head into that soft place under her mama's chin that still smelled greeny fresh from the grass they'd slept on.

"You hang on tight to those shoes, sweetness," Mama whispered. "Whenever you look at them, you think of me."

"Okay."

"And you never forget your beautiful name," Mama said. "Chopine." She said it in that special singsong way Pinny loved. She tilted her head upward and threw her arms up above her head, like Pinny had seen ladies do on TV when they were onstage. She smiled. "You were named after one of the greatest shoes in history. It was a shoe made for courtesans in Venice."

"Curdly sands?" Pinny tried to repeat the word.

"Close enough." Mama laughed. "Your daddy chose that name for you. He didn't realize it, but he did. Shakespeare and your daddy. They both understood that shoes can write poetry. Always remember that."

"Yes, Mama."

Mama stood, dabbed at her eyes with her fingertip, then smiled. "I better go before I miss my chance. If anyone comes up to you, you give them this." She handed her a folded paper from her purse. "They'll know what to do."

Pinny opened it, but she couldn't make any sense of Mama's curvy writing. That was long before she ever learned how to read.

"Wish me luck?"

"Luck!" Pinny grinned.

Mama pecked her on the forehead and walked down the hallway, then disappeared through the glass doors into the sunlight.

Pinny waited. She didn't remember Mama saying when she'd be back, but then, her mind sometimes turned fuzzy over things like that.

While she waited, she tapped her shoes together so the light on their toes jumped cheerfully. When she wondered where the light was coming from, she looked up and saw the sky overhead. Only this sky was different from the one outside—this sky was Tiffany blue with stars all over it. Back then, before she'd come to Texas, she'd never seen stars in the teeny city sky outside. Not ever. And suddenly she knew why. Because they'd been in here this whole time, hiding in this train station! She looked closer and saw that the stars made pretty pictures. There was a horse with wings, some fish, even a big fat cow. She stared up at the sky for a long time, until the windows underneath it went from blazing white to black.

By then, her tummy was rumbling. She remembered thinking that Mama must have had to walk a long way for her audition. When her neck got tired from all the looking up, she watched people walking by. There were more of them, with their heads bent low. Why were they all staring so hard at the ground? The sky over their heads was so much nicer to look at. But none of them looked up. None of them noticed her, either.

Soon, most of the people were gone, and the station grew quiet. That was when the man dressed in black sat down beside her. When she saw the shiny badge on his shirt, her face got hot. Mama always stayed far away from the men with badges.

"You've been sitting here alone for an awful long time," the man said. "Where are your mom and dad?"

"Mama went to an audition," she said. "But I think she got lost."

The man nodded. He had a nice smile. "It's two in the morning. How many hours have you been waiting?"

Pinny shrugged.

"Do you remember where you live?" he asked.

"The dead-end building with the red lights," she said. No, that wasn't right. Not *dead-end*. *Con-con*-something. "A doctor's going to fix it." She hoped that part might be helpful.

"Can you tell me your mother's name?"

She nodded proudly. Of course she could. She never got confused about that. "Mama."

Then she remembered the note. She held it out to the man. He read it quickly, then sighed.

"What does it say?" she asked.

He smiled, but his eyes looked sad. "It says that your mama loves you. And you're right, she must have gotten lost. We'll have to see if we can find her." He stood up. "Okay, sweetheart, have you ever ridden in a police car before?"

"No."

"Would you like to? I'll turn on the flashing lights." He leaned toward her then and whispered, "We only turn those on for very special little girls like you."

"Okay." She hopped off the stairs and slipped her hand into his.

As they walked away, she looked down at her red shoes shining under the magic inside-starlight, thought of her mama, and smiled. It wasn't until later that the Lonelies started up something awful. She kept telling the men at the police station that Mama would come back. She never did.

But now Pinny smiled again, and hugged her red Mary Janes to her chest, walking faster through the night after Ray. She'd waited thirteen years for another chance to find Mama. Tonight, it had finally come.

June 1940
New York, New York

DALYA

Dalya took a deep breath and licked her lips, tasting briny salt. After nearly ten days on the SS *Liberty,* she was finally able to leave her bunk for the deck. The water stretched unbroken to the horizon, and she had the disorienting sensation that if they kept on, they'd sail straight into the heavens. She gripped the rails tighter, feeling their reassuring hardness grounding her to the deck, and fought through a wave of nausea.

"There you are!" a cheerful voice said in German, and she turned to see her bunkmate, Ruth Schwarz, walking toward her.

Ruth smiled, and Dalya was struck by how foreign a smile looked to her now; it seemed like lifetimes since she'd seen one. She'd been introduced briefly to Ruth on the day their boat had left Lisbon, Portugal, and she'd been glad that Ruth spoke German, when so many of the others she'd ridden with on the trains had spoken Polish or Czech. As their ship pulled out of port, Ruth had been chattering enthusiastically, telling her about her family's hurried trip from Munich to France, and how her parents had to stay behind in France to wait for visas. When Ruth had asked about Dalya's family, she had managed to mumble that they, too, stayed behind in Germany. Her voice broke after that, and luckily, Ruth hadn't pushed her with more questions. Instead, Ruth had rambled on about her plans for when the ship docked in America. Thankfully, all Dalya had to do was listen and nod. But from their second day at sea on, they'd hit storms, and seasickness had taken the burden of talking from her.

"I didn't think you were ever going to leave our bunk," Ruth said now. "I stopped throwing up days ago." She frowned. "It's a shame. We're docking later this morning, and you haven't even seen the ship yet. There was a dance yesterday, and we had a table-tennis tournament. You missed all the fun."

"I'm sorry," Dalya said helplessly. She was sure that wasn't the right response to give, but it was the only one she could manage. She felt more relief than disappointment over what she'd missed. There were several dozen children on the boat that were fleeing Europe, like she was. A few were as young as five and six, close to Inge's age, but there were some as old as fourteen and fifteen. Some of the younger children cried and clung to the chaperones constantly, and Dalya wondered if they'd seen the same horrors she had. There were plenty, though, who were happy to be on board and busied themselves with the ship's daily activities. Even though she was invited to every activity, she was older than any of them—ages older, it seemed. If Inge or David had been here, she might have taken part for their sakes. But the games, the dancing . . . it was a distant world, a world she didn't belong to anymore. She wasn't sure she'd ever be able to go back to it again.

"Your hair's gotten a little longer since we left," Ruth said. "It's starting to look prettier."

"Thank you," she said politely, trying not to give in to agitation. The comment felt callous, but Dalya reminded herself that that was unfair. Ruth didn't know anything about why Dalya's hair was shorn. No one knew, except Leonard Goodman and the doctor who'd tended to her in secret while she'd wrestled with illness for weeks in the Goodmans' home. She brushed her fingers through the curls at the nape of her neck. Her hair looked boyish, and she was still getting used to the weight of it against her scalp. But she didn't fuss over it the way she had before Sachsenhausen. Vanity, after what she'd experienced, seemed like a waste of time.

"So, who are you staying with when we get to New York?" Ruth asked. "Are they friends of your parents, or family?"

"No. Their name is Ashbury." The name tripped her tongue. "I've never met them."

"I've never met the family I'm staying with, either," Ruth said. "German-Jewish Children's Aid found them for me. Esther and Herb Blumberg. I think they have a daughter my age, too. They're getting an allowance to care for me until my parents come." She smiled. "I'll give you their address before we get off the boat. That way, we can stay in touch. Maybe we'll be able to see each other once we're settled."

"I'd like that," Dalya said, and realized, with some surprise, that she meant it. Ruth's cheeriness was energizing, and it would be a comfort to have at least one familiar face in a country of strangers.

"I'm sure I won't be with the Blumbergs for long, though," Ruth continued. She looked out at the cresting waves. "I just received a letter from Muti. She hopes they'll be here in a few weeks."

"That would be nice," Dalya forced herself to say through the pinching pain in her heart. She knew she should feel grateful to be on this boat, alive, with an American visa. She'd wondered so many times about Aaron. If he was still at Sachsenhausen, if he was still . . . alive. He'd saved her, but she'd probably never have the chance to thank him. He was a presence she'd always tolerated more out of politeness than pleasure, but now, strangely, she found herself missing him. Not only because of what he'd done for her family, but because he'd been a quiet constant in her old life, and probably a better friend than she'd ever deserved. Looking back, she realized that maybe she'd enjoyed his admiration as much as she'd been exasperated by it, and the realization stung her repeatedly. She hoped—oh, how she hoped!—he was alive. But she knew, also, that was nearly impossible.

Herr Goodman had told her it was a miracle that she'd gotten out herself, and then that her visa had been approved. When she'd been well enough, he had told her the story of how he received word of her family's arrest, how he went to her father's shop the next morning, to find it gutted and burned. He managed to save a few things: one of her father's lasts for making shoes and some of his tools. These she carried with her onto the ship in her one sparse satchel. After the night they were taken, Herr Goodman tried for months, in vain, to have Dalya's family released from Sachsenhausen. He turned to his connections in the Gestapo, connections he explained came from help the Quakers had given Germany during a war before she'd even been born. He tried to explain that her family's internment at Sachsenhausen was a mistake, that it was a place for men who were political prisoners, not women and children. His arguments and attempts failed, and he suspected she'd been taken there, along with the other women and children, as some sort of ghastly camp experiment.

But then came the night when Dalya was delivered to him, barely breathing, in her coffin. She spent weeks verging on death, but Herr Goodman kept her from it time and time again. He told her the visa he'd acquired for her after her family's arrest had long since expired. They'd have to lie and say it was still valid if she was to have any chance of getting out. To complicate matters, she was seventeen, too old to be considered by any of the Jewish-American relief organizations offering aid to refugees. Not that she understood the reasons behind that, or behind any of the other bureaucratic barricades that Herr Goodman tried to explain. The United States had limits on how many refugees it allowed onto its shores. It even had rules about their ages, and where they were coming from. None of it made any sense.

But then her visa was honored, thanks to a family called the Ashburys from New York City, who were privately sponsoring her. She guessed that meant they paid a great deal of money to convince the Gestapo to let her out of the country.

She didn't understand how it had happened, but Herr Goodman said she didn't have to.

"They're not Jewish," he told her, "but they're willing to take you in at your age, which is rare. We can be thankful for that."

Still, she couldn't help wondering why a family she'd never met, a family who had no clear ties to her faith or to her, would want her.

Now, as she listened to Ruth ramble about everything she had on her list to do once she reached New York, Dalya felt only the dullest interest. Her mind was too full of regret that while Ruth could dream of the day her parents would join her, she would forever be without her family. Without anyone.

One of the older boys was the first to see her.

"There she is!" He leaned over the railing, pointing. Shouts and laughter echoed around the deck as everyone crammed the railings to get a better look.

Dalya tried to dampen the thrill that rose inside her when she saw the graceful lady wielding her torch, but it was impossible. The Statue of Liberty had never been something she'd expected, or even desired, to see until this very moment. But she was glorious as she stood in the harbor, outlined by the sprawling city that glimmered silver in the late-afternoon sunlight.

"Have you ever seen anything so spectacular?" Ruth asked, gripping Dalya's arm.

"No," she said. But it was only the beginning. The buildings that, from a distance, seemed to brush the sky became towering giants once the ship docked in the harbor. Dalya couldn't stop looking up, and when the chaperones brought her, along with the other refugees, into the ballroom of the ship for final paperwork and examinations by an immigration doctor, she found herself impatient to see the fantastic skyline again.

Finally, with her satchel and coat in her arms, she was allowed to disembark just as the sun was setting. Some children moving down the gangplank waved enthusiastically to relatives and friends in the docking area below. They rushed forward while others hesitated, scanning the crowd, not sure who they were looking for.

Dalya stepped off the gangplank, swaying unsteadily as her feet adjusted to solid ground. Soon, she spotted a man with skin darker than any she'd ever seen before, holding up a sign with her name on it. She swallowed thickly, straightened her shoulders, and stepped forward.

"I am Dalya Amschel," she said in German. From the man's blank look, she realized he hadn't understood her. She pointed to the sign and then to herself.

"Miss Amschel?" the man said, and she nodded. Together, they waded through the throngs of people hugging, laughing, crying. Ruth called out to her from the crowd, waving good-bye as she walked with a friendly-looking couple toward a cab.

"I'll see you soon!" she said.

Dalya nodded and waved. She followed the man as they quickly made their way through customs and then to a black car waiting amid a slew of yellow taxis. The man held the door open for her, and she took a deep breath and climbed in.

A beautiful woman was sitting across from her, her blond hair pulled into a sleek knot at the base of her neck. She smiled, extending a hand in greeting, but Dalya didn't miss the way the woman's jade eyes widened at her appearance. Her face composed itself almost immediately, but the instant was enough to make Dalya flush in embarrassment. Even though her cheeks had softened since she'd left Sachsenhausen, the gray shadows under her eyes hadn't completely faded, and her still-meager figure swam in her dress. She couldn't stand being pitied, though, and was relieved, when she looked back into those eyes, to see kindness instead.

"Hello, I'm Katherine Ashbury." Her voice had a satin command, and Dalya guessed she was used to being obeyed. The woman kept talking, and Dalya could tell by the slight turns at the end of phrases that she was asking questions, but the words were foreign.

Dalya shook her head, hoping to show that she didn't understand without being offensive. "No English," she said falteringly, but that was all she could manage in this alien tongue. Mrs. Ashbury (as that was how she supposed the woman would be addressed by American standards) stopped talking, looking surprised and disappointed. Then she patted Dalya's shoulder and let her sit in silence for the rest of the ride.

Dalya turned toward the window, grateful to escape questions. Soon, she lost herself in the scenes streaking by the glass. She'd been accustomed to the bustle of Berlin, but it was sluggish compared to the frenzied pace of New York. People hurried by, pushing against each other, the sidewalks, and the streets until the city itself seemed to bulge. Horns blaring, subways rumbling, music wailing, people shouting—all combined into a manic roar that Dalya could hear even above the car's motor. Flowers and fresh produce were piled into vibrant peaks under grocers' awnings, sidewalk cafés teemed with diners, and men in suits scurried about with briefcases. Dalya vaguely remembered hearing of Times Square once in chitchat at school, but nothing had prepared her for the effervescent lights pouring from every street corner, window, and billboard. She stared, awestruck, at a giant electric sign for something called Wrigley's that was full of glowing fish blowing bubbles. Everywhere she looked was dizzying energy, but instead of exciting her, it gave her the helpless sensation of being frozen in other people's spinning, ceaseless lives.

Gradually, though, the streets became less crowded as the tall business buildings were left behind for smaller, more stately homes with curtained windows and gracefully sculpted fronts. Her panic subsided. These streets reminded her of some of the finer ones in Berlin, at least the way she remembered it. She saw women pushing baby carriages and an elderly man walking a dog, and she guessed they were driving into some kind of residential neighborhood.

Finally, the car stopped in front of a cream-colored three-story stone house. The driver helped them out, then held the ornate door open for them before disappearing inside with Dalya's satchel and coat.

Dalya stepped into a marble-floored foyer with a sparkling chandelier and richly carpeted staircase. Branching off from the foyer were, on one side, a dining room with perfectly placed china and crystal wineglasses and, on the other, a wood-paneled parlor with shelves overflowing with books.

Dalya couldn't stop staring. It didn't seem possible that she would be living in such a place. Even the air here seemed to shimmer grandly. How could so much excess and beauty exist in one part of the world, while in another, war was destroying everything?

Mrs. Ashbury beckoned Dalya into the dining room and gestured toward the plates, probably meaning that dinner could be made for her, if she was hungry. Dalya shook her head. She was hungry, but the idea of being scrutinized through an entire meal without being able to make herself understood . . . it was too much. What she wanted was a place to steal herself away from this strange new world, at least for the night.

Luckily, her face must have given her away, because Mrs. Ashbury led her out of the dining room and up the stairs to a second-floor bedroom. Dalya walked into the room to find her satchel sitting at the foot of a four-poster bed. A lovely midnight-blue day dress was draped across the satin bedspread. Mrs. Ashbury held the dress under Dalya's chin, and Dalya blushed, realizing it must be for her. She touched the fine fabric tentatively and said "Thank you" in German, hoping Mrs. Ashbury might understand.

Mrs. Ashbury smiled, said something in a reassuring tone, and left the room.

Once the door was shut, Dalya let out the breath she'd been holding, sinking onto the bench at the foot of the bed. The luxurious bed and furnishings, the plush carpet—none of it seemed real, let alone meant for her. A vision of her humble apartment back in Berlin filled her mind, and longing filled her heart. Here was her body, safe on American soil, but every other part of the person she'd been before—her laugh, her smile, her dreams—had been lost along the way. Who would she become now, without a family or a country, and with a faith that half the world seemed to despise? She didn't even have the right language.

Tears threatened her eyes, but she held them back. She didn't want anyone in the house to hear her crying and think she was ungrateful. Instead, she turned toward the window for a glance at this city that was her new home.

There, perched on the window ledge outside, was a small blue book with a large, round yellow fruit sitting on top of it. Dalya carefully opened the window and brought the book and the fruit inside. The book, much to her relief, was a German-English dictionary. Inside was a note written in German that read: *Welcome to America. Enjoy the grapefruit. Your ally, Henry.*

Dalya smiled. Who was Henry? If Mrs. Ashbury had mentioned him already, Dalya hadn't heard, or understood. But she was so relieved to see the note scrawled in her native language that she felt an affinity for him already.

She ran her hand over the fruit's bumpy rind, and as she did, her stomach whined. She'd never seen or heard of a grapefruit before, and her curiosity (and hunger) was getting the best of her. She peeled off the skin, pulled a section from the fruit, and bit into the rosy pulp. Juice squirted across her cheek and dribbled down her chin as tangy sweetness filled her mouth. It was a flavor unlike any other she'd ever experienced, like rays of sunshine on her tongue. It tasted of newness and promise, and it brought inklings of a smile to her face. The smile didn't break the surface, but even its beginning was enough for now.

• • •

She woke nervously, feeling like a trespasser. The pillows, the satin bedding, the hum of traffic outside, all of it was disorienting. She moved about her room cautiously, afraid to touch anything. She washed quickly in the private bathroom adjoining her room, slipped into her new blue dress, and made her way downstairs.

The house was so quiet that, for a minute, she thought she was alone, and relief swept through her. But then she heard distant splashing and echoing voices. She traced the sounds to an open door at the back of the kitchen that seemed to lead to a basement. Slowly, she made her way down the stairs, and as she did, the air became moist. The white-tiled room she stepped into held a large metal tub filled with steaming water. A woman in a crisp white dress busily adjusted knobs on the side of the tub while a young man, about Dalya's age, sat in the middle of the bubbling water. He was staring at her so openly that she immediately blushed, then hoped he wouldn't notice. But he did, and it made him smile.

"So, you're Mother's new cause," he said in flawless German. "I'm so glad you've finally arrived. Now she'll have a hobby besides me."

"I'm not sure what you mean," she said, trying to avoid looking at his broad, bare chest. He was wearing a bathing suit, but even so, she had never seen so much of any young man before. "My name is Dalya Amschel."

"Henry." He raised a hand in greeting. His steely blue eyes glinted with playfulness, but there was fierceness in them, too, and she wondered why. "Did you like the welcome gift I left you?"

"Yes, thank you," she said. "You speak German very well."

He laughed in a hard way that made him seem much older than he looked. "That's one of the few things I do well. My father wanted me to learn it, along with French, although I don't know why. The only language he understands is money." He leaned forward. "You don't speak any English?"

Dalya shook her head.

"That's really going to muddle Mother's plans," he said, looking pleased. "I'll find her frustration entertaining, but I doubt you will, so that means we have our work cut out for us. If I'm going to help you with English, we'll have to practice in between my water therapy and my tutoring sessions. Oh, and your school schedule."

"School?" Dalya repeated doubtfully. The word belonged to someone else's life, someone who hadn't left childhood behind a barbed-wire fence.

"You didn't think you'd escape it, did you?" Henry grinned. "Mother's at her churchwoman's meeting this morning, but she's planned the rest of your day after that, so prepare yourself. Clothes shopping, and then over to Dalton to register for school." He must have seen shades of panic cross her face, because he added, "Don't worry. You don't start until August, so that gives us plenty of time to improve on your English."

Dalya's stomach screwed up tight. "But I can't pay . . . ," she began.

"It's taken care of," Henry said casually. "You might not see Father around much, but he knows Mother's philanthropic projects are good for the family name. He's made sure she has a hefty allowance for you."

Embarrassment stirred inside her, and she clenched her fists.

"I don't need anyone's charity," she said. "I can make my own way."

Henry's eyebrows arched in surprise. "I'm sure you can, but I bet you'll discover that their way is easier. I did."

The woman in the white uniform brought a towel over to the tub, and Henry propped himself up on his arms and slid backward until he was resting on a submerged ramp. His legs didn't move with the rest of his body. They seemed stiff and ungainly, and he had to slide an arm under his thighs to sweep them over the side of the tub to dry off.

"Polio," he said, catching her staring. "Two years ago, and the reason why I have a full-time tutor and part-time nurse." He smirked. "Mother scours the globe for the latest treatments. Like this—a Hubbard tank, it's called." He banged on the metal tank with his fist.

"I'm sorry," Dalya said, hearing the bitterness in his voice.

Henry shrugged, tying a robe over his bathing suit. "Fortunately for my parents, sitting behind a desk is something even someone in a wheelchair can do. So they still have their heir, and I still have my inheritance." He said it so smugly that she wondered what his parents could possibly have done to warrant that much hatred.

The nurse handed him a pair of cagelike metal braces, which he buckled onto his legs. After slipping his forearms into crutches, he took a few halting steps toward her. "I don't know you yet," he said quietly, "but I'm guessing that you've seen much worse than my pathetic situation. Am I right?"

She couldn't answer over the wailing of blood in her ears. But he kept his eyes on her until the burden of the truth contorted her face, giving her away. She knew he saw every-thing she wasn't saying. He could've pressed her. But he glanced away, leaving her to wrestle her features back into composure.

Just then, footsteps sounded at the top of the stairs, and Mrs. Ashbury called for her.

"Have fun shopping," Henry said as Dalya turned to go. "English lessons start tomorrow, four p.m. sharp."

Dalya felt him watching her as she climbed the stairs, and she wondered if he thought her as much of an oddity as she felt. She hoped not. Instead, she hoped that, in him, she'd found a friend. Because in this wilderness of skyscrapers and commo-tion, that was what she needed more than anything.

PART III

And forget not that the earth delights to feel your bare feet and the winds long to play with your hair.

—Kahlil Gibran

BEA

Bea's first memory was of her parents dancing barefoot in the moonlight.

It was past her bedtime, but she heard her mother's laughter outside and slipped from her covers. She peeked over her windowsill to see her father twirling her mother around until her bare feet flew and her hair caught wisps of silver moonglow. Her father bent forward and grazed her neck with his lips, the whisper of a touch.

Bea smiled. Tonight, her father had taken her mother out for their anniversary. "To the ritziest place in town," he'd said. Her mother had put on her best dress and her pale pink shoes—her wedding shoes.

"Your daddy brought these home for me from the other side of the world," her mother had told her as she dressed. "Aren't they beautiful?"

Bea thought they were the most beautiful shoes she'd ever seen. They sat far below in the backyard, two pearly doves nesting in the grass. They seemed to be watching her parents dance, too, and the way they shimmered in the moonlight made Bea think of Cinderella's glass slippers.

"I have a gal who's sweet on me," her father was singing now. "Evie."

"Hush, Robbie," her mother scolded. "You'll wake Beatrice." But she laughed as she said it.

Bea giggled from her perch high above as she watched her father scoop her mother into his arms all over again.

Bea wanted to dance under the stars like that, too. She got off the bed to go downstairs, then stopped. She didn't want to break the spell. So she stayed, and watched.

June 2013
Jaynis, Texas, to Nashville, Tennessee

RAY

When Ray walked into the bus station, the dawning sky held a few remaining stars. Her clothes were damp from running, her feet throbbed, but she hadn't seen any cops, which meant Mrs. Danvers hadn't noticed she was missing . . . yet. Maybe she could actually pull this off. The small waiting room was empty, but she held her breath as she peered into the ticket booth. Jaynis was the sort of town you couldn't crap in without everybody knowing what you ate the day before, and if Mr. Neener was manning the booth this morning, he'd have her back at Smokebush by sunrise. Thankfully, though, the woman in the booth was someone Ray didn't know. She'd probably sell Ray the bus ticket, no questions asked. Still, it'd be best to lie low until right before the bus boarded, just in case.

She slipped into the ladies' room and wet some paper towels

to cool off her face. After grabbing her wallet from her duffel, she counted the money she'd taken from Mrs. Danvers's stash. She'd get as far as she could on the bus, then hitch the rest of the way. She finished counting, then smiled. Two hundred seventy dollars. Enough to make it to Manhattan, with a little left over for food. She could lift a few bucks from someone's wallet, too, and then she might be able to pay for a place to stay once she got to the city, at least until she figured out what to do next. She'd been checking the fares and timetables for months, ever since she got the catalog from Juilliard. It was an escape route—she hadn't been sure she'd ever use it, but it made her feel better to know it was there.

Confident that the next bus would leave in ten minutes, she stepped into one of the stalls. A few seconds later, the ladies' room door wheezed open, and Ray's stomach seized. Her guitar and duffel, with the cash inside, were sitting on the counter by the sink, where she'd left them. If this was anyone who recognized her stuff, she was screwed. Swearing under her breath, she peeked out from under the stall. There they were . . . a pair of pathetically worn purple Keds shedding glitter all over the floor.

"Pinny!" Ray growled, throwing open the stall door. "What the hell?"

Pinny grinned, clutching Ray's duffel and guitar to her chest. "You can't say no now. I have your stuff. I'm not giving it back unless you bring me along."

Ray lunged at Pinny, making a grab for her bag, but when Pinny opened her mouth like she was about to scream, Ray stopped. The last thing she needed was someone bursting in thinking she was assaulting a disabled person.

"Pinny ... *please*," Ray said through clenched teeth. "You can't come. You need to go back to Smokebush. They can take care of you there."

Pinny stomped her foot. "No! They can't. Not anymore. Mrs. Danvers said." She stared at the tile floor. "I heard her talking to Mr. Sands. They can't keep me anymore 'cause I turned twenty-one. I can't go back to school next year. I'll be too old. I'm a problem now. Mr. Sands says the state doesn't pay for problems." She dug the toe of her shoe into a crack, and glitter rained down. "They're getting me a job at Fricasweet's. In the food line." She scowled. "They have bugs in their burgers there."

"They do not," Ray said. Sure, she'd seen cockroaches the size of small cars in Fricasweet's. But that kind of honesty never did anyone much good. "It might not be so bad."

"*You* work there, then," Pinny snapped, then sighed. "Mrs. Danvers said I have to live at Horizons Assist from now on, too. Starting next month."

"I've heard that's a nice place." Ray made her voice optimistic. Horizons Assist was a dumping ground for people who had issues that no one else wanted to deal with. She didn't blame Pinny for not wanting to live there, but what was she supposed to do about it? *Not my problem, not my problem* was a harping chord in her head.

"It smells like bleach. They make you sleep on plastic sheets in case you wet the bed." Pinny wrinkled her nose. "I have Down syndrome. That's all. I *don't* wear diapers."

"Fair enough." Ray laughed. "So tell them you don't want to go."

"I do. All the time. They don't hear me." Pinny glared at

Ray. "They say there's nowhere else to put me. If I stay, I'm stuck."

Ray considered arguing, but there didn't seem to be a point. Mrs. Danvers called Pinny "high functioning," but even so, Pinny had been in high school for the last seven years. She'd get an honorary diploma at graduation, not a real one, and college would never happen for her. Ray had once overheard Mr. Sands comment on how lucky Pinny was that she hadn't been institutionalized after her mother disappeared. The few foster parents that had tried had only taken Pinny for a month or two at most. The physical therapy, speech therapy, and state assessment meetings had been too much of a nuisance. But after Pinny came to Smokebush, Mrs. Danvers handled everything.

It was sort of impressive, Pinny's ability to nail down a truth most people politely denied, and Ray wondered how much Pinny really understood her own life. Of course, there was a lot Pinny didn't get—like Careena Baddour, for one. Careena knew how to put on the warm-and-fuzzy charade, just like her mother. Careena's family owned the Pennypinch, a thrift shop in Jaynis, and had a reputation for being some of the most charitable do-gooders in town. Careena always had sugary smiles ready for all the kids at school, but hardly any were legit. Maybe it was her smiles that had fooled Pinny, or the shoes she wore that Pinny adored. Maybe it was the way Careena looked at people, like each one was important to her in some unique way that didn't have to be spoken out loud. Whatever it was, Careena became Pinny's object of worship, and Careena milked it for all it was worth.

It was while Careena was running for student-body president last fall that she glommed on to Pinny's adoration. Pinny became her most loyal helper during her campaign, handing out VOTE FOR CAREENA buttons and flyers every lunch period for a month straight.

"Who's my best girl?" Careena would say, slipping an arm around Pinny in the hallway.

"I am," Pinny would respond, beaming.

She'd pretty-pleased Pinny into believing they were friends. Ray saw how warped it was right away, but to Careena it was a harmless game of master-servant. To Pinny, though, it was *everything*. Until the day she found out it wasn't.

Ray's gut twisted now as she thought about Pinny and Careena, and the dance-team tryouts. A speaker crackled to life in the ceiling, announcing boarding for the bus to New York City, and Pinny's eyes bored into Ray's.

"I'm like you. Trapped." Pinny walked toward the door. But when Ray hesitated, she turned back. "You're taking me with you. You know you are."

The certainty of her tone made Ray shiver, as if Pinny knew this was part of a debt that Ray needed to pay for all the times she'd stood by and watched, doing nothing.

But it was impossible for Pinny to know that. It was only the guilt scritch-scratching at Ray's brain, the guilt that she thought she'd be escaping. Turns out, it was following her around in a pair of purple Keds.

Ray shoved her duffel under her feet, then folded herself into the window seat, tucking her legs up so they crossed over into the seat next to her. It was a silent signal to Pinny, a DANGER: LIVE WIRE warning. But Pinny either didn't get it or chose to ignore it. She sat down, her marshmallow hip swallowing Ray's toes.

"Watch it!" Ray yanked her feet free.

Pinny shrugged. "Sorry."

Ray frowned, swiveling toward the window to avoid Pinny's persistent, questioning eyes. She was in no mood for socializing when all the cash left in her wallet was a measly thirty bucks. The rest had bought their two bus tickets. Without Pinny butting in, Ray could've gone all the way to New York on that money. As it was, they only had enough to get them to Nashville. Just fifteen minutes in, and her plan was imploding. Typical.

The bus rumbled to life, then pulled away from Jaynis with a fanfare of spewing gravel. Pinny smiled and heaved her backpack into her lap. It bulged unnaturally, crammed with the countless "treasures" Pinny kept inside. She wore it so much that it was basically an extra limb. "Want to play Go Fish?" she asked.

"No," Ray snapped. Shame swept over her and she added, "Maybe later." But that sounded insincere.

"Okay."

Her relief was only temporary, though, because Pinny pulled out her Polaroid instead. Ray groaned inwardly, knowing what was coming. Pinny dipped toward the floor, taking mental inventory of all the shoes in sight. She fixed her stare on a pair of orange espadrilles, worn by a woman two rows back.

"Pinny," Ray started. "I don't think—"

Too late. Pinny was out of her seat.

"Hi," Pinny said to the woman. "Your shoes are so . . . joyful. Can I take their picture? For my Shoe Hall of Fame."

"Uh—um," the bewildered woman stammered. "Sure."

Pinny clicked her camera, then smiled in satisfaction at the developed photo.

"So," she said, whipping out a pen from her pocket. "How did you two meet?"

The woman blinked, then laughed, her bewilderment replaced with delight. "At a flea market in El Paso. It was love at first sight."

In her professional reporting tone, Pinny said, "Tell me all about it."

Ray held her breath, watching the woman's face for the tolerant smile that masked the underlying annoyance, a signal that Ray'd have to bring Pinny back to her seat. She'd seen the same look cross others' faces before, Careena Baddour's in particular. When Pinny wasn't in class at school, she was on her knees in the hallway or the quad, snapping photos of kids' shoes. She might not get algebra, or the periodic table, but Pinny *got* shoes. On any given day, she could rattle off which king outlawed red heels, how many shoes Imelda Marcos owned, and a whole host of other random shoe factoids. Since Ray only had one pair of shoes, she escaped the Pinnyrazzi. The rest of Jaynis? Not so much. Careena, especially, had an enormous collection of shoes that Pinny found irresistible. At first, while Careena's campaign for student-body president was going on, she'd smiled at Pinny's photography as if it were the finest form of flattery. But once she won the election, and

Pinny had served her purpose, Careena's patience with her ran out. Ray'd witnessed it herself one day while she waited outside Principal Tate's office for yet another lecture on ditching.

"Mr. Tate, you *know* how much I like Pinny," Careena had said sweetly to Principal Tate. "And if it were just once in a while, I'd never say anything. But she follows me in the hallways between classes, taking pictures the whole time. Yesterday . . . she followed me into the . . . *girls' bathroom.*" That part was whispered in a tone of perfected embarrassment. "It's just an uncomfortable situation for me. I mean, isn't it sort of about my privacy?"

"Exactly," Mrs. Baddour said, ever ready to come to her daughter's defense. "Of course children like Pinny should have every opportunity to interact with other students. But surely there's a more . . . appropriate way to go about it."

"Right," Careena seconded. "Why can't she take her photos in the nursery?"

Principal Tate cleared his throat, and Ray couldn't resist glancing around the door to see Careena turning crimson under his gaze. "Surely, by 'nursery,' you don't mean Room 305?"

Some of the kids at school referred to the special-ed room as the "nursery," but no one, until Careena, had ever said it aloud in front of the principal. Ray snickered as Careena, the ultimate queen of fakery, sputtered an apology. "No . . . I didn't mean—"

"I hope not," Principal Tate interrupted. "I expect the student-body president to be an example—"

"I am!" Careena blurted. "You know *I* don't think of it that way. But I've heard other kids call it that so much, it sort of . . . slipped out. I'm sorry. . . ."

"I agree with you, Mrs. Baddour," he said curtly. "Pinny's skills should be afforded a better venue. Which is why I'm appointing her to the school newspaper as a staff photographer. We'll print one of her photos in each issue."

Careena walked out of the office wearing a tight but appeasing smile, and Pinny was left alone to take her photos. Though sometimes, outside of school, Pinny's zealous picture taking was still met with testiness. Thankfully, Ms. Orange Espadrilles seemed happy to share her story while Pinny wrote notes at the bottom of the photo.

Ray sat back, relieved to have Pinny occupied with someone else for a change.

She scoured her insides for patience, but finding nothing but frustration, she gave up with a sigh. Sometimes she had moments where she could step outside of her skin and see herself as a stranger might. In those moments, she hated the ugly sarcasm in her voice. She hated her scowl and smoldering eyes.

But this hardened face was her armor. It helped her slip through days unnoticed. Whole weeks, even. Most of the time, it worked. Most of the time, it kept others distant, minding their own business. It was why kids at school said hi to her in the hallways but never invited her to hang out. Why, at Smokebush, Mrs. Danvers had given up insisting she participate in movie marathons and game nights. Everyone felt some degree of fear around her. Except Pinny. If Ray refused a movie, Pinny came knocking with soggy popcorn. When Ray got arrested for shoplifting a skirt, Pinny offered up one of her own. If anything, Ray's moods made Pinny more insistent, like Ray was Pinny's personal improvement project. Ray had banked on Pinny realizing at some point that she was damaged beyond repair. But here Pinny was, trailing her again.

Ray leaned her forehead against the window's cool glass, watching a lemon-haloed sun inch above the pines. She remembered another face she'd had once, a softer, kinder face. She'd discovered it last summer when she met Carter for the first time, and then again when she'd found the pale pink shoes at the Pennypinch. If she tried, *really* tried, she could probably call that face to the surface. She closed her eyes, drifting back to that day last summer when she'd given in to her softer self, when the air had thrummed with cicadas and her lake had rippled with whispers, calling to her to come.

Her lake was nestled half a mile back from Smokebush, surrounded so thickly by pines that when Ray first discovered it, she felt she'd unearthed an ancient, untouched place of enchantment. Looking back on it, maybe she had. Because when she'd slipped off her shoes and dipped her feet into the water, the pain that was always there, sawing her nerves ragged, suddenly left. The water was the balm that drew her to the lake, and she claimed it as hers alone. The lake was Ray's one reason for staying at Smokebush as long as she had. First, because of the lake itself, and then, because the lake was where she could find Carter.

Ray never came to the lake without her guitar. It was the

lake that taught her the music. It took her years to learn it, years of listening, of playing on her guitar what she heard in the water. The water had a rhythm, bubbly eighth notes tripping over rocks and half-note waves shushing the shore. She didn't know the names of the notes, but she understood how to draw them out of her guitar, matching its tones with those of the water, the birds, and the wind.

It was Carter who, last summer, taught her the names of the notes and how to read them on a page of printed music. The first time she saw him, she wasn't sure he was real. She came through the trees, and there he was, in her lake, dipping and spinning like a water sprite, spraying shimmering droplets behind him. His dark hair was slick, his muscles sleek, his skin golden in the sunlight.

He looked young enough, maybe nineteen or twenty. But compared to the gangly, pimple-pocked boys she'd let undress her under the bleachers at school, he was a god. As she watched, he caught sight of her, then smiled broadly, as if he'd been expecting her. Of course he hadn't. He'd thought all along that the lake was his. But that was until the water brought them together. Or at least that was how she used to think about it.

"Who dares trespass on my sacred lake?" he said. She smiled then, too, because his voice had the most perfect pitch she'd ever heard. A voice you'd want lacing your dreams.

"I should ask you the same question," she countered. "This lake has been mine for the last seven years."

He climbed out of the water and shook himself off, then stretched out on a rock with a satisfied yawn. "Well," he said.

"This lake is my cure, so I can't give it up. But maybe we can work something out."

"Your cure?" she repeated, watching the water running off him in rivulets.

He nodded. "My cure. For nightmares, memories, and monotony." He closed his eyes, tilting his face into the sun. Then his eyes flitted to her feet, where the scars shone wormy pink. A question flickered across his features, but he didn't ask it. Instead, his gaze came to rest on her face. "And *your* cure is . . . ?" he finally said.

"Music." She stared furiously at the ground, not understanding why she'd blurted out such a private truth to a complete stranger. But there was an openness about him that made honesty easy, which was a first for her.

"Music," he repeated. He nodded toward the guitar. "Go on, then. Let's hear it."

Ray's heart unhinged. She'd never played in front of anyone, only in the cleaning closet at Smokebush, where no one would hear her. Or out here at the lake, where only the birds and squirrels could laugh. Still, she found herself strumming the strings, compelled to play for him, even through her embarrassment and stumbling fingers.

"Now I *know* we can make a deal." He leapt off his rock and, before she could protest, swooped up her guitar and played a lick that took her breath away, his fingers prancing over the strings. He handed her the guitar with a complacent grin. "You let me swim here. I'll give you free lessons." He held out his hand. "Deal?"

She hesitated. It wasn't that she didn't trust him, or that she didn't want the lessons. She trusted him more than any other person she'd ever met, even though that didn't make any sense. And she wanted the lessons. No, she hesitated only because of how much she already wanted to put her fingers in his. It was frightening, but she shook his hand. She took the exhilarating heat that shot through her and tucked it away for safekeeping so she could call it up in the darkness of her bedroom whenever she wanted to after that, and she wanted to most every night.

"I'm Carter Hennley," he said, sliding his hand out from hers.

"Ray," she said.

"Have a seat." He patted the rock beside him. "Lessons start today."

That was how it began, their summer afternoons by the lake. They always swam first, and then, when they were deliciously cool and tired, the lesson came. They never talked about their lives outside of the music. Their conversations were barre chords, riffs, chicken picking. Although she would've liked him to, he never touched her, except to correct her fingering on the guitar strings. Most guys would've stared at her chest, squeezed tight as it was into her too-small Goodwill bathing suit. Not Carter. She'd never spent time alone with any guy who didn't have his hand up her shirt or down her pants in record time. But the slightest brush of Carter's hand against her fingertips was more electrifying than anything those other guys had ever done to her. Because of that, she wanted to please him, more than she'd ever wanted to please anyone in her life.

She practiced picking until her fingers first bled and then formed happy little calluses she marveled at. Slowly, she learned how to read the notes on a page and turn them into music. For years, she'd plucked blindly at the guitar, composing pieces that never sounded quite right when she played them. Now her fingers memorized positions, gliding through the notes, until she could play all the songs that wove in endless ribbons through her head. When they swamped her head, she could finally free them . . . writing them out onto walls, bathroom stalls, her music notebook, whatever was handy.

"You're more than a natural," Carter told her after the first few weeks. "You're a phenomenon."

"You're full of crap," she answered, elbowing him, but she was secretly delighted, especially when she got up the guts to show him the catalog for Juilliard at the end of the summer.

"You'd have a shot." He looked out over the lake, then added quietly, "I was supposed to go."

"Really?" She stared at him in surprise. "What happened?" It was the first and only time he'd ever mentioned anything about his life, and an uneasiness crept over her, as if they were stumbling into treacherous territory.

He must have sensed it, too, because he shrugged, his smile distant. "Got jinxed by life, that's all."

He let it go at that, and so did she, happy to finish up the days of summer in a mirage of ignorance. It was a mirage, of course, like every happy event in her life had ever been.

A mirage that turned to shit on the first day back to school.

The pain of the horrible thing that had happened came sharp and quick, and the smile from last summer's memories faded.

She winced as she remembered the stricken look on Carter's face at prom last night, so different from the easy grin he'd always had for her before. She sucked in her breath, opened her eyes, and reoriented herself to the rumblings of the bus rolling over the highway. The sun was higher in the sky now, and the landscape had changed. There were fewer pine trees and more open prairies, with tall grasses and wildflowers sprouting alongside the highway. She was about to point out the flowers to Pinny to make up for being such a witch earlier, but then she realized that the seat next to her was still empty. An instant later, her name was called, and she spotted Pinny grinning from across the aisle.

"Did you have a nice nap?" she asked. "We're in a whole new state now. Ethel says it's Arkansas." She gestured toward an elderly woman knitting beside her. "This is my friend Ethel."

Ethel offered Ray a granny-style smile. "Hello, dear."

"Hi," Ray muttered. Great. So Pinny had moved on from orange espadrilles to, let's see, geriatric moccasins. Cripes. How long had she been asleep? Apparently, long enough for Pinny to bond with half the bus. Oh God, if she'd mentioned anything about Smokebush, there'd be a battalion of red flags raised by now.

"I was just asking Pinny about this trip you're on," Ethel said. "She said you're going to New York City! My goodness, but you two are awfully young to be traveling that far alone."

"I'm twenty-one," Pinny piped up. "And Mrs. Danvers always says Ray was born with an old soul. So she might be even older than me!"

Ethel laughed. "I see. And who's Mrs. Danvers?"

Pinny opened her mouth to answer, but Ray jumped in before she had the chance. "She's our teacher," she lied. "We're homeschooled."

"How nice," Ethel said. "So, the two of you are . . ."

"Sisters," Ray finished for her, then immediately regretted it when Pinny beamed.

"I always wanted a sister," she announced.

"And you got your wish," Ethel said. "How lucky." She smiled at Ray. "I'm sure you're a wonderful sister."

Ray managed a weak smile. How could she have forgotten what a literalist Pinny was? She was leading her into a lie that she would never see. Pinny would believe they'd bonded, or whatever, and Ray would officially be bottom-dwelling scum.

"Pinny was showing me the treasures in her backpack," Ethel said. "What an interesting watch."

"The watch is Daddy's," Pinny said. "Mama gave it to me." She rummaged through her backpack. "Oh!" she cried. "I didn't tell you the story of Mama's shoes yet!"

"I'd *love* to hear the story." Ethel smiled so enthusiastically that Ray rolled her eyes. If Pinny saw anything fake about the woman's eagerness, though, she didn't let on. Instead, she smiled as she slid a dozen crumpled, water-stained sheets from her backpack and attempted to flatten them against her knees. Then, in her thick voice, full of deliberate care, she read:

Thousands of sunsets ago, in a Far East kingdom where magic was as commonplace as water, there lived a great sultan and sultana. Their deepest desire was to have a child of their own. Many years of spent wishes and heart-

aches passed, until at last the sultana gave birth to a daughter. But no bells rang out in celebration, no shouts of joy filled the kingdom. Instead, the sultana's mournful cry filled the palace, for the little princess had been born invisible.

The princess was perfect in every other way. She was tenderhearted, always quick with kisses and hugs. She was joyful, laughing so freely and brightly that fairies followed her wherever she went. She was kind, forever caring for orphaned squirrels, sick dogs, and stray cats. But the only time her parents ever saw the faintest trace of her was during storms, when rain made her shimmer like a million glittering stars. Even the princess's kind and gentle ways couldn't ease her parents' worry. For who would ever wish to marry an invisible princess?

As the princess became a young woman, she grew lonely and heartsick. The sultan invited princes from all over the world to woo her. She charmed many with her sweet spirit, but none of the princes would marry her without knowing what she looked like. After all, what if she was ugly or misshapen?

In desperation, the sultana took matters into her own hands. She traveled for years searching, and finally, at the ends of the earth, she found a prince willing to marry the princess. This prince didn't care that the princess was invisible, because this prince himself was blind.

The prince and princess fell in love, and soon they were married. Every evening, the prince kissed the princess and told her she was beautiful. He told her that she had the heart of an angel, the voice of a lark, and laughter sweeter than a bubbling brook. He told her she had hair as soft as a dove's wings, skin as smooth as pearls, and hands as delicate as butterflies. At first, the princess loved his words. But then she started to wonder if she was truly as beautiful as her husband believed. There was only one way to find out. She had to see for herself.

The princess called on every wizard in the kingdom, asking each if he could use his magic to make her visible. Each said it was impossible. The princess grew more and more distraught. She wouldn't eat or sleep. Her songs withered on her lips. Her laughter turned to sneers. The prince begged her to forget her wish, but she would not. And so, the prince himself sought out the most skilled wizard in the world.

The wizard agreed to help. Using moonlight and fairy dust, the wizard made a pair of magic shoes so beautiful they outshone the stars themselves. The moment the princess slipped on the shoes, her feet appeared, pale and slender. Seconds later, the rest of her followed.

She ran to a mirror, gazed upon her reflection, and gasped. She was even more beautiful than she'd ever imagined. Everyone in the kingdom agreed. Men, women, and children showered her with compliments. They told her that her eyes were emerald seas, her hair was ruby flames, her smile a gift from the heavens.

The princess spent days and days listening to people praise her, and days and days staring at her own reflection. She forgot about her dear husband altogether, until he came to her one day, asking her to leave her mirror and her court full of admirers. He missed her deeply.

The princess refused. She grew angry, accusing the prince of being jealous of her admirers because they could see her in a way he could not. Why should he have her all to himself when he couldn't even enjoy her exquisite beauty?

Heartbroken, the prince left the castle that night. By morning, no one knew where he was. At first, the princess was glad to be rid of him. She had plenty of people who loved the way she looked, and that was more than enough to keep her content. But then she grew weary of hearing the same compliments from her admirers day after day. She longed to talk about something other than herself. She wanted to be with someone who loved her, not her eyes, or hair, or smile. She missed her prince.

She scoured the kingdom for him, but found nothing. She searched countries, but found nothing. In despair, she took a flying carpet from the palace and soared into the night, above oceans and continents, to find him. She called his name, over and over, and at last heard his faint answer on the wind. She found him in a far desert, parched from thirst and dying of a broken heart.

She swept her beloved into her arms, begging his forgiveness and vowing never to let vanity consume her again. He smiled and, revived by her love, climbed onto the carpet beside her. As it flew higher and higher, kissing the heavens, the princess slipped her magic shoes from her feet, letting them fall to earth. For a few moments, her

tears of joy made her shimmer like a million glittering
stars. Soon, those dried in the wind, and the prince and
his unseen princess disappeared forever among the clouds.

"The shoes," Pinny finished with a grin, "landed in a trash can on the corner of Forty-Third Street and Ninth Avenue. And that's where Mama found them."

"Oh, I see," Ethel said. "And did your mother keep them?"

Pinny nodded. "Mama said she was invisible once, too. Like the princess. But as soon as she put on the magic shoes, the whole world turned its head in her direction."

Ethel smiled. "What a lovely story."

Ray fought the urge to scoff. There had been a time when she might have believed that sort of love existed. But not anymore. Not ever again.

"The story's true," Pinny said with conviction. "That's why we're going to New York. Mama disappeared because she lost her magic shoes. When I find her shoes, she'll come back."

Ethel's mouth pursed into a pale raisin. "You poor things." She patted Pinny's hand in a churchgoing, charity way that made Ray want to retch. Leaning across the aisle toward Ray, she whispered, "How terrible to lose a mother at your ages."

Ray nearly snapped a correction, then remembered that she was playing the part of Pinny's sister. So, instead, she nodded.

"Don't be sad." Pinny patted Ethel's hand back. "We'll find her again."

Ethel dabbed her eyes with a tissue, then fingered the cross hanging around her neck. She looked as if she was puzzling through their story, and the pieces weren't fitting. "If your mother is . . . lost, then the rest of your family is—"

"Our father's in Nashville," Ray jumped in before Pinny could say something else that might raise suspicions. Ray could easily imagine the pats on the back the old lady would give herself for reporting a pair of missing girls to the local police station. She wasn't any different from Mrs. Danvers and her crew of do-gooders, always talking about the kids at Smokebush, trying to reroute their futures like they were packages that had been shipped to the wrong destination. Those types of people talked about "God's will" a lot, but Ray had learned early on that "God's will" really meant theirs.

"Our father is meeting us at the station," she said to Ethel now, "and then he's driving us to New York from there." She leaned toward the woman conspiratorially and whispered, "It's really a family vacation for us. Pinny just likes to make things sound more exciting."

"Nothing's more exciting than life itself," Pinny said defensively. "Mama said that."

"Well, I'm glad to hear you're not alone in the world," Ethel said. "I'll keep you darlings in my prayers."

"Oh, no need to waste your time." Ray smiled innocently into Ethel's face, which morphed from astonished to offended. "Pinny, how about a game of Go Fish now?"

"Sure!" Pinny waved to Ethel and plunked down next to Ray. "I deal."

Across the aisle, Ethel cleared her throat several times and then, as if to make a point, pulled a pocket Bible out of her bag and began to read.

"You shouldn't have cozied up to her like that," Ray hissed to Pinny. "She could get us caught and sent back to Smokebush."

"She won't," Pinny said. "She wanted company. That's all."

Ray sighed. "People aren't always nice, Pinny."

Pinny paused over this. "I *know* that. But when I guess them right, it's a good surprise." She grinned. "Being sisters is going to be fun," she added as she slapped a card down on her knee.

Ray focused on sorting her cards to avoid Pinny's gaze. *Sisters.* Pinny better not have too many expectations pinned on that word. Because Ray's days of wishing for a family, real or fake, were over. She wasn't going to string Pinny along with false hopes any longer than she had to. Pinny could never take care of herself in a place like Manhattan, and no way was Ray signing on as babysitter. The first chance Ray got, she was going to drop her. The sooner, the better.

DALYA

It was as if she were half a person, as if she were watching a fragment of herself moving through this new life. But in a city where chaos drowned out the chance for too much thought, forgetfulness came easily.

Her first months passed in welcome muteness. Mrs. Ashbury combed the floors of Bergdorf Goodman and Saks, choosing fine dresses and blouses for Dalya while she watched helplessly. Dalya had tried to protest. But because Mrs. Ashbury didn't speak a word of German, Dalya's arguments for simpler, less expensive clothes fell on deaf ears. In the beginning, she felt self-conscious in the fabrics, but then she discovered she could hide in them.

Her thin body slowly grew softer and fuller, and soon she looked as if she belonged in her new clothes, as if she'd always been wearing them. As if her body had never known hunger or illness at all.

At first, the calendar was a raw reminder of what she'd left behind. Each Friday night at sunset, she found herself at dinner with the Ashburys, trying not to think about Shabbos. There were usually candles lit on the table, but there were no blessings, no kiddush, no breaking of the challah bread. A few weeks after her arrival, she'd had Henry ask Mrs. Ashbury for a pair of candles to use privately for Shabbos in her bedroom. Her mother had always lit the candles and said the prayers back in Berlin, but now Dalya would do it alone. Mrs. Ashbury had agreed right away, smiling graciously, but there was also an unease on her face that made Dalya regret asking. Just once had she excused herself from dinner to light the candles and say the prayers in her bedroom. But it felt wrong without her family around her, wrong to assume her mother's place. There'd been a subtle shift in the mood of the Ashburys' house afterward, too, more awkwardness than disapproval. For Dalya, though, it kindled fear. She understood now that being Jewish was dangerous, and she had no more bravery left for it. She wanted acceptance, no matter what its form. So, she tried to be someone safer.

School was another place for pretending. She was thankful her English wasn't any better, because it made her silences in class excusable. No one pushed her with questions, or even tried to make friendly conversation. Aside from the curious stares the first weeks, hardly anyone noticed she was there. She was placed in tenth grade, even though she should've been in eleventh. The teachers decided this was necessary until she learned better English, and to make up for the school she'd missed in Sachsenhausen. It would've been embarrassing for the Dalya of Before. But for the Dalya of After, it wasn't. The very idea of blackboards and chalk, of math problems and essays, seemed ridiculous now. Even more ridiculous was that anyone should expect her to care about these things. She was tossed into a tide of students that eddied and swirled around her. Their words were foreign, but their laughs sounded like her own might have, if she'd still been the Dalya of Before.

School was another joke in a life full of absurdities. But the routines kept her busy, kept the memories from dropping her to her knees. For that, at least, she was grateful.

She was grateful, too, for Henry. Mr. Ashbury owned a financial firm downtown and didn't get home until late at night, and Mrs. Ashbury was often gone for charity meetings and teas at the Plaza. Both of them acknowledged her politely, but neither ever made a great effort to talk to her because of her laborious English. Henry was the only one who understood her, and he became her life preserver, keeping her afloat in the sea of strangeness. He was unpredictable, teasing and playful one day, edgy and critical the next. Sometimes his moods were determined by his pain, and on those days he forged through the lessons with gritted teeth. Sometimes there was no pain, just the bottled rage, threatening to explode at the slightest provocation. His anger was a version of her grief, and when she looked in his eyes, she understood the story behind them.

He'd taught her the rules for the city grid in her first week, and she learned to navigate the streets of their neighborhood quickly. She'd walk the blocks from her school to the Ashburys' home at Seventy-Third and Fifth Avenue to find him waiting impatiently at the dining room table.

"What took you so long?" he'd demand to know. "*I could've walked faster than that.*"

He couldn't walk far, but he usually had the Ashburys' driver, Thomas, and one of the family cars at his disposal. Each day, they went someplace different, like a bench in Central Park or a gallery at the Metropolitan Museum of Art. When she met him for an English lesson, a new piece of the city came along with it.

On the September day she ran into Ruth Schwarz, Henry had taken her to the Lexington Candy Shop for her lesson and her very first egg cream. When she admitted she had no idea what an egg cream was, Henry smiled and immediately ordered two.

"You'll love it," he said.

"Do you love them?" Dalya asked in German. Henry glared at her, and she slowly repeated the question in English.

"I love anything my parents hate, especially this place, and egg creams." Remembering softened his expression. "When I went to Dalton, I came here with my friends after school. But when I got sick, Mother blamed the subways and soda fountains, among other things. She probably would've blamed my friends, too, if it hadn't meant stepping on some of the richest toes in town. Mother's careful never to acquire enemies of influence."

"So why can't you still see your friends?" Dalya asked.

"Oh, I could, if they'd agree to see *me.*" He laughed, but his smile bordered on a sneer. "Funny how polio can turn you into a social pariah overnight."

"Like being Jewish," Dalya blurted, then sat motionless, numbed by what she'd said. Even Henry looked surprised.

"Is that really what it feels like?" he asked.

Dalya stared at the counter. "It did," she said quietly. "In Germany, before ..." She couldn't say the rest, and an instant later, the shop owner brought over their egg creams, saving her from having to explain.

She stared at the foamy brown liquid filling her glass, then frowned when Henry slid a pretzel rod into the middle of it.

"Why'd you do that?" she asked.

"There's only one right way to drink an egg cream," he said. "Take a sip ... then a bite of pretzel." He demonstrated. "Repeat."

She sipped, and creamy chocolate fizzed over her tongue. "Mmmm." She smiled. The pretzel's saltiness made the drink even sweeter. "That *is* good."

She took another sip, then heard her name being called. It was Ruth, arm in arm with another girl and heading directly for her. Dalya shrank into her stool, wishing she could disappear.

"Dalya!" Ruth smiled, but the curl of her lips was slighter now, less enthusiastic than the last time she'd seen her, on the SS *Liberty*. "I've been waiting for you to write me."

Heat prickled her cheeks. "I'm sorry," she said. "I meant to, I just ..." *Couldn't bear it* was the truth. But she couldn't admit that.

"It's all right," Ruth said. "I'm sure you've been as busy as I have." She glanced at Henry, and Dalya introduced them. Ruth introduced the girl she was with as Ann Blumberg, her foster sister, and Dalya noticed Ruth was speaking with some short, halting English phrases now, too. But she often slipped back into German as automatically as Dalya did, and she seemed relieved to realize Henry could understand her either way. "So," Ruth said. "Where are you going to synagogue? We're part of a congregation downtown. Do you have plans for Rosh Hashanah?"

"Well, I—I haven't found a synagogue yet," Dalya stammered, then dropped her eyes in shame when Ruth raised her eyebrows in surprise. "I'm looking, though," she lied.

"You can come to synagogue with us on Rosh Hashanah," Ann volunteered, and Ruth nodded enthusiastically. "You could join us for dinner afterward. My parents won't mind."

Dalya's heart constricted. "Thank you for the invitation." She stumbled over the English words, hoping they sounded polite enough. "Can I let you know in a few days?"

Ruth looked at her quizzically, but Ann nodded kindly. "Of course," Ann said. "My mother loves to have company, so it's no problem at all."

Dalya stared into her egg cream, desperately seeking a change of subject. "How are your parents?" she asked Ruth. "Have they arrived yet?"

Ruth's smile tightened. "I haven't heard from them in over a month, but . . . I'm sure they're fine." Her strained cheerfulness was disquieting. "We got word that they're being held by the French government at Camp de Gurs. It's probably some ridiculous precaution because they're German. I know they'll be released any day."

"I hope so," Dalya said, but doubt trickled into her voice. Ruth must've heard it, too, because panic pinched her face.

"We have to go," she said suddenly, uncomfortably. "We're going to watch *Rebecca* at the Strand." She glanced from Dalya to Henry, then added, "Would you like to come along?"

Dalya hesitated. She hadn't been to a movie here yet, but with the tidbits of English she was finally picking up in conversations, she'd understood from other girls' chitchat at school that they were a wonder to see. She wasn't sure she wanted to get to know Ruth any better, though. It would only lead to more questions, and more invitations she'd have to turn down. "No thank you," Dalya said. "I should work more on my English before I see an American movie. I'll enjoy it better then."

Ruth nodded. "Well, it was wonderful seeing you. Let us know about Rosh Hashanah."

"I will," Dalya said. She wouldn't, though, and she knew Ruth would be relieved.

She waved as Ruth and Ann left the shop, arms linked companionably. But when she turned back to her egg cream, she found Henry studying her.

"You lied," he said simply. "About everything." He leaned closer. "I think you'd be happier if you never saw her again. Why?"

"I don't know." She expected to find judgment in his face, but what she saw was curiosity. "Because . . . I can't do any of it. It's . . . too much."

She closed her eyes. Grief beat against their lids, but the warmth of Henry's fingers closing over her own pulled her back from its abyss.

"You're a lot like me," he said matter-of-factly. "People see us breathing, eating. They think it means we're full of life, like they are. They don't know that on the inside, we're just dried-up souls."

He smiled at their shared secret, but Dalya shuddered, not wanting it to be true. She hated what he saw in her, but she knew it was there, all the same. Still, she liked the firmness of his fingers over hers, the way his eyes sent tremors of heat through her perpetually chilled skin. She realized, too, that a callused heart could still do its job, even if it beat stiffly, poorly. Maybe this was what she was now. This was the Dalya of After.

So she let her hand stay in his as they talked of everything else—the city, his parents, egg creams. He made forgetfulness easier.

That night, she slid her Shabbos candles back into their drawer in the Ashburys' dining room. Then she tucked her father's bag of shoemaking tools into the deepest corner of her bedroom closet, where the shadows would swallow it whole.

The Friday after that, on her walk to school, the Ashburys' car pulled to the curb beside her. Henry peered out of the rolled-down window, his eyes bright with excitement.

"No school for you today." He jerked his head toward the car. "Climb in."

"My classes," she started, but he held up a hand.

"Don't try to tell me that you care."

She wanted to argue that she did, but what was the point? Henry could see right through her, and he, of all people, seemed to understand the joke no one else did. She slid into the backseat to find him grinning mischievously. He looked more his age—the way he should've looked without his anger. She liked it much more than she cared to admit.

"Where are we going?" She eyed him suspiciously. "And what about your tutoring?"

"My brilliant and illustrious tutor thinks I'm at home in bed with a fever," he said, "and we are going somewhere absolutely forbidden. At least, forbidden by my mother, that is. It's a secret."

She peered into the front of the car, where Thomas was driving, his face solemn as usual. "What about Thomas?" she said softly.

Henry leaned toward her, whispering conspiratorially, "Thomas is on our side. You wouldn't know it to look at him, but he's a big believer in renegades."

Dalya smiled. As they passed Dalton, she felt a delicious anticipation, knowing that wherever Henry was taking her had to be better than the solitude she faced among her classmates each day. The car wove through traffic for blocks as it headed away from the New York skyline that had become so familiar over the last few months. The landscape gradually changed to smaller buildings and less congestion, until finally Thomas turned into a grass parking lot full of cars. Before them stretched a sprawling fairground clustered with buildings and amusement-park rides, a large white dome and spire nestled at its center. The smoky scent of roasted peanuts and hot dogs wafted in the air. People's chatter mixed with rumbling motors and music to create a magnetic chaos that made Dalya's pulse sing.

She glanced at Henry as Thomas helped him settle into his

wheelchair. He beamed. "Welcome," he said with a theatrical bow at the waist, "to the World's Fair."

It was something she never could've imagined until it unfolded before her eyes. The theme was "Building the World of Tomorrow," and that's exactly the way the fairground felt, like a dream of the future created for people to taste, touch, and explore.

They wandered through the Town of Tomorrow and around the Lagoon of Nations, then wove their way through the gardens, which even in late September brimmed merrily with flowers. In the RCA building, they saw a demonstration of something called a television, which played a splendid picture on a screen with sounds at the same time. After watching a fashion show at the Special Events Center, Dalya ran her fingers over a pair of stockings made out of some silky material called nylon.

Everything was so astonishing that she didn't know where to look, which exhibit to choose next. She talked eagerly for the first time since she'd arrived, questions bubbling out of her as fast as she could think them. She stumbled over the English words dozens of times, but Henry waited patiently, then corrected her pronunciation and answered her questions with an enthusiasm she'd never seen in him before. His face had a passionate animation so different from the dullness it held when he was hunched over his schoolbooks or eating dinner with his parents. She wondered if this was a glimpse of what he'd been like before the polio.

"Come on," he said, urging Thomas to push him faster and motioning for Dalya to hurry, too. "We have to see everything."

He led them into the Amusement Zone of the fair, right up to the base of the Life Savers Candy Parachute Jump. He lifted himself out of the wheelchair, shrugging off Thomas's help, and walked haltingly toward the entrance to the ride.

"Dalya." He waved her closer. "Ride it with me?"

"Henry." Thomas had hardly spoken over the course of the day, except to marvel at exhibits along with them. Now his voice held a warning.

"I don't want to hear it," Henry snapped, and Thomas sighed, giving up. Henry focused on Dalya. "Are you coming?"

Dalya looked up at the metal tower, taking in a parachute as it rose, pulled by a cable, hundreds of feet into the air. Once at the top, it bulleted down as passengers suspended in their seats shrieked with delight. The Dalya of Before would've thought it looked fun. She might've begged her parents to let her ride it. But these days, fun didn't seem right, or fair, anymore.

"I don't think I should," she said.

A grimace clouded Henry's face, and his eyes were cobalt cyclones. "Not you too." He jabbed a finger at the tower. "This is why Mother never let me come here. Dangerous rides aren't meant for people with my . . . condition." He shook his head, and the sadness in his eyes made her falter. He spoke again, this time with pleading. "Don't you want to remember what it feels like? To be the way you used to be? Just for a few minutes?"

Remember. Remember being normal. Yes, she wanted to remember what it felt like to laugh without guilt, to have nothing to grieve over except some silly homework assignment, to have a ridiculous argument with her mother over a skirt she wanted to wear. She desperately wanted to remember, but she wasn't sure she could.

"Yes." She stepped to his side. "I do."

The cloud on his face disappeared, and his smile came back, but it only lasted until they reached the front of the line.

"Sorry, kids." The ride operator nodded at Henry's braces. "Can't let you on."

It took a few moments for Dalya to mentally translate what he was saying, but by the time she did, Henry was exploding. "Why?" he barked. "I might have an accident? Maybe it would cripple me for life? That would be awful."

"Henry." Heat rose to her cheeks as people stopped to stare at them. Every muscle in Henry's body was clenched. She'd seen him angry, but this was the first time she'd seen him looking dangerous, and it terrified her.

The ride operator held up his hands. "Hey . . ."

"Here." Henry yanked a fold of bills from his pocket. He hurled them in the operator's face. "I'll pay you to let me kill myself."

The man flinched as the bills hit him, but then, seeing how much they were, he mumbled a grudging "Get on."

Henry stormed through the gate, his chest and arms swinging wildly in his effort to move his legs faster. Suddenly, he lost his balance, and Dalya lunged to catch him before he fell.

"I can do it!" He straightened, roughly grabbing her shoulders like he might push her away. She shrank back, and instantly his grip softened. He blinked and breathed, the fury on his face thawing to shame.

"I'm sorry," he said awkwardly. "Thank you."

Her heart was thundering and she could still feel his wiry tension, but she offered him a cautious smile. "It's all right."

They climbed into the seat of their parachute in silence, and it shot rapidly upward.

"You didn't have to be so . . . so rude," she said. "That man didn't do anything to you. It doesn't help to treat people like that."

Henry stared out at the buildings below as they receded into miniature. "I know. I just . . ." He sighed. "I used to be able to run. Run fast. And now I can't get the wrongness of what happened to me out of my head. Sometimes I want other people to feel it, too." There was an icy hardness in his gaze. "Don't you think that way sometimes, about what happened to you?"

"No," she said quickly, shuddering. "I don't ever want anyone to feel what I did."

"Then maybe we *are* different," he said. "More than I thought."

The parachute stopped at the top of the tower, swaying in the cool breeze. Dalya stared out in wonder. Rising into the cloud-flecked horizon, the city gleamed. From here, New York looked like a magnificent tomorrowland of its own. Henry had been right. There was a lovely liberation in being suspended above reality, if only for a moment.

Then the parachute plunged, and even though she hadn't thought it possible, her body reacted the way any other seventeen-year-old's would have. She shrieked with exhilaration, clinging to Henry as her stomach sprang to her throat.

When she opened her eyes, her head was tucked protectively

into the nook of Henry's arm, her face inches from his. His fingers held tightly to her waist, kindling her skin to a blaze. "Sorry," she murmured as the parachute slowed to a lazy drifting. Embarrassed, she pulled herself away.

"Don't be," he said quietly, and she saw something new in his smile, something that made her heart quicken all over again.

They left the fair at dusk, tired but also energized by what they'd seen. She and Henry chatted easily on the ride back, recounting every detail of the day. They were smiling when they walked in to find Mrs. Ashbury waiting in the parlor, frowning.

"What do you think you were doing, disappearing like that?" she snapped. "What if you'd been injured?" Her glare was leveled at Henry, but Dalya immediately stepped forward with apologies. Henry interrupted her.

"It was my fault, Mother," he said. "Dalya didn't want to come along, but I made her. Don't be angry with her."

Mrs. Ashbury's eyes bored into Dalya's in an unspoken reprimand. It was the first sign of disapproval Mrs. Ashbury had ever shown her, and Dalya felt humiliation at disappointing her. How could it have slipped her mind that Mrs. Ashbury might worry about Henry? Especially after all Mrs. Ashbury had done for her.

"Very well, then," Mrs. Ashbury said. "Dalya, please leave us, and close the door on your way out."

Dalya paused in the doorway, not wanting to leave Henry with the brunt of the blame. She glanced at him uncertainly, but he gave her a confident wink and grinned. Dalya nearly laughed from sheer nerves, but after Mrs. Ashbury stiffened, she didn't dare. Instead, she closed the door and instantly heard Mrs. Ashbury's voice grow louder and Henry's rise to match it.

Upstairs, she sank onto her bed, staring at the ceiling. For a few minutes, she relived the day, and it brought a smile to her lips. But as darkness stretched from her window across the floor, fear scuttled into her. Fear that she'd never get out from under her own wrongness, the wrongness she felt over staying alive. Fear that even a day like the one she'd had with Henry couldn't erase.

PART IV

She's a rich girl.
She don't try to hide it.
Diamonds on the soles of her shoes.
—Paul Simon, "Diamonds on the Soles of Her Shoes"

BEA

Bea pulled her legs up into the folds of her bathrobe, turning to stone. She made her toes rigid, then her feet and legs, moving upward until even her eyes were frozen, unblinking. It was all part of Princess Bea's fairy tale, the one her father used to tell her every night before bed. Princess Beatrice was turned into a statue by an evil sorceress. Trapped in a labyrinth with impossibly high walls, Beatrice waited, in her stone body, for a prince to find her and break the spell with his love.

When her father had been alive, they played the game in their tiny backyard in Ohio. Bea made herself still as a statue in the grass, waiting for Prince Daddy to find her, grab her, and tickle her back to life.

But Daddy was gone now, and her new father, Benjamin, didn't play fairy-tale games. He never wanted to rumple his suits and dirty his shoes. So Bea played the game by herself. Their new house in Connecticut was so big, it *was* a labyrinth. The morning they'd moved in, her mother had galloped her through the empty, echoing rooms on piggyback, neighing like a horse and declaring, "What a fine castle for Princess Bea!"

She was trying to play the game, and Bea didn't have the heart to tell her she wasn't anywhere near as good at it as Daddy had been. But when the two of them burst, prancing and laughing, through the doors of Benjamin's study, he'd looked up frowning from his desk.

"This room is for conducting business," he said. "It's off-limits, Bea. Understood?"

Bea glanced at her mother in confusion. Her mother planted a playful peck on Benjamin's cheek. "We were just taking a tour of the kingdom, right, Bea?"

When Benjamin's face didn't soften, her mother dropped her arms from around his waist and ushered Bea quietly out of the room.

"He's too grouchy," Bea blurted when the study door clicked shut.

"Shh." Her mother knelt to her eye level. "We're so lucky to have Benjamin in our lives. Without him, we'd be . . ." She bit her lip, then smiled. "It's only that he hasn't been around children much before." She smoothed Bea's hair from her forehead. "This is a big change for all of us. I'll help you through it, and we'll both help Benjamin. 'Cause we're partners. Princess Bea and her trusty steed. Okay?"

"Okay," Bea said, then giggled as her mother scooped her into a tickling hug.

For months since then, Bea had lost herself in the maze of rooms. It was easy to pretend she was the stone princess here. Just like she was doing tonight, as the jumble of shoes and loud voices invaded her hiding place.

The lace tablecloth dipped down to the floor, giving Bea the perfect unseen refuge underneath.

After her mother had tucked her into bed, Bea had waited until she'd gone to dress for the dinner party, then tiptoed downstairs. Slowly, the dining room had filled with guests, and laughter and the tinkling of china rang in the air.

A pair of lemon-yellow high heels appeared at the edge of the tablecloth now, followed by a pair of blue ones with pink-painted toenails peeking out of the tips.

"This place is incredible. Twenty acres. A driving range, a pool atrium out back," whispered Lemon Shoes. "Evie has quite the catch. It was worth the drive from Ohio to see all this."

"Oh yes," Pink Toes said. "Benjamin's worth millions. Evie certainly found her safety net."

"Well, she deserves it after losing Robbie," Lemon Shoes said. "He was the love of her life."

"I heard that after it happened, Evie wouldn't leave her bed for weeks." Pink Toes was whispering. "Her mother nearly had her committed. And there was the poor little girl, wandering around the house, practically orphaned. But Evie pulled through."

Bea clutched her doll tighter, tears welling up under her eyelids. She remembered the bad time. When her mother had met Benjamin, though, she'd stopped wearing her bathrobe every day. She'd stopped crying, too. And now she was always smiling. But her smiles were plastic like a doll's. They weren't like the smiles she used to give Daddy.

"Well, it was such a tragedy," Lemon said. "A heart attack at thirty-two. It doesn't even seem possible."

Bea's eyes wouldn't stay frozen anymore. Tears streamed down her face, and there was a sob inside her threatening to burst out.

Pink Toes made a tsk-tsk sound. "He fought in the war. Who knows what that could've done to his heart?"

"Bad hearts can run in families," Lemon said. "If I were Evie, I'd have that little girl examined by a doctor right away."

The sob ripped out of Bea's throat, and she brought her doll's head down as hard as she could on Lemon's foot.

Lemon jumped back from the tablecloth in alarm as Bea charged out from underneath, screaming.

"Daddy did *not* have a bad heart!" she cried. "You take it back right now!"

Bea used her doll as a battering ram, swinging at the woman wearing the lemon shoes. The woman's wineglass tipped sideways, and a red fountain sloshed onto the carpet and Bea's pajamas, but she didn't care. The other grown-ups pulled away from her, staring.

A pair of strong hands gripped her shoulders, holding her down.

"That is *enough,* young lady." Benjamin's stern face loomed over her, and then her mother's appeared next to it.

"Beatrice, what on earth?" Concern creased her mother's forehead. "Why aren't you in bed?"

Her mother reached for her, arms extending into a hug. But Benjamin whispered, "Get her out of here, Evelyn. She's causing a scene."

The arms froze halfway to Bea, then shrank back. The concern was rewritten as anger and embarrassment. "Of course, Benjamin," her mother said. "Right away."

Bea was crying so hard that the faces around her turned watercolory. Her mother shuffled her out of the room, making apologies to her guests. "Please excuse her. She's not feeling well today."

Once they were back in Bea's room, her mother stood over her, frowning.

"That exhibition was embarrassing," she said briskly. "I won't tolerate such unladylike behavior. Benjamin has important business partners here tonight."

"I wanted to see the party," Bea started. "Everyone was dressed so fancy and—"

"What are you wearing on your feet?" her mother whispered, her cheeks graying. "Are those the shoes your father . . . " Her voice trailed away.

Bea looked down at her mother's pale pink wedding shoes. She'd found them earlier when she'd been playing dress-up. She loved them. They were elegant, and she had wanted to be an elegant princess at the party.

"I was just trying them on," Bea said. "They're so pretty. . . ."

Her mother bent down, staring. Bea saw it, too. A dime-sized dot of red wine across the toe of the right shoe.

"I'm so sorry, Mommy," she whispered. "I—"

The slap came across her cheek suddenly, sharp and stinging.

"Don't ever wear these shoes again." Her mother's voice broke, tears swimming in her eyes. "Never. And you are not to leave this room. Do you understand?"

Bea nodded, but she didn't understand at all. When Daddy was alive, her mother had never even spanked her, let alone slapped her. There were no dinners where she didn't belong. Only backyard barbecues and sticky fried-chicken fingers. Her mother had never used the word "ladylike" around Daddy. She'd never worried so much about other grown-ups before, either.

Bea crawled into bed and waited for a good-night kiss. It never came. Her mother left the room with the shoes, snapped the door shut, and locked it from the outside.

Bea's tears trickled onto her pillow and away into the darkness. There was no prince coming to save her or her mother. Suddenly, Bea could feel the stillness overtaking her again, turning her into stone. It didn't stop until it reached her heart, sealing it in cement for good.

RAY

Ray hadn't banked on rain. It was only a light tapping on the bus's roof when they crossed the state line into Tennessee. By the time they reached Nashville's city limits, it was the sort of summer squall that brought driving walls of rain.

Her eyes were sandpapered with exhaustion, but she forced them to stay open as the lights of downtown Nashville appeared in neon rivers on the window. As soon as the bus pulled into the station, Ray nudged Pinny awake and grabbed their stuff.

She stepped into the aisle before the bus stopped, hurrying toward the door. Pinny moved more slowly, rubbing her eyes and yawning.

"Come on," Ray said through clenched teeth. They had to get out of here before any cops came checking for missing persons, or their "friend" Ethel realized Daddy Dearest was a no-show.

Inside the station, Ray spotted a vending machine, fed two bucks into it, and grabbed two packs of peanut butter crackers.

"Here you go." She tossed a pack to Pinny. "Breakfast."

"We didn't eat lunch or dinner!" Pinny protested. "Today is Sunday! Cheesy-macaroni day!"

"It's one in the morning on Monday now," Ray said. There was a freak-out coming, and she was so not in the mood for another holdup. "That's breakfast."

"I . . . I never miss cheesy-macaroni day." Pinny sagged.

"Hey, you wanted to leave Smokebush, remember?"

"Yeah, but . . ." Pinny clutched her backpack like a security blanket. "Sundays, cheesy macaroni. Mondays, meatloaf. Tuesdays, chicken and biscuits—"

"I get the picture!" Ray snapped.

Pinny's eyes toppled into panic, and sympathy overruled Ray's impatience. Pinny had been so hell-bent on leaving Jaynis, but it was only a matter of time before reality kicked in. "Look," Ray said, as gently as she could manage. "We're sort of . . . over the rainbow now. Like Dorothy in Oz. So we have to be flexible about food." She grinned and elbowed Pinny. "At least it's not a bug burger from Fricasweet's, right?"

Pinny giggled a bit. "I knew you thought their burgers were gross, too."

Suddenly, Ray spotted an opportunity. Her life could be easier in a matter of minutes if only Pinny agreed . . . "You know," she tried, "you can get on a bus back to Jaynis, no problem. You don't have to stay."

Pinny's brow furrowed, her glasses slipping a fraction. "No

way," she said. "Face it. You're stuck with me." She took a deep breath, tearing open her pack of crackers. "Monday, crackers." She stared at the water racing down the windowpanes of the station. "But . . . where are we going to sleep?"

Ray shrugged. "Not here." She looked over her shoulder at Ethel, who was watching them with that Good Samaritan gaze. "I'll find someplace. Let's go."

They pushed through the door and into the downpour, getting drenched within seconds. The rain hammered the streets as they started running. Pinny protested, but Ray ignored her. She cursed herself for not grabbing a city map while they were in the station, because now they were racing blindly through the deserted streets. Where could they go? The only places still open were bars; they'd never get in.

They turned corner after corner, until Pinny tripped, collapsing onto the sidewalk. Helping Pinny to her feet, Ray squinted through the rain to make out the sign on the lamppost above them: OPRYLAND DRIVE.

She'd heard of that. . . . Suddenly, she remembered why.

"Come on," she said, just as every light on the street blinked out. "I know where we can go."

With a tremendous flash of lightning, the Grand Ole Opry lit up like a white fortress in front of them, an inviting shelter from the storm. The parking lot was empty, and with the power out, Ray thought they stood a chance of getting into the building without alarms blaring.

She led Pinny past the front entrance and around the side of the building, looking for some other way in. Finally, she spotted a door under an awning labeled ARTIST ENTRANCE.

She pulled out her pocketknife and jimmied the door. After

a few seconds, a click reverberated up through her hand. She tested the handle, and the door eased open. She set a cautious foot inside and waited for sirens. But there was nothing but silence. The next flash of lightning illuminated wood-paneled walls and a sitting area.

"Where's the stage?" Pinny whispered.

"We came in a back way," Ray said. She rummaged through her duffel for the lighter she'd taken with Mrs. Danvers's camping gear. She flicked it on and walked into another room filled with rows of mailboxes.

"What are those for?" Pinny asked.

"That's where the Opry members pick up their mail," Ray said. "The musicians, when they come to perform." She'd read about it on the Internet. She wasn't a fan of country music, but she'd always wanted to come here anyway. This was a place where nobodies became somebodies, and that counted for something.

She moved through the rooms on tiptoe, afraid that at any moment the lights would come on and they'd find a guard plowing toward them. When it didn't happen and the minutes passed, she forgot they were trespassing. She forgot Pinny. She forgot everything . . . except music. Music had built this place, and she felt its thrum in the walls, its tendrils on the air, waiting to be given life.

When she found the auditorium, she stopped in the doorway as peace settled inside her. Surely, this was the way believing folks felt when they walked into church. The way people felt in the midst of something precious.

She walked past the rows of seats and onto the stage. Standing in the six-foot circle of wood on the center of the stage made Ray breathless, and her fingers craved to move. Her guitar was slick with rainwater, but she slid the strap over her shoulder, closed her eyes, and played. It was a melody she'd been working on for months, soft, slow, woozy.

She'd woken up humming the notes the day after she found out about Carter. She'd gone back to school thinking she'd see him again. He'd promised her as much that last afternoon at the lake. But she'd never expected to see him where she did.

On that first day back at school last September, she overheard Careena talking to Meg at the lockers.

"Have you seen the new music teacher?" she'd said. "He's adorable. I heard he's an ex-marine."

Meg laughed. "Maybe I'll pick up a new elective this semester."

Ray rolled her eyes as she walked away, not thinking anything of it. But then, when she rounded the corner and saw Carter standing outside the office, a wrecking ball gutted her. Carter. They'd been talking about Carter.

In that second, the secret imaginings she'd kept close to her heart all summer, the sweet kisses she'd wished for, crumbled into reality.

She turned away, hoping he hadn't seen her, but then he called her name. He walked toward her in those slacks and that button-down shirt that made him look older and her feel like a ridiculous child.

"Ray." He smiled. "I was hoping I'd run into you."

"So . . . you're a teacher?" The word spat out like an insult.

"Crazy that they're going to let me mold young minds,

right?" He laughed, but then grew serious. "I got injured when I was deployed in Iraq two years ago, and I couldn't go back. I . . . didn't want to go back." His eyes took on that glazed expression she'd seen before at the lake, the look of someone saddled with memories he didn't want but couldn't get rid of. Then he shrugged. "So here I am."

She nodded mechanically. "You didn't say anything. . . ."

"I know," he said. "I didn't want to rehash it. And I didn't want to spoil your lake for you either. Teachers in summertime . . . totally uncool."

"Definitely." She fell back on her smart-ass routine, hoping the tremor in her voice wouldn't give her away. She'd spent the summer treating him like an equal. If she acted any different now, a red flag would go up. "If you'd told me, I would've kicked your ass."

He laughed. "I believe you. But hey." He leaned closer. "Don't let the other teachers hear you say that. Spare yourself the detentions."

His smile was the same easy one he'd had at the lake, but it was misplaced here under the fluorescent lights.

"So . . . maybe you'll take my music-composition class this semester?" he asked. "Work on some new songs to play for me?"

Her mind said no. It said to save herself while she could. But her mouth answered yes. She wanted to be near him, every day, because there might still be a chance. She was stupid enough to believe in the possibility of his love. Screw taboo.

Her music knew better, though. The next morning, it had woken her up with the bittersweet melody she was strumming in the middle of the Grand Ole Opry stage right now. The song had tasted so sad in her mouth that the notes became a sound track to her tears.

PINNY

She knew Ray had forgotten about her. It wasn't Ray's fault. It was the music, and what it did to her.

The song sounded exactly the way Pinny felt when she thought of Mama—like she needed to cry, or laugh, or maybe both together. It made her glad she hadn't gotten on that bus back to Jaynis. Ray had wanted her to. She could tell. Oh, she'd thought about it. All she had to do was say yes to the Life Plan. Horizons Assist had cheesy-macaroni Fridays. Mrs. Danvers had told her so. But then every day would be Fricasweet's and Horizons Assist. That wasn't enough. That's why it made her itchy like a too-tight shirt. Even with a zillion jitterbugs fizzing in her stomach, even with the bigness of the world, the bigness of everything she didn't know about, she was staying. And Ray's song helped her remember why.

She clapped as loud as she could when Ray finished playing. When she did, Ray's eyes flew open, and her eyebrows shot together like one long caterpillar.

"Stop," Ray said.

"But it was good." Pinny dropped her hands to her sides. "Way better than anything else you've ever played."

Ray glared at her, and Pinny's cheeks warmed. "I don't play in front of anybody, except Ca—" She shook her head like she was hoping something she didn't want in there would fall out. "I don't play in front of anybody," she said again. "You don't know what I play."

"Do too." Pinny sniffed. Why did Ray argue so much? It was a puzzle. Especially when she was wrong, like she was now. "You played all the time at Smokebush. In the cleaning closet."

"That's none of your business," Ray huffed.

"Then try playing softer." Pinny shrugged and stood up from her seat. "Why do you write songs, anyway?"

Ray was quiet for a minute. "I guess I . . . I want to be heard."

"That's plain backward." Pinny shook her head. "I hear you. But you just said that makes you mad. So you *don't* know what you want."

Ray laughed. "Maybe not."

"See?" Pinny said, feeling proud of herself. "Everyone thinks I can't pay good attention. Mr. Sands. Mrs. Danvers. In my Life Plan meetings, they talk *about* me. Not *to* me. But I know lots of things nobody else does."

"Like what?" Ray sat down at the edge of the stage, with her legs dangling over the side.

Pinny grinned. "Mrs. Danvers keeps funny-smelling cigarettes in the shed at Smokebush. She sneaks out Sundays to smoke them. Careena throws up after lunch in the school bathroom. And I know that singing is your More."

Ray stared at her. The caterpillar on her forehead was having a downright tantrum. "What are you talking about, my More?"

"Mama used to call it that. It's not like having more black jelly beans. Mama said it was like . . . being Sunny-Side Up all the time. Like when Dorothy sings about the More that's over the rainbow. With the lemon drops and happy bluebirds." Pinny climbed onto the stage and settled down next to Ray. "Your face usually knots up tight, sort of pruny. But when you sing, it goes smooth and quiet. Like you believe in the More of things, same as me and Mama. That you'll find it. And it makes you happy."

Ray stared down at her feet. "I don't believe in anything anymore," she barked.

Pinny glared at her. "You're lying. The More is why you got the Julie School book. It's why Mama had auditions. Why I can't work at Fricasweet's. I think my More maybe has to do with Mama's shoes. And I'm scared of it, too."

"Don't you *ever* quit?" Ray grabbed her guitar, clambering off the stage. "I'm *not* scared. I don't need some lame pep talk about it, either."

Pinny snorted. "And *I'm* supposed to be the stupid one." She followed Ray up the aisle and out of the auditorium. "If you're not scared, then you're a . . . a grouch for real!"

"Bingo!" Ray snapped her fingers. "Don't say I didn't warn you."

Pinny stopped, letting Ray stomp ahead of her. She didn't want to be around her. She didn't like her like this. Not even a smidge.

Ray's lighter turned the corner, disappearing, leaving Pinny with the growling storm in the dark.

She pushed the button on the hand dryer, then sat back down underneath it. The hot wind blew so hard, her cheeks flattened into her face. Maybe this was what a tornado felt like. She'd hit the button on the dryer five times so far. Another three would do it.

The tornado died, and she was about to start it again when the bathroom door creaked open.

"Pinny?" The lighter made Ray's face a jack-o'-lantern. "Pinny . . . I'm . . ." She sighed. "What are you doing in here?"

"Drying off." Pinny turned her back. She was still sore at her, and Ray might as well know it.

Ray came to stand beside her. "Good idea," she said. Her voice was soft, not snappy like before.

"Are you done?" Pinny asked her. "With the tantrum?"

Ray tried to frown but a laugh busted it open. "For now."

"Then I'll let you use the dryer." Pinny moved over, and Ray worked on her own clothes for a while.

Then she elbowed Pinny and headed for the bathroom door. "Come on. I found something you need to see."

Pinny followed her down a hallway lined with posters and glass display cases.

"Check it out." Ray raised the lighter over one of the cases. "The people who run this place must've known you were coming. They put out some shoes for you."

Pinny peered through the glass and sucked in her breath. There was a pair of black Mary Janes with MINNIE and PEARL spelled out in brass buttons across the sides. Her heart practically danced right out of her. "Minnie Pearl's Mary Janes," she whispered. "They're legend. Famous like Dorothy's ruby slippers."

"Bizarre," Ray said. Her voice was teasing, and Pinny wasn't sure she liked it. "How did you know that? You're like a fount of shoe trivia."

"You know music," she said. "I know shoes." She leaned closer to the shoes, longing to touch them. She settled for snapping a photo. "She went all over the world wearing these shoes. Just to make people laugh." She straightened up and looked at Ray. "So the people you say you hate . . . they were her More."

Ray coughed and shifted on her feet. People squirmed like that when some bad thought was bugging them deep inside. *Well,* Pinny thought, *Ray could do with some squirming.*

"It's late," Ray finally said. "We should sleep. We've only got a few hours before daylight, and we'll have to be out of here by then."

" 'Kay." A yawn pulled at Pinny's mouth, and her body felt slow as a slug.

She followed Ray back to the room called the artists' lounge. Ray pulled cushions off the armchairs and laid them on the floor like beds, then spread her sleeping bag on top.

"Climb in," Ray said.

But Pinny couldn't yet. She sat down and opened her backpack, careful not to let Ray see the pale pink shoes inside. If Ray knew Pinny had them, she might turn grouchy again. It was better to keep them a secret. She pulled out Daddy's watch. Then she slid her red Mary Janes from around her neck. She fixed the shoes and watch together on the floor so they hugged up against each other. She nudged them even closer, till they looked cozy. Then she flipped through her stack of shoe photos, making sure each one was there.

"What are you doing?" Ray asked, watching.

"Getting ready for bed," Pinny said.

Ray sighed beside her. "Do you have to mess with that stuff now?"

"Every night." She squinched her eyes to double-check her photos. "So I can sleep." She pointed to her Mary Janes and Daddy's watch. "They keep each other company. Like you and me." She put the photos away and lay down. "You want to know what I'm scared of?" she whispered.

There was a long quiet, then, "What?"

Pinny swallowed. She'd never said it out loud before. "That I'll find Mama's shoes, but not Mama." Her hands went sweaty. "Maybe the magic won't work."

"I don't know squat about magic." Ray rolled over to face her. "There's no point worrying about it yet anyway. Let's just get to New York first."

"I guess," Pinny said. But she wasn't so sure.

Ray stayed still for so long Pinny thought she'd fallen asleep. Then her voice came trembly. "You were right," she whispered. "I'm scared, too. Of . . . myself. Not ever being who I want to be."

"Well, I'll never want to be somebody different." She shook her head. "How would Mama know me when she saw me, then?"

Ray laughed at that. "You got me there."

Pinny nodded. "Don't not be you. Maybe just get rid of something you don't want. Like all that mad. You for sure don't want that. It'll use you up." She sighed. "I've got lots to be mad over, too. And people to be even madder at."

"For what?" Ray whispered.

She shrugged. "Things they do they think I won't get. Like

Careena calling Room 305 the nursery, like me and all the other kids in there are babies. Bet you didn't think I knew that."

Ray's face was dough-white. "I . . . I wasn't sure. . . ."

Pinny snorted. "I know. Other people figure I'm too dumb to see mean. It took me a long time with Careena. To see her mean. But I did. Anyway, my mad can't fix mean. So I don't bother with it."

Ray opened her mouth, like she wanted to say something else. But then she shut it, and Pinny figured she was all talked out. She settled onto her side. Her clothes were still a little wet, and she wished she had a blanket. But that was like finding sugar ants in the honey. They didn't matter when you had a whole pot of sweetness in front of you. "Thanks for bringing me along," she whispered to Ray's back. "I've never had a sleepover before."

The room was quiet for a few minutes, and then Ray's voice came, muffled and stale-bread tough. "You're welcome."

"I knew you were the right person to help get Mama's shoes back," she said. "You believe me, don't you?"

Ray heaved a sigh. "Good night, Pinny."

"Good night," Pinny whispered around her smile. She closed her eyes and heard Ray's song again. In her dreams, she saw Mama, dancing in the sunlight in her silver shoes, in perfect time to the beat.

November 1940
New York, New York

DALYA

She never planned to talk about it. Not with anyone. Then came the afternoon when Dalya left school to find Mrs. Ashbury waiting for her. Henry, Dalya knew, had gone for an admissions interview at Columbia University, and she'd been planning to walk home alone. But here was Mrs. Ashbury, waving her to the car. Ever since the World's Fair, Mrs. Ashbury had cooled. She'd never mentioned it to Dalya again, but Dalya sensed her subtle disapproval. Today, her polished-silver smile made Dalya's palms damp, although she couldn't say exactly why.

"I'm meeting a few ladies at the Plaza for tea this afternoon," Mrs. Ashbury said as Dalya slid into the car. "I thought you might like to join us."

Questions brimmed in her mind, but she nodded without asking any of them. "I'd like that, thank you," she replied in carefully pronounced English, and was gratified when Mrs. Ashbury's smile broadened.

"I've just attended a meeting at the school," Mrs. Ashbury said as the car wove through the streets. "Your teachers all agree that your English has improved in the past few months. They tell me that some of your schoolwork now seems too easy for you." She patted Dalya's hand. "They think you may be able to move up to the eleventh grade, with students your own age, sometime next spring."

"That's wonderful." Dalya made her voice swing up enthusiastically, but she felt nothing. What did it matter what grade she was in, when her presence at school was shadowy at best? Yes, she did her work well and tried to answer clearly when called on in class. Understanding English was easier now, though speaking it was still a challenge. In spite of that, to other students she only amounted to mere whispers in the hallway, and even those had died down as her novelty wore off.

"I hope you're feeling more at home here," Mrs. Ashbury said as the car stopped before a grand white high-rise with a green steepled roof. "You and I haven't spent much time together yet. Now that we're starting to understand each other a bit better, I hope that will change."

"Me too," said Dalya. But she felt as if one of them was lying, though she wasn't sure who.

Mrs. Ashbury touched a gloved hand to Dalya's elbow, leading her through the Plaza and into the Palm Court. Bright light showered down from an enormous domed glass ceiling so beautiful that Dalya had a hard time looking away, even when Mrs. Ashbury motioned her to a table. Three other ladies as finely dressed as Mrs. Ashbury smiled as she sat down with them.

"Dalya," one said, squeezing her hand sympathetically. "It's a true honor to meet you."

As Mrs. Ashbury made introductions, the other women, too, gazed at Dalya much the same way, until she longed to stare at the ceiling to avoid their placating eyes. Thankfully, a waiter came with tea and a menu she could lose her face behind.

"Order anything you'd like," Mrs. Ashbury said.

Dalya couldn't muster an appetite through her nerves, but out of politeness, she decided on a pastry cake. Once it was ordered, though, her menu was gone, and all eyes again turned to her.

"Dalya," Mrs. Ashbury began, "we wanted you to join us today because we have something important to ask you." She took a sip of tea. "We've been searching for ways to help more wartime refugees. Certain laws make it difficult for refugees to come to America. We're fighting to change those laws, but we're hoping to help in other ways, too, through private charities and aid societies."

One of the ladies leaned toward Dalya, speaking conspicuously slowly and loudly, as if to help her make sense of the English words. "There are stories about camps in Germany . . . places where horrible things are done. Some people believe they're just rumors."

Camps. Rumors. The words made her mind sluggish and her lungs burn, like she was listening underwater.

"We thought if you told your story," Mrs. Ashbury said, "if you shared what happened to you and your family with some key people, it might make a difference." The other ladies smiled with satisfaction, and Dalya realized this was the appeal they'd been waiting for. "It might help the cause."

"The cause," Dalya repeated, her voice garbled. Somewhere deep in her mind, she vaguely wondered why Mrs. Ashbury had said "cause" instead of "people." But her thoughts couldn't go any further than that, because she couldn't get out from under the weight of it all, and the pressure was unbearable.

A waiter slid Dalya's food in front of her, and she blinked, baffled that things remained in motion around her while she sat frozen. Mrs. Ashbury's smile tarnished as silence settled uncomfortably over the table.

When she spoke again, her voice held a sliver of a crack. "I'm sure it's difficult to talk about these things," she said. "And you're still working on your English, but Henry could translate for you, if you'd like. You would be doing such a service. When you came to us, this is what we hoped for."

There was compassion in Mrs. Ashbury's eyes. But something else, too . . . expectation. As if Dalya wasn't being asked, but commanded. She suddenly wished Henry were here beside her, because even if she didn't need him to interpret words for her anymore, there was so much about Mrs. Ashbury that she didn't understand.

In the last months, she'd come to rely on him for more than his friendship. When he wasn't fixated on his anger, his kindness and humor shone through. Since the World's Fair, she'd felt a shift in the air between them. When they talked, she caught him staring at her with an expression of more than camaraderie. With tender affection. It thrilled her. It terrified her. It brought her comfort, and the closest connection she'd had to anyone since Berlin. He was her distraction and her protector. But Henry wasn't here to shelter her from this, and Mrs. Ashbury was waiting for her answer while her friends watched.

Dalya drudged her voice up from the depths. When it surfaced, it was barely a sigh. "Yes," she said. "I'll do it."

"You don't have to," Henry said that night as they listened to the radio in the parlor. "She should never have asked. Or dragged me into it. I don't want anything to do with her agenda. It's wrong."

"She wants me to," Dalya said. "Maybe it *will* help, like she says."

"Maybe," he said grudgingly. "Or maybe she only wants you to be her latest philanthropic showpiece."

Dalya studied the pattern on the rug. "She said that this was what she'd hoped for when I came. What did she mean?"

"It means you are the perfect diversion. With you here, she can be a social crusader instead of the wife of a crook. Rich people don't like mud on their faces, especially when it comes from dirty money. If you can't make her look clean, at least you can make her look generous."

"A crook?" Dalya repeated. "Your father?" She didn't see Mr. Ashbury very often, but the severe, driven man didn't match her idea of a swindler.

Henry smirked. "My father's not always an honest investor, and everyone knows it. I'm sure he's already bought my admission into Columbia, even though he'll never admit it. It's our name that matters anyway, not my merit."

"You want to go to Columbia, don't you?" she asked.

He shrugged. "Columbia's convenient. Mother's planning for a companion to help me get around campus. They've arranged it perfectly. I'll get my degree and then step right into my father's shoes." He laughed, rolling his eyes at his braces. "Or at least sit at his desk."

"But . . . that's what you want."

"When your life's mapped out by someone else, what you want doesn't matter." He sighed. "What I want is for this"—he motioned to his legs—"never to have happened. I couldn't stop that, could I?" He grimaced and unstrapped his braces, his forehead beading with perspiration.

She watched as he rubbed his legs. "Do they hurt tonight?"

"They hurt every second of every day," he snapped. Then his face softened, and he smiled. "Don't you know by now that you're the only one who has any real chance of helping me?"

Dalya's cheeks warmed. "How?"

"You could teach me to ignore the pain, like you do. I know it will never really go away, but I could shut it up at least, put it under lock and key. Keep it from wailing all the time, right?"

"I don't know what you mean," she said. But, oh, she did, and the relief she felt at his words frightened her. He knew her secret, that this was how she survived each passing minute, and she loved that he knew and didn't judge her for it. Even if she didn't recognize her own self anymore, he saw something in her worth admiring.

"I suppose that helps, too? All that pretending. But no one can pretend they don't see these." He frowned down at his legs, then reached for the bottle of wintergreen oil on the table beside him. His hands shook so badly with pain, though, that the bottle slipped, spilling onto the table.

"Dammit!" he breathed, but Dalya was already setting the bottle straight, saying, "It's all right. It's all right."

He slumped against the back of the chair, pale and tired. Before Dalya could think, a wave of affection surged through her, and she was kneeling before him. She reached for the cuffs of his pants, but he grabbed her hands.

"Don't."

She smiled up at him and whispered, "Let me. Please." He tensed, but didn't fight her as she rolled up his pants to his knees and slipped off his shoes. She poured some oil into her hands. He gave a soft sigh as she laid her palms against his skin, kneading the oil into his calves, ankles, and feet. His muscles were soft and small, his legs and feet thin. He closed his eyes as she cradled his feet in her hands, and a peaceful silence settled between them.

She studied the structure of his feet, memorizing their brittle angles and unnatural curvature, and her mind drifted to a place it hadn't in years. The Dalya of Before could've helped him. With the right type of arch support and more comfortable braces, his pain might be less. A vision of tall leather boots formed in her mind, but the instant it did, she dismissed it. Making shoes again, touching her father's tools . . . Her own pain clawed the surface, threatening to break free, to break *her.*

She yanked her hands back, gasping. No, the Dalya of After didn't make shoes. She couldn't . . . wouldn't.

Henry sat up, staring at her, the peace on his face replaced with humiliation. "It's disgusting. I know."

"No!" she protested. "It's not that. . . ."

He jerked his pants down over his legs, and even as his features twisted angrily, she kept her hands clenched in her lap, letting the impulse to touch him again pass.

"It's not you. Don't ever think that, not for a second. I couldn't stand it if I hurt you. You have to believe me. Please."

She said it so adamantly, with such urgency, that she startled the anger out of him. He nodded, believing her, and his face softened. "What is it, then? Tell me."

"It's me. It's being . . . close to you. To anyone. I . . . can't," she said weakly, standing to go upstairs. "I'm sorry that I'm . . . like this." She looked down tenderly at his legs. "I'm sorry it's so painful. That I can't do more."

"Everyone's sorry," he said, his face sagging. "Helpless, but sorry. People's shallow sentiments are about as effective as these braces." He shoved his braces, sending them clattering to the floor. "They're not going to cure a damn thing. America's sorry about the war in Europe, but not enough to fight the Nazis. When people hear your story, they'll tell you they're sorry, too. But 'sorry' doesn't change laws or save people." He reached for her hand, his fear for her showing on his face. "You shouldn't have to rip out your heart to ease their consciences."

"I won't," she said truthfully. Her heart was already scabbed over, drained of blood. "I'll be fine."

She was fine, perfectly fine, one week later as she walked into a throng of the most elegantly dressed people she'd ever seen to make her way into Madison Square Garden. Or that's what she told herself. Mrs. Ashbury braced her arm with a steady, white-gloved hand as they started toward the entrance, but Dalya craned her neck, looking for Henry. Thomas was helping him out of the car and into his wheelchair, and Henry lifted his hand with a smile.

"I'll see you inside," he called to her. "I have to use the secret entrance," he added as Thomas wheeled him past. "It's reserved for only the *most* important people, you know."

She smiled, but couldn't bring herself to laugh. The fur coat she was wearing was one that Mrs. Ashbury had lent her, and its bulky warmth made her claustrophobic among the waves of people. She longed to follow Henry through whichever quiet door he'd entered, but that was impossible. The Night of Stars, as Mrs. Ashbury had explained to her, was a fund-raiser for Jewish refugees, one of the largest in Manhattan. It was the "ideal opportunity" for Dalya's story to be heard by the most influential people in the city. She'd told her what a privilege it was to be able to share what had happened to her, so that other victims might find refuge, too. Dalya had agreed, and now she felt herself being caught up in Mrs. Ashbury's enthusiasm. There was a nervousness concealed in Mrs. Ashbury's poised face tonight, though, as if she wasn't convinced that Dalya would be true to her word.

Mr. and Mrs. Ashbury led her swiftly through the crowd, not giving her time for second thoughts. "Stay by my side," Mrs. Ashbury whispered. "I'll introduce you to everyone you need to know." She squeezed Dalya's hand, smiling at her with something akin to pride.

Stepping into the main lobby, Dalya entered a gilded world of tuxedos and candy-colored gowns. Women with coiffed hair were draped on the arms of men sipping martinis at the bar, trailing elegance like perfume. It seemed so impossible to her that this world could exist parallel to the one she'd come from, that while these people fluttered about in their brilliance, others shivered in threadbare clothes and filthy barracks, starving. She might've stood staring all night, but Mr. Ashbury brushed her shoulders to remove her coat, making her start. He and Mrs. Ashbury were immediately drawn into conversation with some couples standing nearby, and Dalya was left awkwardly on the edge of their circle, waiting for Mrs. Ashbury to introduce her.

She tucked her bare arms to her sides, afraid that the golden air might corrode on contact with her impostor skin. But it didn't, and a moment later, she took a relieved breath when she spotted Henry across the room, leaning against the counter of the Coca-Cola soda fountain. With his wheelchair tucked discreetly behind the counter, and his braces hidden underneath his tuxedo, he looked like every other able-bodied man there. She stepped toward him, and his eyes found hers. Astonishment was a look she hadn't seen on his face before, and it made him look younger, more vulnerable, and very handsome.

"I feel like everyone is staring at me," she whispered, smoothing her pale green gown self-consciously. "Do I look out of place?"

Henry shook his head, struggling to speak. Finally, he said quietly, "You look more like you belong here than anyone else."

"Because I look like a refugee?" she said.

"No." His eyes swept over her gown and came back to rest on her face. "Because you look beautiful."

Her cheeks flared, and she smiled shyly. She had an urge to

move closer to him, to stand beside him for support. If she did, would he slip his arm around her waist like she wanted him to? She leaned forward, her feet ready to take another step, but then Mrs. Ashbury was at her side.

"Here you are." She tucked an arm around her. "Come. Both of you. Dalya, I've been telling Mr. and Mrs. Cavendash about you, and they'd love to talk with you."

As Mrs. Ashbury steered her away, Dalya glanced back to see anger in Henry's eyes. She knew how he felt about what his mother was asking of her, but she hoped, for all of their sakes, he wouldn't make a scene.

"I won't do this." He leaned toward Dalya, whispering, "I won't translate your pain." Shaking his head at his mother, he added a brisk "I'll go find our seats inside." Mrs. Ashbury flushed with embarrassment as he turned away.

"No." Dalya tried to keep the panic from her voice, but Henry must have heard it, because he stopped. "Please . . . stay. I need you here with me." Yes, she needed his words for the English she still had trouble forming smoothly. But more than that, she wanted him beside her. She couldn't do this, any of it, without him.

He hesitated, but as he looked at her, his eyes turned tender, until finally, he nodded and followed her through the crowd. She straightened her shoulders as her resolve returned, then extended her hand toward Mr. and Mrs. Cavendash. "I'm Dalya Amschel," she said in slow, careful English. "It's a pleasure to meet you."

Then, because she knew it was what they were waiting for, she began.

There was a moment when anguish threatened, strangling her breath. But her body took over, forming the words it needed to say, while she watched from somewhere outside herself. As she talked and Henry translated, the words sounded more and more like they belonged in someone else's story, to someone else's life, until she almost believed it hadn't happened to her at all. Almost. Her family's faces grew blurry and distant, losing their familiar curves and colors, becoming more and more like strangers.

When she finished and looked up, it was into horror-stricken faces. Mrs. Cavendash was wiping her eyes with the handkerchief Mr. Ashbury had offered her, mumbling, "Oh, my dear, my heart breaks for you."

Dalya nodded politely, but their sympathetic words slipped from her skin, falling to the floor to get trampled. After they'd apologized to the point of embarrassment, silence settled over the group, as if no one knew how to move on from what they'd heard. Mr. and Mrs. Cavendash filtered back into the crowd but were soon replaced by others. Some were strangers, but others were famous people who might have inspired awe in the Dalya of Before. Ethel Merman paused to take her hand and shed some lovely tears, and Danny Kaye offered her his kind smile. They promised to dedicate their performances to her; they told her *she* was the star tonight, not them. The Dalya of Before would've swooned, would've asked for autographs in her girlish, giggly fashion. But the Dalya of After was numb as she mechanically gave her own performance again and again.

Finally, it was Henry who ended it, interrupting Mrs. Ashbury during another round of introductions to announce that the show was about to begin. Mrs. Ashbury, for a moment, looked disappointed. But she recovered with "Of course. Let's go sit down." She clasped Dalya's hand. "You were brilliant, my dear. You've done such a service. You should be proud."

Then she drifted away on Mr. Ashbury's arm.

Dalya put a hand out to steady herself against the wall, but instead, Henry took it gently into his own. She hadn't dared to look at him while she'd talked, afraid of seeing pity. Now she did. What she saw was her own calm face mirrored as a statue in his eyes.

"Well, you did it." He studied her worriedly. "Was it horrible?"

With anyone else, she would've lied, because the truth made her seem too warped, too unnatural. But because it was Henry, she answered honestly. "No. I didn't feel a thing."

"Good," he said. "It's better to distance yourself. You didn't need to relive it."

She stared at him, wishing he hadn't said that. Didn't he realize *that* was the most horrible part of it? If she couldn't feel pain anymore for the ones she'd loved the most, what hope did she possibly have?

She helped him with his wheelchair and they made their way to their orchestra seats. Soon, the lights dimmed and the show began to the cheers of the thousands of people filling the arena. There was a speech by Eleanor Roosevelt, and Glenn Miller conducting his swing band to "In the Mood." There was laughter, toe-tapping music, and applause that made the floor quake. But the music and lights were a faint buzzing in Dalya's ears, an acute reminder of a joy she couldn't be part of.

The trembling didn't start until the evening finally ended, and then it came suddenly and ceaselessly. Mr. and Mrs. Ashbury had decided to join some friends for drinks, sending Dalya and Henry back to the house with Thomas. The ride was blessedly short, but as Dalya pressed into the seat, drained of the adrenaline that had sustained her through the night, the trembling began.

She tried to hide it in the folds of her coat, but once she stepped into the foyer and Henry took her coat, he startled at her shaking shoulders.

"What is it?" he asked, but when she tried to speak, no words would come. He led her to the elevator at the back of the house.

Numbly, she followed him to her room, and when he lay down on her bed and opened his arms, she went into them without a sound. His arms encircled her as her head dropped to his shoulder in exhaustion. She gave no thought to judgments, or their recklessness, only to his warmth and the steadiness of his heartbeat in her ear. He didn't move to touch her or kiss her, but if he had, she would've given herself to him without hesitation. She wondered if he'd soften under her touch, if he'd give up his own anger if their bodies met. She wondered if it would bring her own feelings, *any* feelings, to the surface. But he didn't move. Instead, he held her, for hours it seemed, until her violent trembling stilled and she drifted into soundless sleep.

When she woke later to the shuffling footsteps of Mr. and Mrs. Ashbury passing her door, her limbs were sore and stiff, her bed empty and cold.

But over the next months, as winter stretched into spring and then to summer, the memory of Henry's heartbeat stayed while memories of her family slipped further and further from her mind. There were more talks, at Mrs. Ashbury's teas and church meetings and fund-raisers. Each time, Dalya's tale got easier in the telling. And because she could almost believe it hadn't happened to her, her lack of tears didn't feel so much like a betrayal.

PART V

Be it resolved that all women . . . that . . . betray into matrimony any of His Majesty's male subjects, by scents, paints, cosmetics . . . high-heeled shoes, or bolstered hips, shall incur the penalty of the laws now in force against witchcraft, sorcery, and such like misdemeanors.
    —1670 Marriage Act under Charles II of England

BEA

Bea couldn't go through with it. She stood in front of the full-length mirror, staring at the terror-stricken face peering back at her. There was no expectant awe washing over her, like her mother and friends said it would. There was only suffocation as she was sucked under a flood of silk and pearl beading. This was not her dress; it had been handpicked by her mother, altered and delivered to their front door without Bea ever once uttering a word about it. This was not her engagement ring; it had belonged to Gerald's grandmother, a family heirloom that he'd had resized to fit her finger. It felt foreign on her hand—heavy, cold, and impossibly tight. And these pale pink shoes on her feet. They would never be hers. They would always belong to her mother. Her mother, who'd worn them on the day she married her father. Who'd worn them for him on every wedding anniversary until he died. These shoes belonged to a woman who loved. And there was one thing Bea knew with certainty. She did *not* love Gerald Hawthorn. She never would.

When her mother had brought her the shoes, Bea had hesitated. The last time she'd seen them, her mother had slapped her for getting a red wine stain on one toe. The shoes had been cleaned since then, and there was only the faintest trace of the wine left. To the untrained eye, the stain would never be noticeable.

"Here," her mother had said, all business. "Your father would've wanted you to wear them on your wedding day."

"No, Mom. I can't. They're yours. They mean too much to you."

Her mother had shaken her head. "No." Her glance skimmed over the shoes. "I don't know why I held on to them, except to keep them for you. Ridiculous, really, to get attached to a silly pair of shoes."

Her mother's nonchalance when she gave Bea the shoes made wearing them even more excruciating. Had she forgotten what true love felt like, or had she just buried the memory so deep it had become distorted in her mind?

Bea glanced at herself in the mirror again, cringing at the sight of the shoes. The nausea came on violently, sending her flying to the bathroom. She barely made it in time. She was patting her face with a towel when her mother came in.

"Nerves?" She arched her eyebrow in a way that dared Beatrice to offer up another explanation.

"Yes," Bea muttered. She knew her mother had noticed her rounded waistline, tightening skirts, and lack of appetite. Her mother also knew about Bea's short-lived fling with Harvard-dropout-turned-musician Luke Tannen. Benjamin, her stepfather, hadn't been home from his business travels often enough to notice the romance or the effect it had on Bea's waistline. And Bea was positive her mother had never mentioned it to him. Instead, her mother had pushed the idea of marriage to a "more acceptable" young man, and she'd done it with such subtlety that Benjamin had never questioned the lightning-fast courtship and hurriedly arranged wedding. Of course, her mother had made sure that Bea invited Gerald into her bed so that Gerald would never doubt when Bea told him she was expecting his child. Her mother's capacity to mask deceit never ceased to amaze Bea.

"Here." Her mother offered her a package of saltines. "They help."

"Mom," Beatrice started. "I can't . . ."

Her mother's eyes flashed with impatience. "Yes, you can. You will. That's all there is." She turned away, then stopped. "You'll need more rouge to hide the paleness."

"I'll put more on." Bea gripped the edge of the sink, swallowing thickly.

"Guests are arriving," her mother said. "I should go downstairs. You . . . collect yourself. In time for the ceremony."

Bea nodded, holding her breath until the door clicked shut. Then she deflated against the counter. She gathered her waterfall of skirts, squeezing them back through the bathroom door and into the sitting room. From the window, she could see her mother on the back lawn greeting guests.

She was perched on Benjamin's arm, chatting politely with

his business associates. She knew each of their names and the intricacies of their families, and she played the perfect hostess flawlessly. But as Bea watched, that sculpted woman blurred into the mother of her early childhood—the mother of bare feet and untamed hair, of water-gun fights and three-legged races. The mother who had been loved by her father for spontaneous kisses and Christmas carols in July. The mirage was over in a blink; that mother turned to stone again, gone.

The whine of the string quartet began. The several hundred seats were nearly full, and Gerald was standing with his groomsmen at the front of the crowd. He looked handsome. Bea could practically hear the ladies on the lawn whispering as much to each other. He *was* handsome, but her body never had the right response to him. Her heart never trip-trapped happily at the sight of him; she never felt heat sparking when he touched her. His hand on her back may as well have been a cold marble wall, no more. She'd tried to force her feelings, to talk herself into love. Her mother had said it was possible—to choose to love someone. But Bea's heart wouldn't cooperate.

Her mother would be coming for her any minute. Suddenly, Bea felt a shortage of oxygen. There wasn't enough air, and her dress was drowning her. She flung open the sitting room door, ran through the hallway, and grabbed Benjamin's car keys off his bureau and the cash from his wallet. Three hundred dollars. She'd make it last long enough to get where she needed to go. She flew down the back stairs to the kitchen and out the side door. Everyone was gathered out back for the ceremony, so no one saw her in the driveway. She pulled Benjamin's Rolls-Royce out of the garage just as the string quartet played the opening chords of the Canon in D.

She drove for hours and hours, stopping only to check into cheap motels to sleep and to buy herself some clothes somewhere in Pennsylvania. Five days later, right before she crossed the border into Mexico from El Paso, the baby moved within her for the first time. The tiniest bubble popping under her skin, there was no mistaking the sensation of an alien being inside her. She pulled over, threw her wedding dress over a cactus, and tossed the pearly pink wedding shoes onto the side of the road.

She wished she could shed the little life twirling inside her, but she would bring it into the world. That was the least she could do for it before she let it go. She'd stay in Mexico until she was sure her mother wouldn't force her to go through with the wedding. Luke had once mentioned an artists' commune near Parral where he'd lived for a time. Maybe she could live there for a while. Then she'd figure out where to go until the baby was born. It wouldn't be home, that much was certain.

She took a deep breath, hit the gas, and entered a new world, never looking back as the tires spewed her dress and shoes with baby-fine dust.

PINNY

Her stomach was whining. It had woken her up, and no matter how she shifted on the cushions, it wouldn't hush up. She closed her eyes, trying *not* to think about the eggs and waffles the girls back at Smokebush would be eating this morning. The more she tried *not* to think about them, the more she did, and the worse she felt. She loved those eggs with the stringy yellow cheese melted over the top.

She flipped onto her stomach and reached into her backpack for her jelly beans. The bag came up empty. Then she remembered. She'd finished them off last night.

The whining was a lion's roar now. She sat up. Ray was curled tight, her hands in fighting fists, even in her sleep. Pinny looked out the window. The storm clouds were gone, and moonlight was turning the soaked streets blue. Daylight was probably a ways off; she wouldn't last till then.

An idea zinged through her. Ray had done so much for her. She'd fix her a surprise. She got her backpack ready and put it on, then slid Ray's duffel over her shoulder. She knew where their money was. She'd seen Ray tuck it inside after they'd bought the crackers at the bus station.

Ray wouldn't mind if she used some. She'd sneak out quiet-like and be back before Ray woke up. Ray would be so proud of her, bringing back breakfast! She'd make sure she'd only be gone a few minutes.

She tiptoed to the door, pushed it open without making a sound, and stepped into the soupy night.

She glanced around the parking lot, trying to remember the way they'd come here before. Her jitterbugs started up. Everything looked different coated in midnight. Everything felt different without Ray beside her. But she could do this. Horizons Assist . . . ugh. She didn't need the "Assist" part. No sirree.

She hugged her red Mary Janes to her chest and started walking. Sooner or later, she was sure, she'd run across a donut shop, or maybe, if she was lucky, a grocery store where she could buy donuts *and* more jelly beans.

RAY

It was the first time she'd slept since the horrible thing happened. She woke up crying, sweat trickling down her neck. She pressed her palms against her eyes until they hurt, trying to black out the picture of Carter, trying to forget the one horrible instant that had ended their friendship. It was her fault, that instant. Maybe she could've done something different.

But even now, she didn't know what. As that stricken look had crossed his face on prom night, her mind had had time to think a thousand thoughts, but her body hadn't moved. A thousand thoughts, no motion. It all came down to a second of inertia.

Inertia. It was the one vocab word she'd bothered remembering from sixth-period English. She'd wanted to write a song with that word as the title, and she'd scribbled it on the back of her hand so she wouldn't forget. She'd never written the song. Instead, when the horrible thing happened, she'd become the word. Now she wondered if she'd ever do anything that mattered again, or if she'd stay stuck in her head, reliving the humiliation.

She brushed the sweat off her forehead and flipped over, listening for Pinny's light snore, hoping it would ease her back to sleep. There was nothing but silence.

She jerked up, staring at the empty cushions. She whispered Pinny's name, then yelled it. Nothing. Alarm jabbed her insides, and she grabbed at the darkness, frantically searching for her duffel.

Her duffel was gone, and so was Pinny.

PINNY

She had just stepped out of the twenty-four-hour mini-mart when she saw the woman on the corner. Her skirt was caked in mud, and her white hair reminded Pinny of the thistles she'd accidentally stepped on once in the field behind Smokebush.

There were enough lines on her face to fit out a road map. But what made Pinny stop was her moaning.

"Old Mabel's hurtin'," she mumbled, rocking back and forth. "Yes, she is. Hurtin' somethin' awful."

Pinny stepped closer. She might've been scared, except the woman's back was hunched like a turtle's. Pinny had never been afraid of any turtle in her life, and she wasn't about to start now.

"Who's Old Mabel?" she asked.

"Me, myself, is Mabel," the woman said. She rocked faster, hugging her knees. "Got me some aches in these bones, I tell you. The grave's callin', but I ain't answerin' yet."

Pinny inched closer. "What . . . what should I do?" she asked. "To help with the aches, I mean?"

Old Mabel's one eye opened wider, its milky-brown eyeball swirling like a marble. It was exactly the way Pinny imagined a witch from a fairy tale looking. She bet Old Mabel could pop that eyeball right out if she had the mind to. Luckily, she didn't.

"Could use me some food," Old Mabel said. Her staring eye stuck fast on Ray's duffel. "Some money to get me a place to sleep for the night. Soak these bones in a warm bath, maybe."

Pinny's breath caught as a memory hit her square in the face, a memory of her and Mama camping in the grass in Central Park.

"Spare some change?" Mama'd asked a man in a suit passing by.

"Trash," the man had muttered, and kept right on walking.

Afterward, Mama'd hugged her extra tight. "Never be stingy

with your heart, Chopine," she'd whispered. "You never know when God's gone undercover."

Pinny smiled at that Mama in her mind. She turned to Old Mabel. "I can help you." She unzipped Ray's duffel and reached inside.

RAY

She heard the security guard at the exact moment he saw her. He started whistling when he rounded the corner to the artists' lounge. By the second note, a flat G, Ray was throwing open the exit door.

She barreled down the sidewalk, slamming straight into Pinny, nearly knocking her over.

"Where have you been?" she cried, yanking Pinny toward the parking lot.

Pinny opened her mouth, but the security guard gave a shout before she could say anything, and Ray pulled her into a run. "Never mind. We're leaving . . . *now*."

For once, Pinny didn't argue. Ray took off, willing her screaming feet to move faster, while Pinny brought up the rear. The guard gave it a good effort for a block or so, pouring out a string of curses. Pinny couldn't run as fast as Ray, but even so, they left the guard bent over in front of a bluegrass bar, puffing and red-cheeked.

As soon as he was out of sight, she spun on Pinny, who was looking back the way they'd come, bewildered.

"Where *were* you?" She shook Pinny's shoulders. "You took my duffel!"

"I bought us breakfast," Pinny said. "But then I met Old Mabel. She was hungry. Way more than us. So I gave her the food."

Ray stared at her, too astounded at the pride she heard in Pinny's voice to speak. Then panic gripped her. "Pinny. Where's the rest of the money?"

There was danger in her voice now, and Pinny heard it, too, because her eyes skittered apprehensively.

"She didn't have any place to sleep." She raised her palms helplessly. "She said so!"

Ray ripped the duffel from Pinny's shoulder and tore it open. The pocket where the money had been was empty. So this was her payback for sticking her neck out. . . . Crap! She threw the duffel on the ground, fury coursing through her veins. "You gave it away!"

"She needed it." Pinny's cheeks purpled.

"*We* needed it!" Her ears rang, her pulse bellowed. "How are we supposed to get to New York? What are we supposed to eat?"

"I . . . I . . ." Pinny's lower lip quivered, but she raised her chin stubbornly. "I thought . . ."

"No, you didn't." She spat the words. It was only when she heard their venom and saw Pinny's face crater that she felt shame. But by then, she couldn't stop. "I can't believe I felt sorry enough for you to bring you along."

She'd wanted it to hurt, but she couldn't look at Pinny again to see if it'd worked. Voice hoarse, throat burning, she picked up her things and walked away. She wanted Pinny to give up, to leave her alone for good. But she heard shuffling feet behind her and, finally, a loud sniffle.

"I'm gonna pretend you didn't say that last thing." Pinny's voice was muffled, like she might be wiping her face on her sleeve. " 'Cause pity is the only thing I hate."

They walked in silence after that. It should've made Ray happy. But instead, queasiness cramped her stomach, the kind that comes from having said something beyond hurtful—something truly cruel.

December 8, 1941
New York, New York

DALYA

The day the war came to New York City was the day Henry kissed her for the first and last time. At school that morning, perspiration staled the hallways, and the students' chatter was hushed and frantic. Then came the crackling of the loudspeakers in her classroom as President Roosevelt announced the declaration of war, and the sober, helpless silence that followed. Dalya had seen it all before, and even though it was a familiar scene, the fear still felt as raw.

A few girls began to cry in their seats, and probably because some of the teachers felt like crying themselves, school was dismissed minutes later. Afterward, Dalya wouldn't remember her walk home, the way her feet plodded through the streets to the Ashburys' like they had hundreds of times before. But she would always remember how Henry's pale face looked when she walked into the parlor.

"Did you hear?" she asked, even though she could tell that he had.

"The whole world heard," he said.

"What about your class at Columbia?"

"The other professors canceled their lectures," he said. "But not Dr. Vanson. He didn't think the president's speech was as important as economics. He said as much. So I told him to kiss my ass."

"You didn't." She flinched. It wasn't the first time that Henry'd gotten careless with his misery. He'd pushed the limits with professors before, even openly cheating on exams. He'd hoped one of them would have the courage to fail him. None of them did.

"Your father won't be happy."

"No," Henry said. "And I don't care." He grabbed his crutches and made his way over to his father's liquor cabinet, where he poured himself a tumbler of amber liquid, then drained it.

"Don't do that." She watched him fumble with the bottle again.

"Why not? I've got nothing else to do today." He smiled, and it was so close to a leer that Dalya shuddered. "Guess where my friends went after class? Downtown to enlist." He finished his second drink in one swallow. "They'll all be deployed soon, off to do heroic deeds on the front lines." He stared into his empty glass. "And I'll be here . . . counting Father's money."

He pulled something round and gold out of his pocket and tossed it to her. It was a watch. "Father gave that to me when I started at Columbia. It has our family creed on it. Take a look."

Dalya read the inscription: TIME WASTED IS MONEY LOST.

"Words my father lives by." Henry snatched it back. "How's that for heroic?"

Dalya frowned. "You sound hateful. I don't like it."

"Maybe I am. Maybe that's what they've made me."

"No," Dalya said. "No one can make you hate like that unless you want to."

He looked at her, his eyes pools of bitterness. Then his glance softened. "I wish I could be like you. You have better reasons for hate than me, but you can't. You're not capable of it."

She hesitated at his words. The night her father's shop was destroyed, the freezing nights she'd spent huddled with her dying family at Sachsenhausen . . . there had been moments when she'd felt the thorns of hatred. But she'd never given herself over to it. "I'm capable of more than you know," she said now. "But I don't let it consume me. And you don't have to either."

Faster than she'd thought possible, he crossed the room until he stood so near she could feel the heat of rage coming off his body.

"Don't you see what I am?" He grabbed her roughly by the shoulders, and she lost her breath. "Look at me! I'm only nineteen and I'm half a man! What do I have to look forward to? I'll never be able to do what I want. Or *have* what I want."

"You have your family," she blurted. "They can give you everything."

His eyes bored into hers. In them, something unexpected flickered. Longing. "Not . . . everything."

His kiss was sudden and harsh, with anguish behind it. It felt dangerous, like he was pulling her toward a darker place. But her body responded, wanting more, her arms sliding around his waist, her face lifting to meet his.

Then he pulled away, so abruptly that she stumbled backward.

She didn't understand why until he said, "Hello, Mother."

Mrs. Ashbury stood in the doorway, her mouth taut, her eyes flitting from Henry's face to hers.

"We're at war," she said flatly, and then disappeared up the stairs.

Dalya sank into the nearest chair, trembling.

"Don't worry." Henry broke into a triumphant smile. "I'll talk to her."

Dalya nodded as he left the room, her mind spiraling, her body still liquid and tremulous from his kiss. She thought back to Mrs. Ashbury's words, and she had the unsettling feeling that they were meant entirely for her.

Mrs. Ashbury made sure Henry was out of the house when she did it. Of that much, Dalya was certain. She came home from school the next afternoon to find Mrs. Ashbury sipping tea in the parlor. The house was so quiet Dalya could hear the clock ticking in the dining room.

Mrs. Ashbury smiled, but her eyes had a catlike glint that made Dalya uneasy.

"Dalya," she said. "Join me?"

It was made to sound like a question, but Dalya knew better. She sat down across from Mrs. Ashbury, shaking her head at the tea she was offered.

Mrs. Ashbury draped her arms across her lap. "It's time we talk about your future."

"Yes," Dalya said, hanging on Mrs. Ashbury's words, wondering what was coming next.

"We've loved having you with us." Mrs. Ashbury's voice was a model in sincerity. "And I'm so grateful for your help with the refugee relief efforts. Your story made an enormous impact. You should be proud. Your family would be proud."

"Thank you." Dalya nodded as nausea crept over her.

"You'll be graduating this spring." Mrs. Ashbury patted her hands lightly in her lap. "Have you given any thought to what you'll do afterward? Where you'll go? With your English so improved, I'm sure you could find work easily. You're eighteen now, and I suspect more than ready to be living on your own. We'll continue paying your tuition at Dalton, of course, but perhaps we can start looking for an apartment share for you right away, if you'd like. . . ."

Dalya stared at her. There they were. The words she'd known were coming. Mrs. Ashbury made them sound so sweet, too, as if Dalya would be a fool not to see the appeal of it. As if it were Dalya's choice to make.

"I understand," she said. "You don't want me around Henry. I see what you're doing."

"Oh, please don't misinterpret," Mrs. Ashbury said in a wounded tone. "This is my fault, really. It never occurred to me that this could happen." She sighed. "I only want what's best for you. I don't want you to get hurt in one of Henry's childish games."

The lie sounded empty and absurd.

"What about Henry?" she asked.

"Henry knows what's best for him. He just hasn't accepted it yet."

"Maybe he never will," Dalya countered. She hoped saying it might make it true, but Mrs. Ashbury shook her head.

"If you keep believing that, you'll be heartbroken," she said. "None of us want to see that after what you've already been through. Wouldn't it be better to find someone who can share your history and understand? Someone like you, who knows what it's like . . ."

"Someone Jewish," Dalya finished. The word tasted bitter on her tongue. It was a word that used to taste sweetly of family, of comforts and pride. Now it tasted only of loss. When her manicured politeness was stripped away, Mrs. Ashbury disliked the word, too. For Mrs. Ashbury, "Jewish" wasn't a faith or a culture. It was a label. One she didn't want sticking with her family.

Dalya could've screamed, or fought. She could've spit in her face. But her marble heart didn't flare as it might've years before. It didn't see the point. She stood quietly, and said simply, "Goodbye."

She gathered her schoolbag from the foyer and walked out the door.

For a moment, standing in the doorway, she couldn't think where to go. Then she remembered Ruth Schwarz and the Blumbergs. She dug Ruth's address out of her schoolbag, where she kept it, mostly out of guilt that she'd never used it, and started walking downtown.

She imagined Henry coming home from his lectures for dinner, and Mrs. Ashbury coolly explaining what had happened.

She wanted to be with her own people, Dalya could hear her saying. *We'll miss her terribly.*

Henry wouldn't believe it, and it would only make him hate them more.

That caused her the most pain . . . knowing what it would do to him. And something else, too. Something she didn't realize until later, as she lay under a blanket on the Blumbergs' couch after an exhausting night of fielding worried glances and giving awkward explanations.

She'd left her father's bag of tools behind, tucked in the back of the Ashburys' closet, unwanted and abandoned.

Only then did she feel truly sick. Sick of everyone, sick of the world and its traitorous promises of human kindness and love that, in the end, amounted to nothing.

PART VI

"The Silver Shoes," said the Good Witch, "have wonderful powers. . . . They can carry you to any place in the world in three steps, and each step will be made in the wink of an eye."

—L. Frank Baum, *The Wonderful Wizard of Oz*

PINNY

Pity. It tasted sour in her mouth, and she bit into a black jelly bean to wash it away. *Forget, forget, forget,* her head chanted in time with her steps. Ray was a speeding train in front of her, and Pinny panted to stay close. Not too close, though, not with Ray steaming the way she was.

Pity made Pinny's heart black and blue. It made her think of her birthday party, 'cause that was when she saw it scribbled across Mrs. Baddour's face. Her real birthday was in the middle of summer, but she'd wanted her party to be in August after school started, hoping more kids would come then.

"Twenty-one is a big birthday," Mrs. Danvers had told her. "We can't afford much, but you can invite a few kids over for the party, if you want."

"Careena Baddour!" she'd blurted, not even needing time to think about it. "I'm inviting Careena and the dance team!"

"Careena's a busy girl," Mrs. Danvers said. "She's got dance competitions, and her boyfriend. . . ."

"But I'm her best girl. She said so," Pinny said. "Plus, she's the dance-team captain, and captains support their team."

"You're not on the dance team," Mrs. Danvers said.

"I'm going to be," Pinny said. "After tryouts next week."

Careena never used to talk to her, but right before Careena became the president, that changed. On account of Pinny being so helpful handing out the VOTE FOR CAREENA buttons and all. Careena walked with her in the hallways. She gave her jobs to do. Careena needed her. "I'd be lost without you, Pinny," she'd told her. "Honestly."

"But I could always find you," Pinny told her. " 'Cause of your shoes." Careena had more shoes than anybody she'd ever met. She wore a different pair practically every day. Pinny had tons of photos of Careena's shoes, and she knew them all by heart. Careena was pretty, too, the way Pinny remembered Mama being. A sparkle sort of pretty that made other kids look at her and smile. Like she was a flower and they were the bees. Flowers like Careena had lots of friends. Pinny thought she was one of them.

Not the sorts of "friends" the special-ed kids always had, either. Principal Tate made announcements about those kinds every week.

"Don't forget, people," the intercom ordered, "our fellow students in Room 305 deserve our hellos in the hallways. Eat lunch with them, invite them to the movies, be their friends. They are part of the student body."

What part? Pinny wondered. Not the eyes, the smile, the

hair. Not a part people noticed much. More like . . . a belly button. There, but usually tucked under something and forgotten about.

Pinny got "hi"s in the hallways, but no phone calls after school. She worked with other kids on the school paper, but never got asked to the movies. She wasn't a friend kids shared secrets with. When people called her "friend," they meant the belly-button Room 305 kind. They called her "friend" because they had to. Not Careena, though. She meant it.

And after Careena came to her birthday, after Pinny made dance team, Pinny would have more real friends, 'cause then Careena's friends would be hers, too.

She'd given the invitation to Careena in the cafeteria, right when she was talking to Principal Tate about the dance-team tryouts.

"The party's this Saturday," Pinny told her. "I made the invitations myself." She pointed to the cutouts she'd made of Dorothy's shoes. The red glitter she'd used was rubbing off a little. "Want to come?"

"Oh, wow, Pinny. This looks fun." Careena's cheeks pinked right up as she brushed some red glitter off her shirt. "I have to check the date. I have some stuff coming up—"

"How nice, Pinny!" Principal Tate jumped in. "Careena's such an exemplary leader at our school, and after all the hard work you two did together on her campaign, I'm sure she'd love to." He looked at Careena. "Wouldn't you?"

"Um . . ." Careena gave her shiny smile. "Sure. Sounds fun!"

On the day of the party, Pinny waited for the doorbell. She waited until the pizza Mrs. Danvers made got cold and chewy, until the *Wizard of Oz* DVD played four times in a row. The doorbell rang late, and when Pinny opened the door, Mrs. Baddour was standing there.

"Happy birthday, Chopine!" Mrs. Baddour smiled. "I came by to drop this off for you." She placed a present in Pinny's hands. "We had a, um, family function today. It came up suddenly . . . you know how it is. Careena's so sorry to miss your party, though." She stepped off the porch, waving. "I hope everyone else had a great time!"

"No one else came," Pinny said. Of course, Ray, Nancy, Mrs. Danvers, and the other Smokebushers were at the party, but they *had* to be. They lived there.

That was when Pity showed up, squashing Mrs. Baddour's cheeks into dried red apples. She looked at Pinny the way she'd look at a dead dog flattened on the road.

"Oh, I'm sorry," she croaked. "If I'd known . . ." She sighed, then smiled sunnier than before. "Well, I'm sure Mrs. Danvers made you a delicious cake." She checked her watch. "I *must* run. I'm late—"

Pinny shut the door on the rest of her words.

When she turned around, Ray was in the hall, holding two plates of cake.

"I heard." She shrugged. "It's like drowning in a bucket of cat piss. It stinks, and there's no way out."

Pinny wrinkled her nose, giggling through her tears. That's what she loved about Ray. Ray was no faker. She didn't try to convince Pinny that she wasn't a lousy belly button. She only told her how much it stunk to be one.

"I'm still trying out for dance," Pinny said forcefully, wiping her eyes. "Careena will see how good I am, and then . . ."

Then what? Pinny didn't know. She wasn't ready to quit, that much she knew. Ray handed her the cake.

"Come on," Ray said. "You know I hate *The Wizard of Oz*. But today, for you and only you, I'll watch it."

Pinny smiled. She'd been wrong. A friend had turned up at her party after all. Ray.

That was the Ray from the birthday party, though. Not the Ray steaming ahead of her on the sidewalk right now. That other, kinder Ray was in there, but she didn't pop out much these days. And Pinny was getting downright tired of waiting for her to come back.

RAY

She found the campsite by accident. She'd been walking for several hours, drifting down streets without seeing them. Furious, but emptied out of fight. *No money. No money. No money.* Two words that pounded through her head, and no way to get rid of them.

Pinny was somewhere behind her, her footsteps keeping a safe distance. A good thing, too. Because Ray didn't trust herself right now.

Her burning feet finally forced her to stop, and when she did, she blinked, taking in her surroundings for the first time since they'd left the Opry. There was a freeway to her left, humming with traffic, but the street they were on was less congested than the downtown area they'd been in before. Ahead of them, a sign sticking up from a brick column read JAMBOREE CAMPGROUND. An overstuffed cartoon bear wearing a cowboy hat pointed down a lane bordered by trees. RVs and tents dotted the campground, which was crowded enough that they stood a chance of sneaking in unnoticed.

"Follow me," Ray said to Pinny. "And *don't* say a word to anybody."

Ray skirted the welcome center, thankful there weren't any campsite employees hovering near the entrance. She steered away from the main buildings and sites bustling with families, where parents might get curious about two girls on their own. Farther back were remoter sites, where the trees thickened and RVs had planters and recliners alongside them. She took this as a hopeful sign that these RVs "lived here" permanently, and that this part of the campground wasn't monitored as closely.

A small, empty site butted up against the tree line on one side and a rusted RV on the other.

"Here," she said, and began setting up Mrs. Danvers's tent. Pinny sat on the ground a few feet away, watching, but Ray avoided her gaze. She wanted Pinny to stay angry with her. In the end, it would be easier that way.

She was kicking the last stake into the ground when a voice behind her said, "Well, what do we have here? Two lovely little ladies for new neighbors. It's my lucky day."

She turned to see a bristly, leather-faced man in snakeskin boots and a sweat-stained T-shirt. His smile oozed across his lips, making Ray's skin crawl.

"I'm JT." He extended his hand while his eyes started at her feet and worked their way up, stopping in all the wrong places.

Ray held up her palms in a helpless gesture. "Sorry." She shrugged. "Dirty."

But Pinny grabbed his hand. "I'm Pinny and this is Ray," she said with a smile that Ray wished she could've stopped. "I love your boots."

"Thank you," he said. "Genuine cottonmouth. A four-footer. I have his head on my hat in there." He nodded toward his trailer.

"Really?" Pinny gaped. "You killed him yourself?"

"Yes, ma'am," JT said proudly. "Had to. Found him in the shower one morning. It was him or me." He winked.

"Wow," Pinny said, awestruck. "I have to get a picture of these." She grabbed her camera, but Ray stopped her.

"Pinny," Ray said. "We should go find the bathrooms. . . ." It was the best she could come up with to end the chitchat before Pinny got too friendly.

"Oh, you can use the one in my trailer if you need to." JT smiled. "Everyone's like family here."

"No thanks," Ray said quickly, her insides squirming. "We wanted to check out the rest of the campground anyway. . . ."

Her voice died as a tan car wielding a JAMBOREE banner pulled up and a security guard climbed out of it.

"Hey, JT," the guard said. He smiled friendly enough, but his eyes were focused on their tent. "Girls." He tipped his hat, then shifted his gaze to Ray. "Did you miss the welcome center on your way in? I don't recall you paying for your stay."

Ray opened her mouth, lies ready. But before she could utter a sound, JT was talking, nice and easy. "That's my fault, Earl," he said. "I was so excited about my nieces coming to visit that I forgot to swing by to get them squared away."

"Your . . . nieces?" the guard repeated doubtfully.

JT nodded. "My sister dropped them off earlier. Guess it

was before your shift started." He clapped a hand down on Earl's shoulder. "It's a mite early, but we're fixin' to sit down to some barbecue. Got to eat before I go to work downtown. Could I drop the money off tomorrow with my rent? I figured that wouldn't be a problem."

"Course not," Earl bumbled. "No problem. Only doing my job. You know how it is. There was a break-in at the Opry during the blackout. Some punk kids spent the night inside, looks like."

"Really?" JT raised an eyebrow. "Any damage?"

Earl shook his head. "Nope, not that anybody can see. Old Charlie didn't get a good enough look at 'em to do anything. Just put the word out to watch for strays." He looked at Ray and Pinny long and hard, then smiled, as if he wasn't sure what he believed but wasn't about to challenge JT. "You gals enjoy your visit with your uncle, now."

"We will!" Pinny waved as Earl drove away, and Ray could guess what she was thinking. *A sister and an uncle in two days' time! Jackpot!*

"See?" JT's eyes steadied on Ray's. "Like family."

"We . . . we don't have any money." Her face burned.

"I figured as much. I recognize fellow nomads when I see them. I wouldn't be where I am unless somebody did me a favor once, so don't you worry about it." He clapped his hands loudly and rubbed them together. "Now, how 'bout that barbecue? You girls look hungry."

"Starving!" Pinny piped up.

"Then you've got a feast coming your way," he declared before disappearing into the trailer.

"Isn't he nice?" Pinny looked after him. "He smells like sardines, but he's nice."

Ray opened her mouth to argue, then shut it again. She didn't like JT, and no way in hell did she trust him. It didn't matter, though. She'd only be here for one night, and she hadn't been planning to sleep anyway. Not after what happened last night.

JT reappeared with paper plates piled high with pulled-pork po'boys, and for the next half hour, the three of them ate in happy camaraderie. Ray wished Pinny wouldn't gab the way she did, spilling their business to JT like he really was their long-lost uncle. But that didn't matter much either. Not anymore. And even she had to admit the barbecue was delicious.

Once they finished eating, JT announced that he had to go downtown to sell some of his snake merchandise.

"I won't be back till late," he said. "You're welcome to join me for breakfast in the morning. I cook a mean omelet."

Ray was relieved to see him go, but the second his truck disappeared, a tense silence wedged its way between her and Pinny. Later when it got dark, they squeezed into the cramped tent and spread out the sleeping bag like a makeshift mattress underneath them. Ray bit her tongue when Pinny used the better part of a corner for the creation of her nightly shoe-and-watch shrine. Ray even scrunched down so her head wouldn't knock the Mary Janes and screw up their "hugging." She could do that much for Pinny, as a parting gift.

The heat was stifling, but every once in a while, a breeze blew, cooling things off enough to be bearable. Ray lay still, listening for Pinny's snore to start. It didn't, and after a few minutes, there was a soft whisper.

"Ray? Are you awake?"

"Yes."

There was a sigh, and then, "I'm sorry. About the money. My numbers just get . . . mixed up sometimes."

"I know. I'm sorry, too. About what I said."

"Hey!" Pinny nudged her grudgingly. "I can't forget it if you bring it up!"

Ray snorted a laugh. "Right."

"Anyway, you didn't mean it," Pinny said. "It was only your mad side. . . . It wasn't *you*."

"God, Pinny!" Ray threw up her hands. "I don't have some . . . secret sap identity. I'm never going to turn into Glenda the Good."

"Maybe not. But you can't stop me from waiting for it." Pinny shifted, and Ray was sure she was smiling in the dark. "I'm glad you're here with me."

Ray clenched her eyes shut against the guilt squeezing her heart. "I am too," she whispered.

Then she waited, barely breathing, barely moving. When Pinny's breath grew deeper and smoother, she eased herself off the sleeping bag and grabbed her stuff. Tearing a page from her music notebook, she wrote the phone numbers for Smokebush and the police. Then she added instructions for what Pinny should do when she woke up in the morning.

Go straight to the welcome center. Call the police, then Mrs. Danvers. Wait for someone to come and take you back to Jaynis.

It was as simple as that. Pinny would do it. She'd have to do it. Because by then, Ray would be long gone.

DALYA

Henry was waiting for her at school the next afternoon. His eyes seemed to have hardened overnight, and his face had a determination that she found frightening and flattering all at once. Her mind told her to walk right past him, to make Mrs. Ashbury's lies about her seem true. But her heart made that impossible.

"You shouldn't have come," Dalya said, with much less conviction than she'd intended.

"*You* shouldn't have left," he said. "And don't try to tell me it was your idea."

Dalya stared at the ground, but her trembling lip gave her away, and an instant later, he'd wrapped her in his arms. She wanted to bury her face in his shoulder, to never move again. Instead, she pulled herself away.

"I need to go." She turned, but he caught her arm.

"It doesn't have to be like this." It was a plea. "They don't have to win. I can move out, quit school. We can be together."

"How?" she asked. She knew he didn't have the answer, and neither did she.

He gripped her hands like lifelines, so tightly his pulse seemed to beat in her own skin. "We can go someplace where it doesn't matter what we are, or who we are."

"I've stopped believing in places like that," Dalya said, and as soon as she did, she felt her soul aging. She wanted to swallow the words back down, but it was too late for that.

"Please." His voice shook. "I can be a good person with you. You'll make me better than I am."

His heart beat in her hands, and hers matched it, with certainty, like it had always belonged there. Even though she'd never experienced it before, she recognized what she saw reflected in his eyes, because she felt it, too. This was love. The rare kind that never comes for most people, and only once for those lucky enough to find it. The passionate, hungry kind that could make people great, or destroy them. But there was anger in his eyes, too. Too much of it, hovering, ready to consume everything else. Because of the anger, she knew what he asked was impossible.

If she took it on, with the griefs already in her own heart, she might become all anger, too. Her heart was probably beyond repair, but she wasn't ready to give up on it entirely.

"I—I'm . . . not strong enough," she stammered. "Not for both of us. I can't."

A shadow spread across his face, and he threw her hands back at her. "You don't know what I'll become."

"You'll become whatever you choose." Her heart strained against its cage, but stayed in it, barely. "You can be just as good without me. Maybe even better."

"You're wrong," he whispered. Grief twisted his features, and a single sob escaped his throat.

He climbed into the back of the Ashburys' car and left without another word. She'd hurt him badly, maybe even irreparably, and fear gripped her as she watched him go.

PART VII

They went into my closets looking for skeletons, but thank God, all they found were shoes, beautiful shoes.

—Imelda Marcos

May 1968
El Paso, Texas

DANIEL

Danny loved the brokenness of abandoned things. He didn't know why Officer Newton couldn't understand that. Here he was, in the back of the squad car again, slumped down in the seat, waiting for his house to come into view. The first time he'd ridden in the squad car, Officer Newton had flashed the lights and turned on the siren for him. Not anymore. Today, his frown stretched the entire length of the rearview mirror.

Luckily, Danny had hidden the pale pink shoes before Officer Newton picked him up. They were safe at the bottom of his backpack right now. He'd been walking home from school when he saw them. He'd dug through the Dumpsters near the trailer park first, but finding nothing but rotten food, he'd decided to give Highway 10 a try. People were forever tossing stuff out car windows. He'd spotted the shoes between two cactuses by Exit 18. That dust kicked up from passing cars coated their tiny, fragile flowers and pearls infuriated him. How could anything so precious get thrown away? They were perfect in every way, and he had to have them.

He'd gotten lucky and found a wedding dress, too. It was tattered, but he could see it had once been beautiful. He'd been holding it when Officer Newton had pulled onto the shoulder beside him. Now the dress sat in the front seat next to Officer Newton, held hostage.

"All right, Danny." Officer Newton stopped the car alongside the curb. "Let's get you inside."

Danny skulked behind Officer Newton, his stomach pinching, preparing for the interrogation.

When they stepped into the marble foyer, Suki, his nanny, was looming on the staircase, her stare formidable.

Officer Newton explained everything while Suki clucked her tongue and muttered, "Lordy, Lordy," and Danny bore holes in the floor. Finally, Officer Newton left, but not before giving Danny a talking-to.

"Look, son," he said. "I know your mom and dad aren't home much. But you can't keep losing track of yourself this way. You've got no business roaming that highway. You could get hit by a car, or picked up by some lunatic." He gave him a manly slap on the back. "And for God's sake, stay out of people's trash. You stink like a mound of pig slop."

The door clicked shut, and Danny waited for Suki's scolding to kick in where Officer Newton's had left off. But there was only a sigh and then, "Come on. Let's get you upstairs for a bath."

The wedding dress was banished to the back porch as if

it were contaminated, but Danny had time to hide the shoes in his closet before his bath. Knowing that they hadn't been discovered made what came at dinnertime a lot easier to take.

When his parents got home from work, Suki motioned them into Danny's father's office for a hushed conversation. Afterward, his parents sat down across from him at the dinner table, exasperated.

"Really, Daniel," his mother started in. "This is the third time in a month you've been caught digging up garbage in the bad part of town. What has gotten into you?"

"It's not garbage," he said. "I'm using what I find to make art."

"To make messes, you mean, " his father said. "Those piles of junk you piece together in the garage are an eyesore."

"It's not a productive use of your time," his mother added.

The lecture went on, but Danny didn't dare defend himself. The collages he made from old skirts, hats, and jewelry looked odd to most people, but putting them together made him feel peaceful all over. Still, he had to be careful. He knew what happened when boys who came from "decent people" got into trouble. Boarding school. His friend Eric had disappeared that way, and he was not about to suffer the same fate.

So, he listened. He promised not to go near Highway 10 anymore, or to dig through Dumpsters. Finally, when his parents had bored even themselves with the lecturing, they sent him to his room. Once he shut the door, he smiled. He was free.

He ran to his closet and dug out his two newfound treasures—a pair of broken clip-on earrings he'd unearthed from his teacher's wastebasket last week, and the pale pink shoes he'd found today. He locked his door and carefully laid the earrings on the bed. He caressed them, admiring the way the silver teardrops fractured the light. Then he stepped into the shoes. They were too big for his feet, but that didn't matter.

He arched his ankle, examining himself in the mirror. His legs were too knobby and hairy—not the way a woman's sleek legs should look. The shoes were beautiful, though, even on his awkward feet.

He dug for these buried treasures in trash cans always, because he could never take anything from his mother's room. When he was smaller, he'd loved watching her get dressed. He loved the silkiness of the fabrics she wore, how her skirts flowed when she moved. He loved beautiful clothes; he loved watching women wearing them. As he got older, his mother told him it wasn't proper for him to be in her room, playing in her closet. His father told him it was freakish. They told him . . . told, told, told. So much talking, without ever understanding. But he couldn't explain that he felt more normal around high heels and jewelry than he did playing cops and robbers or Lone Ranger. He couldn't much understand it himself. But somehow, it felt as natural as breathing to him.

He could never tell anyone. It wasn't right—a boy collecting women's trinkets. Everyone said so. Pastor Marshall, Suki, his parents. It wasn't right. It wasn't normal.

Tonight, though, he held the pale pink shoes as their pearl beading shimmered, and he smiled. All those words were lost on him. They didn't change a thing. But the shoes—the shoes gave him a glimpse of who he wanted to be.

PINNY

Pinny woke to good-morning voices, sleeping bags unzipping, and a crackling campfire. But none of those cozy sounds were coming from her tent. Her tent was so quiet she could hear a shushing from her sleeping bag whenever she breathed.

"Ray?" she called, sitting up.

Then she saw it. The note in the corner where Ray's duffel and guitar had been. Ray was gone.

"Ray!" Heat filled her belly. She'd been so sure Ray would do right by her. And now here she was, without Ray. Without anybody.

She beat her fists on the ground, but that only made her hands sore. So sore that she felt like crying. Then she *was* crying. Droopy tears that dribbled off her chin and made her nose a river. That made her even madder, because crying like this always gave her the hiccups.

"Everything all right in there, darlin'?" a voice called from outside. A person-shaped shadow loomed over the tent.

"JT?" she said through her hiccups. She unzipped the tent to see him smiling down at her, a steaming frying pan in his hand.

"None other." He tipped his hat. "I hate to hear a pretty gal like you cryin'. Why don't you come on outta there and tell me what the problem is?"

Pinny nodded, dressed quickly, then climbed out of the tent, wiping her eyes. JT handed her a plate brimming with scrambled eggs, biscuits, and gravy.

"JT's all-you-can-eat breakfast." He winked. "On the house." He motioned to the folding chair next to his grill. "You eat while you tell me what's eatin' *you.*"

She took a bite of eggs and sniffed. "Ray up and left. She promised to take me to New York, but she lied. Her note says I should go back to Smokebush." She gave her eggs a grumpy shove with her fork. "I won't do it! She thinks she knows what's best for me. Like everybody else. But I can decide my own self!"

JT patted her shoulder. "Of course you can. You seem like a gal who knows how to take care of herself just fine." He sat down next to her. "But what's so special about New York that you need to get there so bad?"

Pinny smiled, and before she'd finished her eggs, she'd told JT everything. About Mama's shoes. Daddy's watch. The invisible princess. She'd even told him about the pink high heels she had hidden in her backpack. He was a good listener. He said she was right to be mad, and that made her feel better.

"You know, I'd love to see those pink shoes," he said. "Why

don't you come on inside the trailer and show me? Then we'll see about gettin' you to New York." He opened the door to the trailer, waving her inside.

"Really?" Pinny stood up. "You can help me get to New York?"

"Sure," he said. "We're friends, right? Friends help each other out."

Pinny nodded. She'd thought Ray was her friend, too, until this morning. Well, she'd show her. Maybe she'd even get to New York before Ray did. 'Cause together she and JT would figure out a way to get Mama's shoes back.

She smiled, then swung her backpack over her shoulder and climbed the steps into the trailer.

RAY

Ray stood on the side of the road with her thumb in the air as car after car passed her. So far, no one had even slowed down. She checked her watch. Eight o'clock. Pinny would probably be awake by now. Had she seen the note yet? What if she hadn't? Ray's stomach churned. Pinny wouldn't go looking for her on the streets of Nashville, would she? What if she left the campsite and couldn't find her way back?

Stop it. Ray pushed the thoughts away. It wasn't her job to look after Pinny. But the pitching of her insides wouldn't quit, and she knew why.

There'd been other times, lots of times, when she'd looked the other way.

She closed her eyes and tried to shake the memory out of her head. But it stuck there, until she could smell the bitter bleach in the bucket, feel the weight of the mop in her hands. Until she was back in the gym last fall, swiping halfheartedly at the bleachers with the mop, watching the dance-team tryouts. She'd been sentenced to scrubbing the bleachers after getting caught ditching English. She didn't care. Punishment was her comfort zone. Without it, no one would notice her. Not even Carter anymore.

To Carter, she'd become another blurry face at a desk. It was torture, being near him in "teacher mode," when he acknowledged her politely but without the easy openness of summer. A single smile, though, or a casual question about music . . . she could live off that for weeks. She gnawed the bones of hope Carter threw her, but her frustration over him, over the dead-end, small-town future closing in on her, was what fueled her. If she wasn't lashing out at the world, she couldn't control her corner of it. Scrubbing bleachers was just the lame price she paid.

Besides, she'd been getting a good laugh out of the dance tryouts. Careena and her co-captains were running them with all the bitchability they could muster. Careena was trying to be diplomatic in her Miss Politician mode, offering compliments even to the worst dancers, but they were too sugarcoated to sound even remotely sincere. Meanwhile, Meg was whining that every candidate danced like a stripper or a Bible-beating revivalist possessed by the Holy Spirit (apparently, neither one qualified as Jaynis Dancette material).

That was the moment when Pinny walked in, with her

shoelaces untied and her ponytail slipping messily out in every direction. Ray gripped the mop in a choke hold, fearing she was about to witness a slaughter. Pinny'd been gushing about the tryouts for weeks. Not one of those Dancette drama queens had bothered coming to Pinny's birthday, but that had only made Pinny more obsessed with winning their friendship. Ray didn't get why Pinny had to reach for the upper crust to feel like she belonged. Then again, Ray was reaching for Carter. God, maybe they both had delusions of grandeur.

"I'm next," Pinny announced happily.

Careena's mouth opened in a silent O, but she recovered a second later, smiling. "Great!" she crooned, nodding to Meg and Kim. "Show us what you've got."

She perched her head on her hands, her expression one of polite, coddling interest, as Meg turned on the music and Pinny began her routine.

Pinny's movements were slow and clumsy, and she stumbled a few times. She kept smiling, though, even as her cheeks blotched with sweat. But it was on her first high kick that everyone saw the blood. A red blemish blooming in the crotch of her shorts.

Careena covered her mouth, blushing. Meg turned to Kim, mouthing, "Oh my God," and an uncomfortable giggle followed.

Ray watched it happen. The smirk on Meg's face made her want to vomit. But still, she didn't move a single inch.

When the music ended, Meg leaned toward Careena as they clapped.

"Shouldn't you say something to her?" Meg whispered,

snickering. "I mean, you're so close to her and everything. Bes-ties, right?"

"No!" Careena hissed, keeping her eyes on the notepad in front of her, her face puckered with mortification. "No. She helped me out with campaigning, but . . . we're not friends or anything." She shrugged. "I'm sure the special-ed aides will deal with it. That's why we have them." Then she stood up quickly, smiling at Pinny. "That was incredible!" Her voice gushed enthusiasm. "Thank you so much."

"So, I made the team?" Pinny asked hopefully.

Careena dropped her eyes, acting very busy scribbling notes. "Um . . . we'll see. We won't know anything until after the rest of the tryouts. We'll post the new team members next week."

Pinny walked away beaming, waving over her shoulder. And Ray let her go. She stayed as Careena sat back down, blowing out a breath.

"That was completely awkward," she said with a stilted laugh after Pinny left. "I don't know why Principal Tate said we had to let her try out, when she didn't stand a chance." She crossed Pinny's name off the list on her notepad. "Well, nobody can say we didn't do our part." She shook her head. "At least, it's out of the way."

In the moment, Ray could've done so many things. She could've told Careena off. She could've gone after Pinny. She knew what was right, but she didn't have the momentum to follow through. "Inertia," the word of cowards.

Later, when she saw Mrs. Haley, an English teacher, lead Pinny from her locker to the restroom, whispering in her ear, a gnawing started in her gut. It stayed with her for days, making her want to strangle the memory of that afternoon right out of her body.

The gnawing gave her inspiration for the very unflattering picture she drew in permanent marker on every stall of the girls' bathroom the next day. A piece she coined "Queen Careena." But it didn't get rid of the gnawing.

It was with her now as she stood on the side of the road, waiting to abandon Pinny. She straightened her shoulders, determined not to give in to it.

A car slowed, pulling up next to her. A friendly-looking girl in her twenties leaned over the steering wheel.

"Need a lift?" she said.

Ray put her hand on the car door. She wouldn't get another chance like this. Besides, the sooner Pinny realized that she couldn't rely on the world to come to her rescue, the better. Ray had learned that long ago, and now it was Pinny's turn. After that, Pinny would be fine. Maybe not as happy, but fine, all the same.

DALYA

Dalya had been sleeping on the couch at the Blumbergs' apartment for a month when the knock came at the door. They'd invited her to live with them until she graduated and could find steady work, but she'd told them she'd stay only until she found an after-school job and a place to live. She'd reluctantly accepted the Ashburys' offer to continue paying her tuition, knowing she needed to graduate to have any chance at all of supporting herself in the future. Even so, she didn't want to rely on anyone's charity—the Ashburys' or the Blumbergs'—for a second longer than she had to. That afternoon, she was studying with Ruth at the kitchen table when she heard the doorbell and the click of Mrs. Blumberg's heels as she went to answer it.

Then Mrs. Blumberg was in the kitchen, looking baffled. "Dalya. Someone's here for you."

Dalya stood, worry pulsing through her. If it was Henry, she didn't know if she'd be able to refuse him this time. But when she rounded the corner of the kitchen, it wasn't Henry she saw. It was a ghost, time worn, all trace of boyhood gone, but with the same unwavering eyes.

"Aaron?" she choked, bracing herself against the doorframe. He smiled slowly, sadly. "I told you I'd find you."

The Blumbergs were full of questions, but Dalya couldn't breathe, let alone fathom explanations. So after making some vague excuses, she and Aaron left the apartment and started walking uptown. Dalya paid no attention to the blocks that passed. Instead, she walked beside him, too stunned to say anything except one repeated word: *"How?"*

Once they were seated on a bench on the outskirts of Central Park, he told her. He told her of how he'd been put on a train from Sachsenhausen to Auschwitz but had jumped from it in the middle of the night. How he'd limped through the countryside, hiding in the forest, camouflaging himself with mud and leaves and living off insects, wild berries, and anything else he could find. How with the help of a few brave people willing to hide him, he'd worked his way out of Europe and then to Argentina. There, he'd waited for months for an American visa.

"Finally, I got on a boat to Texas," he told her. "But they kept us aboard in Galveston Bay for a week before they let us come ashore, even with our approved visas. They told us it was for our own safety, but really it was the government." He shook his head. "Everybody in America wants to be sympathetic to the plight of refugees, as long as we don't move here."

"But they let you off the boat," Dalya finished, "and you came to New York?"

He nodded. "My mother has a distant cousin who lives here," he said. "They own a kosher market at Ninety-Second and Broadway. I've been working there and sleeping on their floor. Until I can afford a place of my own."

"But . . . how did you find me?" she asked. "How could you know I was here?"

"I didn't," he said, almost in a whisper. "I hoped that you'd found a way to stay alive. It seemed so . . . impossible. But then I remembered your father's friend Leonard Goodman. I wrote to him, hoping he'd heard from you, if you were alive. He gave me the Ashburys' address."

Dalya swallowed hard, her pulse roaring. "You went to them?"

Aaron nodded. "I talked with Mrs. Ashbury first, but she told me you'd left without telling them where you were going." His expression turned thoughtful. "Then Henry came to the door."

At the mention of Henry's name, Aaron looked at her cautiously. Even though she tried to hide the tremor that ran through her, she saw an unhappy question answered on Aaron's face.

Understanding came into his eyes, and then pain, but after a few seconds of silence, he continued. "Henry remembered you running into Ruth Schwarz and Ann Blumberg. I tried a dozen other Blumbergs on the Upper West Side, but today I went farther downtown and finally found the right ones. Still, it doesn't seem real."

"No, it doesn't," she whispered. He leaned forward on the bench to stare at the ground, his elbows resting on his knees. His once-familiar face was a canvas of cracks and creases that made him look older, and infinitely sadder than she'd ever seen him. "But . . . you found me."

"Yes. I promised your father I would." He focused his eyes on hers, and he reached out his hand, like he was about to slide it into hers. Instead, he dropped it helplessly to his knee. He sighed and straightened. "I've told you my story. Now, will you tell me what happened to you?"

She wrung her hands in her lap, weighing the heaviness of what he was asking, trying to gauge if she'd come out alive on the other side of the question. But she couldn't say no. He'd followed her halfway around the world. She owed him an answer.

"Do you remember that night in the camp when we talked about being born as another person, and the choices we might make?"

Aaron nodded.

Shame crawled under her skin. "I tried it," she whispered. "I tried becoming someone else, just to forget. I wanted to see if things might be . . . easier."

"Were they easier?"

"At first," she admitted. "But then . . ." She clasped her trembling fingers. "Then it felt like I wasn't anybody anymore. And that was worse." She bowed her head, unable to meet his eyes, and then, slowly, she told him her story. She was terrified he'd judge her. That he'd hold her accountable for the many months she'd hidden with the Ashburys, the months she'd spent talking about her family as if they were made-up characters in a book, the months she'd never set foot in synagogue or said a Shabbos prayer. But he had no anger or shame for her. At least, not that she could see. He only listened carefully.

As she talked, she felt a few of the scabs on her heart flaking off, turning to dust. Tentatively, she spoke of her parents, her sister and brother. She whispered their names as if they were made of the most fragile glass and would shatter at the faintest breath of wind. She knew she didn't have to tell their story to Aaron. He'd borne witness to it. Instead, she could talk about them and see the light of recognition in his eyes. In their shared memory, the people she'd once loved that had become strangers slowly drew closer to her again. They emerged from the murky shadows, and the curves and colors of their faces solidified.

The pain she'd kept at bay, the grief she'd built a barrier against, ripped the callus from her heart, leaving it scarred but beating furiously, and her tears fell, for the first time, on Aaron's shoulder, mixing with his own.

When she was sapped of tears, Aaron stood up.

"Will you walk with me?" he asked. "There's something I want to show you. Something in this city I don't think you've seen yet."

She didn't recognize the blocks they walked through on the Upper West Side, with their narrower, less austere buildings, their corner markets and colorful coffee shops and delis. But soon enough, she heard it. German, Yiddish, and Polish peppered the streets, drifting from corners and open doorways. Words she hadn't heard spoken in lifetimes, it seemed, words that she herself hadn't thought or dreamt in months, words that sang deliciously in her ears. And with them came other things, wonderful things. The smell of freshly baked challah bread, butcher shops with their names painted in Hebrew on their windows, and kosher delis selling matzo ball soup.

She closed her eyes, letting the familiar sounds and smells take her back to another country, another time. When she opened them again, Aaron was watching her, smiling.

"This is where they're coming," he said. "All of us who had to leave, who survived. It's still a strange land, but it's closer to home than the Ashburys'."

"I can't believe I never came here before," she said. Of course, even back in Berlin, she'd heard about pockets of New York that were like this, teeming with immigrants, welcoming to all. But she'd never wanted to explore on her own to find them, always afraid of the memories they might stir. So much time in this city, and she'd stayed confined to the parts of Manhattan the Ashburys had shown her. Even Henry, intent as he'd been on hating his parents and their world of wealth, had never taken her here.

She didn't want to be anywhere else. They walked for hours and hours, until her feet burned fiercely, but she only wanted to keep going. The streetlights winked on and the sky purpled, but she didn't care, until, suddenly, an air-raid siren ruptured the night.

She froze midstep on the sidewalk and squinted past the glow of the city, searching the sky for planes, listening for their ominous drone. A second later, the lights went out, and the street pitched into darkness. In the blackout, beams from the searchlights downtown in Bryant Park scanned an empty sky.

"Just a drill," Aaron muttered when the streetlights flickered on again, and it was only then that she realized his arm had gone around her shoulder, firmly and protectively. She didn't pull away, but a moment later, his arm slipped to his side.

"The drills are all the time lately," Dalya said. "But look at them." She glanced toward Broadway, still bustling with people and traffic. "No one's screaming or running for shelter. I'm not sure any of them actually believe the war will come here. It must be wonderful, to feel that safe."

"I don't think the war *will* come here," Aaron said. "Even if it does, it could never be the way it was for us."

"I wish I could believe that." Dalya shivered, then straightened. "I should get back to the Blumbergs'. They'll be worried."

Aaron nodded, and they began slowly making their way back downtown.

"Are you glad?" he asked, his voice tentative but hopeful. "That I found you?"

"Yes." She smiled with more genuine happiness than she'd allowed herself since she'd come here, more than she thought she deserved.

"And"—he paused, digging his shoe into the sidewalk—"what about Henry?"

"Henry?" His name stabbed her heart.

Aaron's brow knitted. "Something happened with him. I saw it in his face when I mentioned your name. It's in yours now. Did you . . . ?" He swallowed. "Did you fall in love with him?"

Dalya hesitated, thinking that the truth would be too unkind after what Aaron had done for her. Finally, she settled on a softer, gentler piece of the truth. "I can't make Henry happy," she said. "No one can."

Aaron frowned, and she knew he'd wanted to hear a different answer. Then he sighed, and his frown dissolved into reluctant acceptance.

"This place"—he raised his eyes to hers—"is where I'll make my home. You don't have to share it with me, but I can help you make a home of your own here, too. If you'll let me."

She sensed the rest of what he wasn't saying, the rest of what he was hoping for, but she was thankful he didn't push for more.

"I . . . I can't promise anything," she said quietly. "But I'd like to have your help, and your company."

She waited for him to shake his head, to give up and walk away. Instead, he smiled. "Good." He held out his hand, waiting.

She slipped her fingers into his, and together, they walked through the filmy golden streets, not knowing what the city held for them, but feeling, for the first time since they'd come here, that it could be home.

PART VIII

Between saying and doing, many a pair of shoes is worn out.

—Iris Murdoch

1980
El Paso, Texas

DANIEL

When Daniel came home from the Rhode Island School of Design, he brought his boyfriend with him. It was the first time he'd ever introduced his parents to someone he was involved with romantically. His parents never asked questions about his personal life, and Danny never offered up information. They'd reached an unspoken agreement years ago that Danny's attraction to other boys never had to be acknowledged.

The day Danny brought Pete home changed everything. He needed it out in the open. Pete wasn't just another relationship. The two of them were in love, and Danny wanted to share his happiness with his parents, his friends, the whole world, judgment be damned. Instead, the moment Danny walked through the door with Pete, a curtain fell on his parents' faces. His father didn't extend his hand to Pete. Then there was an awkward dinner, followed by an announcement. His parents thought it best if Danny moved out and got a place of his own. He was nearly through with college. Soon, he'd be on his own anyway. Why should his mother keep up his boyhood bedroom anymore? They'd wanted to convert the room to an office for quite a while.

It was all presented to Danny with deadening calm. Yelling wasn't his parents' way. They were skilled in desensitizing.

After dinner, Danny told Pete to go outside while he got his things, not wanting him to suffer through more of his parents' silent condemnation. When Danny walked into his bedroom, he discovered his mother had already placed a dozen boxes in the room, ready for packing. Danny held back his tears. If this was what they wanted, then he wouldn't waste one tear on them.

He quickly tossed his trophies and books in the boxes. The more he lingered over his things, the more repulsed he became. The very floral and Lysol-infused scent of his parents' house was sickening. He couldn't stand another second here, in this place where he'd always been misunderstood.

But he paused when he unearthed the pale pink shoes from the recesses of his closet. He ran his hand along their sides. How many hours had he spent with these shoes? They'd offered him comfort when he held them, no matter how many disappointments he'd given his parents through the years, how many times they'd misplaced their love for him or forgotten it altogether. The shoes had given him a window into his future. He'd always admired the designs of women's shoes and clothing. And for this summer, he'd landed an internship at one of the top fashion magazines in Manhattan, as a wardrobe assistant. Someday, if he worked his way up, he'd be a full-fledged fashion designer.

He tenderly tucked the shoes into the last box, then let himself out without saying goodbye. Pete was waiting in the car with a hug, and Danny kept his eyes straight ahead as they left town.

They drove by the thrift shop a few hours later. It was in the middle of a nowhere Texas town called Jaynis—a pit stop on the way to Pete's sister's shore house on the Gulf. Danny hadn't given any thought to the boxes, until he saw the tiny little shop. The Pennypinch.

"Stop the car," he told Pete. Hurriedly, he carried the boxes into the shop.

"Are you sure about this?" Pete asked him. "There are memories here."

"Not many good ones," Danny said. "I want it gone. All of it."

When the shop owner, a Mrs. Baddour, pulled out the pale pink shoes and set them on her counter, Danny felt the urge to take them back. Then Pete slipped his hand into Danny's, and Danny smiled. No. Better to leave them behind. Maybe the shoes would find their way onto someone else's feet. Someone who needed them as much as he had. He grazed their flowers with his finger one last time, and then walked away, without looking back.

PINNY

Pinny was pulling the pale pink heels out of her backpack when JT's hand went where it shouldn't.

"Please stop." She gently pushed his hand away. Why did he want to touch her there? It was a private place where no one was allowed. Mrs. Danvers had taught her that. Ray let boys touch her there. Once, Pinny'd seen her under the bleachers with Travis Ross, practically naked. Ray hadn't looked like she liked it much, though.

And Pinny didn't like this. Not one bit. JT smelled like sardines and cigarettes, and being this close to him made the smell worse. He smiled and put his hand on the private place again.

"Come on, darlin'," he said. "I helped you and your friend out yesterday. You owe me a little sugar."

"Stop!" She tried to move past him. But the trailer was small, and he blocked her way, laughing.

"I thought we were friends," she said. "But you are not nice. Not nice at all."

His smile turned crooked in an ugly way. Like the sort of smile a snake might have, if snakes had smiles, which she wasn't sure about. He grabbed her wrists hard, holding them against her sides. "Now, don't fight me. You be nice and quiet and I won't hurt you."

He pushed her backward, toward the bed. He pressed his whole body onto her, squeezing the air out till she couldn't holler, and a storm of jitterbugs rose inside her, filling her with fight. She wiggled under him, but he pressed harder. She wiggled again, and one of her hands sprang free. The hand reached for her backpack, feeling for it somewhere above her head on the bed.

While JT tried to pull down her pants, her fingers scrambled inside the backpack, searching. Brushing against a cluster of smooth bumps on silky softness, her hand made a fist around the shoe.

He was undoing his belt when the shoe hit him. She hit him with it again, then stabbed its heel as hard as she could into his eye.

His scream broke the silence. She clambered off the bed, clutching her shoes and backpack, and slammed into Ray. She was standing by the door, holding her pocketknife.

Ray jabbed the knife in JT's direction, but he was bent over the bed, clutching his eye and moaning. "If he hurt you—"

"No," Pinny said quickly. Ray's eyes were wild, and Pinny was scared of what she might do with the knife.

"Come on," Ray urged. "Before he gets up."

She scuttled down the trailer stairs after Ray. "What about

our tent?" If they left it, Mrs. Danvers would be grumpy. Especially after the magnolias, too.

"Forget it!" Ray said. "We've got to go. Now! Hurry!"

They ran through the campground and out the entrance to the main road. She looked over her shoulder once, thinking she'd heard shouts. It was probably JT. She wondered if he could see out of his eye. She hoped not, at least not until later, after they were gone.

They ran faster, turning corner after corner. Soon, her breath was whooshing in and out like her chest was catching fire.

"Ray," she panted. "I can't run anymore."

Ray glanced back at her, then nodded, slowing down. A minute later, they ducked into a diner that smelled like French fries and burnt coffee. It made her think of Fricasweet's, and she wrinkled her nose. But this smell was better than sardines and cigarettes. For sure.

"Sit down." Ray sank into a booth with red seats. "Even if he followed us down the street, he won't risk a scene in here."

Pinny shook her head. She didn't want to sit. Not right now. Her face was hot and sticky, tears stung her eyes, and her feet burned like firecrackers. She'd left her purple glitter Keds back in the tent. So here she was, barefoot in a diner. But that was fine by her. The tent could keep her Keds, as long as she stayed far, far away from JT. Besides, she still had the pale pink shoes. Those were the ones that really mattered.

She set them on the table, then rubbed her arms. She'd been clutching the shoes so tight, they'd left red dents all over her skin.

"Watch those for me," she said. "I'll be back." Without giving Ray a chance to say anything, she marched straight to the bathroom. She bent over the sink and turned on the faucet, then let the tears loose. She wasn't sure she'd ever understand the meanness of some people. It seemed to stick to certain folks, the way goodness stuck to others. But she never could see it. Not at first, at least. Not until someone did something so nasty to her that she *had* to see it. Like with Careena. She'd kept on giving Careena chances, hoping she'd end up as pretty on the inside as she was out. Well, that'd been one hope wasted. It was the only thing she hated besides pity: the meanness. Why couldn't the world ever manage to get by without it?

She sighed, put her hands into the steaming water, and scrubbed. Her face, her neck, her arms. Everywhere JT had touched. His trash-stink of sardines was still in her nose, and she wanted to get rid of every last bit of it.

RAY

Ray sat in the booth, staring at the pale pink shoes that, a few days ago, had belonged to her. They were haunting her, no doubt about it. She chided herself for not being able to hate them more. Even after the horrible thing and the promise she'd made to forget the shoes, she felt their familiar pull. It was as strong as the very first time she'd seen them.

She'd stolen from the Pennypinch before. She'd stolen from every shop in Jaynis at one time or another. Her fingers always knew she was going to steal before the rest of her did, grabbing and pocketing treasures quicker than a darting dragonfly. Her fingers took small things, mostly. Guitar picks or sheet music, once a pair of junk earrings on clearance at the Wiggly Pig. Doing damage in increments. A few times getting caught; most of the time not.

That day in October at the Pennypinch had been different, though. That day she'd gone to the Pennypinch wanting to take something from Careena and her parents, wanting to wipe the holier-than-thouness off their faces, to rattle their McMansion world. Wanting to pay Careena back for Pinny's birthday, and the dance tryouts, wanting to keep her from making Pinny look like a fool ever again.

When Ray walked into the store, Careena smiled from behind the counter, where she stood beside her mother.

"Ray!" Mrs. Baddour clasped her manicured nails together in a miniclap. "It's always lovely to see you."

"Ray." Careena's voice dripped friendliness. "We got a fresh batch of clothes in this morning. I'd be happy to show you—"

"Don't need you to," Ray muttered, breezing by. She headed for the back of the store, where odds and ends were stuffed helter-skelter on shelves, and clothing racks bulged against the walls. Crumpled, water-stained shoe boxes, probably decades old, teetered in crooked towers along the walls. Everything in the store was tossed together so chaotically that Ray had the impression that Careena and her mother touched the merchandise as little as possible, wanting to avoid contamination. Mrs. Baddour did her Christian duty to help the needy, but only up to a point.

She didn't notice Careena following her until she brushed her arm in a customer-service "I'm here to help" way.

"So ... can I do something for you?" she asked reluctantly, and Ray guessed her mom had sent her back here on a do-gooder mission that Careena wanted no part of.

"Actually, you can," Ray said, mirroring Careena's smile. She drew out each word as she stared at Careena. "Leave ... Pinny ... alone."

Careena blushed, whipping toward a rack of clothes, focusing on organizing them. "I don't know what you mean."

"You do." Ray stepped in front of her. "She's not some ... some project to add to your community-service tally for your college applications."

"Of course not!" Careena gave a tight, awkward laugh. "She's great! She helped me so much with the election and everything. I like her—"

Ray snorted. "Not enough to come to her party."

"Come on," she whispered, avoiding her eyes. "That was months ago. Anyways, what was I supposed to do? She probably doesn't even remember inviting me. And you know she was never going to make the team." She shrugged. "Look, I already put up with her following me around school with that camera. That's more than anyone else would do. I'm sorry if she thinks we're best friends. But I can't help it if she's got the wrong idea."

Just then, Mrs. Baddour called out, "Careena, I need your help!"

Careena glanced toward the front of the store. "I have to go." She started to turn away, then paused. "Were you the one who drew those pictures of me on the stalls in the girls' bathroom?"

Ray gave her a look of doe-eyed innocence. "Oh, right, I saw those. Who knows who did it? You have so many admirers."

Careena's smile cratered, and underneath was anger. "You think you're so much better than me, but I don't think you want her hanging around you either. Not really. Nobody does."

Ray watched her walk to the register, hating Careena for her complacency, and hating herself for not being able to deny what she'd said. Now more than ever, she was on a mission. She scanned the shelves, looking for something that she could slip easily into the pocket of her pants, or under her shirt. She was flipping through the racks when a flash of cherry-red caught her eye. She shoved a pair of puke-brown trousers aside, revealing a satin sheath dress just her size. She stared at the dress with one thought and one thought only: Carter. The dress would make her look older. Prom wasn't until June, but she could wait until then . . . and hope. Maybe if he saw her in the dress, he wouldn't see her as his student. Maybe if he saw her wearing this dress, instead of her ripped tees and worn jeans, he'd see her as someone he could love.

As she pulled the dress off the rack, she jostled some fraying ancient boxes with her elbow, and a shoe fell out from the shadowy depths of one of them, toppling to the floor.

The shoe was old-fashioned, but elegant, with pearl beading at the throat and faded flowers embroidered along the toe. The pale pink fabric was yellowing slightly, and there was a scuff mark along the back of the heel, but that only made its grace more surprising, and appealing. Ray traced the flowers with her fingers, wondering why the shoe had ever been left, forgotten, in this store. It had a displaced, wounded look to it. Like it had been deeply cared for once and was never supposed to have ended up here. It was exactly the way Ray felt about her own life, and a sudden sadness overwhelmed her. She had the strangest sensation that it was coming from the shoe itself, as if it were trying desperately to tell her what had happened, what twists of fate had brought it to this place.

Out of some inexplicable urge to comfort the shoe, Ray pulled off her ratty sneaker and slipped on the pale pink heel. She closed her eyes, waiting for the pain to start. It never did.

The shoe was a pillow cradling her foot, embracing it. Never had a shoe felt so good. Staring down in disbelief, she smiled.

Just then, the front door chimed, and in breezed a troop of Girl Scouts holding bags of donations. Ray sucked in her breath. This was her chance. She shoved the dress down the leg of her baggy cargo pants, then dug through the boxes until she found the pink shoe's mate. She slipped that one onto her other foot, sighing with relief as her pain vanished entirely. With her Reeboks under her shirt, she glided out of the store unnoticed.

Now, in the booth at the diner, Ray squirmed. They were only stupid shoes, for cripes' sake! But she could swear they looked accusing, like they were scolding her for abandoning them back at Smokebush. God, this was completely deranged! No way was she letting shoes make her feel guilty! She slapped one of them roughly, and it fell onto its side. As it did, she noticed that the heel was broken and bent back at an odd angle, exposing a small chamber inside.

Ray tipped the heel upside down and tapped it against the tabletop, and a slip of paper and two shiny objects tumbled out. Ray leaned closer, staring. They were rings. One was a diamond ring. Her heart galloped through her chest. Diamonds.

Diamonds she could pawn once she got to Manhattan. Diamonds that could pay for rent and food, at least for a while. Diamonds that could buy her a comfortable first few months in the city.

She swept the rings swiftly into her pocket. Then, once they were hidden, she picked up the slip of paper. A handwritten message was scrawled across it:

יְהִי רָצוֹן מִלְּפָנֶיךָ ה׳ אֱלֹהֵינוּ וֵאלֹהֵי אֲבוֹתֵינוּ,
שֶׁתּוֹלִיכֵנוּ לְשָׁלוֹם וְתַצְעִידֵנוּ לְשָׁלוֹם
וְתַדְרִיכֵנוּ לְשָׁלוֹם. וְתַגִּיעֵנוּ לִמְחוֹז חֶפְצֵנוּ
לְחַיִּים וּלְשִׂמְחָה וּלְשָׁלוֹם.

It was a language Ray had never seen before. She nearly crumpled the note and tossed it under the table, but hesitated. Someone had put it in the shoe with the rings for a reason. She was taking the rings, no matter what, even if the shoes haunted her for the rest of her life. It was tit for tat, after all the trouble they'd caused. But the note? The shoes could have it. She could care less. She tucked it back into the heel, then set the shoes upright on the table.

As she did, the bathroom door swung open and Pinny emerged with puffy eyes and swollen cheeks. She'd been crying. Ray felt a stab of guilt. If she hadn't left Pinny before, none of this would've happened. Still, though, she'd gone back to get her before JT could really hurt her. Today, she hadn't been part of the Careenas, those everybodies who pretended to like Pinny but then pushed her aside. A peace came over her, like she'd done the right thing. And since she didn't get that feeling much, she went with it.

PINNY

Pinny sat back down, relieved to see that the shoes were exactly where she'd left them. She was worried Ray might want them back, but that wouldn't be fair. Ray'd thrown them away. She didn't deserve them anymore. No . . . Ray should definitely let her keep them, as a way of saying sorry. She made squinty eyes at Ray, to match the mad inside.

"You left me." She squinted harder.

Ray nodded. "Yes." She sighed.

"Why?" Pinny swallowed, staring at the table. "Is it because it's hard? Being with me?" She didn't want to say the next thing, but it was hankering to get out, so she let it. "People . . . they don't always know how to be around me."

"What are you talking about?" Ray blew out a breath.

"You know." Her voice was cranky now. "Remember my dance-team tryouts? I saw you there, cleaning the bleachers. I got my . . . you-know-what." Her face turned steamy thinking about it. "There was blood . . . on my shorts. Careena kept smiling at me, real biglike. I forgot about how she didn't come to my party. I thought she loved my dance. But I heard what she said after about not being my friend. And about letting special ed deal with me. I didn't get that other part until Mrs. Haley took me to the bathroom." She watched Ray's cheeks go cherry. "You were there, too. *You saw.*"

Ray's face shrank, and she slowly nodded.

"You didn't tell me. You let them . . . laugh." She slapped her hand down on the table, and her fork crashed to the floor. "Why?"

"I don't know why!" Ray cried, tugging at the spiky hair hanging over her forehead. "I'm ... I'm a chickenshit, okay? Is that what you want to hear?"

"No." She picked up her fork and gave it a pat by way of apology. "I wanted you to say that you didn't see the blood. Then I'd believe you would've told me about it."

She folded her arms, staring out the window. She didn't want to look at Ray. She was afraid she'd look too ugly. Meanness always made people look uglier. Ray leaned across the table and tapped her arm.

"Look. I ... I used to be brave. I used to fight. But then I got hurt too bad, so I stopped." She sighed. "It wasn't worth it." She said it small and tired, looking down at those safety-pin shoes of hers.

Pinny wondered if Ray was thinking about those scars on her feet. *She* might've given up, too, after scars like that. There was no telling what could wear a person down. "Maybe some people can't hack it," she said. "Being brave. Maybe that's why I never met Daddy. He had a *K* name. Ken, or Kent, or something. Mama told me it, but it's hard to remember it right, 'cause I don't *know* him. He could've been afraid, of how I am." The words were hot in her throat. "Sometimes ... sometimes I think Mama lost her magic shoes on purpose. That maybe she wanted to disappear. Maybe that's how hard it was for her ... taking care of me." She bit her lip before it went quivery.

"You shouldn't think about things like that," Ray said quickly, looking away.

"Why not? Could be true." Pinny shrugged, fiddling with her napkin. "Everyone wants to disappear sometimes. It's only wrong if you don't come back. That day, after the dance try-outs, I wished I could disappear. I saw the mean in Careena. I knew she'd never be nice to me really. I told her so, too."

"You did?" Ray's eyes went big with surprise.

"Yup." Pinny's chin jutted out. "I gave her back her birthday present. The one she got me. It was a good one, too."

"I remember," Ray said. "It was that *Wizard of Oz* doll, right?"

Pinny nodded, thinking about the Dorothy doll Mrs. Baddour had given her, and how pretty it was. It wasn't a doll for babies. Mrs. Danvers had called it a "collectible" and said it was made out of something fancy. "Porchlean," she thought it was called. But whenever Pinny looked at it, it made her stomach hurt, the way it did when she ate too many jelly beans. When the tryouts were over, after school that day, she'd gone to the Pennypinch. Careena was at the counter when she walked in. She was smiling, like always, but Pinny couldn't find the nice in it anywhere this time. Come to think of it, Careena's smile was kind of like JT's that way—all teeth. Not much else.

"Here." She'd put the doll on the counter. "I don't want this."

Careena's smile wobbled. "But . . . it's for you. You should keep it. Please . . . keep it."

"Why? So you feel better?" Pinny gave the doll a little push toward Careena. "Give it to your next best girl."

Then she walked right out of the shop with her stomach doing some happy growling, telling her it was ready for some jelly beans again.

"I thought you loved that doll," Ray said now.

"I never missed it," Pinny said. "Not even once." She leaned toward Ray, making up her mind to push her anger clear out and away. 'Cause she sure didn't want the meanness infecting her, no sirree. She took a deep breath and smiled. "You were a chickenshit yesterday. But you were brave today. You came back for me."

"Don't say that." Ray dropped her eyes to the table. "It's not true."

"Suit yourself. But it's in you."

"What?"

"Goodness," she said. "You can't get rid of it, even though you keep trying."

Ray snorted. "Goodness won't get us to New York. It can't buy food. Or a hotel room."

"But it makes you happy," Pinny said. She could tell by the brightness in Ray's eyes. It was the sort of sparkle people got from doing right, and it looked pretty on Ray.

Ray shrugged, then tapped the toe of one of the pale pink shoes. "How did these get here?"

"I found them in the Dumpster at Smokebush," Pinny said. "They don't like being thrown away. You hurt their feelings. They don't want you to take them back."

"Don't worry. I don't want them back. You didn't have to drag them along to New York, though."

"Did too," Pinny said firmly, giving the shoes a hug. "They needed to come. They belong there."

Ray rolled her eyes. "Yeah . . . right." Her laugh sounded like a goose choking. It was a hard sound. Not a real laugh at all.

Pinny crossed her arms at Ray. "You don't have to believe

me, but they told me so. And I *know* shoes, remember?" She smiled. "I'm a good listener."

"Except when *I'm* talking, for some reason." Ray smirked. "So, what, the shoes tell you secrets?"

"I have an extra chromosome," Pinny said. "It took points off my IQ, but maybe it added something, too. That's what Mama used to say." A waitress came over with menus and water, and Pinny took a big gulp. "I don't know what a chromosome is. How come the right number makes other people smarter than me. Numbers don't matter much anyway. Because sometimes smart people sure act stupid." She raised an eyebrow at Ray and locked eyes with her. "But I don't know any people like that."

Ray's eyes ballooned, and then she laughed. This time the laugh was full of bubbles and hiccups, and it made Pinny laugh, too.

"Okay, I deserved that." Ray shook her head, muttering, "Chopine Miller, the Shoe Whisperer." She waved her hand at the shoes. "Well, if they talk to you, then you should keep them."

"Thanks." Pinny grinned. "'Cause I left my other ones back in the tent." She slid the pale pink shoes onto her feet.

"Do they fit?" Ray asked.

When she wiggled her toes, her bones rubbed together. "They're tight," she admitted. "And one heel wobbles. But I love them."

"You're not going to be able to walk far," Ray said. "We'll have to hitch."

She nodded. "What about food? I'm starving."

Ray slapped the menu shut. "Toast," she said. "That's it.

We're down to the five bucks I had in my pocket from yesterday."

"Toast and jelly beans." Pinny grabbed her bag of black jellies from her backpack. "I gave the other food to Old Mabel. But she didn't want these. Said licorice made her tongue go itchy." She slid them across the table to Ray. "Delicious."

Ray stared at her, and then they both burst out laughing. They ordered and a few minutes later, their toast arrived. Pinny smeared hers with apricot jelly and ate it in three bites. Her stomach was rumbly, though, and jelly beans didn't shush it.

"I'm still hungry," she started to say, but Ray motioned for her to be quiet.

"See that woman over there at the counter?" Ray whispered. "She's a trucker."

Pinny looked toward the counter. The woman who sat there had rivers of wrinkles running over her face, but her body was as thin and curvy as the dance-team girls'. She had a mess of blond curls piled high on her head and shimmery purple eye shadow. Then Pinny saw the woman's boots over her tight jeans—turquoise cowboy boots studded with rhinestones. "Ooh," Pinny exclaimed, "she looks like Dolly Parton, only prettier!"

"Who cares what she looks like?" Ray said. "I heard her tell the waitress that her next delivery's in New York." Ray pointed out the diner window to a red truck being unloaded across the street.

"I've never been in a truck before," Pinny whispered. She clapped her hands. "And it matches my red shoes!" She held up the Mary Janes around her neck as proof.

"I don't know," Ray said. "What if she's some kind of crazy and we get stuck in the cab with her?" She narrowed her eyes at the woman. "She looks whacked."

"So do you," Pinny said. "Your hair is a raccoon nest, and you make it look that way on purpose!"

"A raccoon?" Ray touched her spiky hair. "Really?"

Pinny nodded. "She's not whacked. We can trust her."

"How do you know?" Ray asked.

Pinny grinned. "Her shoes. I love her shoes."

"Are there any shoes you don't love, Pinny?" Ray said. "You liked JT's, remember?"

"I can't always be right," she said, glaring at Ray. "You're not perfect, either, you know."

Ray laughed, then looked at Dolly Parton again. "I like her shoes, too." She shrugged. "That has to count for something."

Just then, Dolly Parton finished her coffee and asked for her bill.

"Okay," Ray whispered. "Let's do it." She threw their last five dollars down on the table, and then they left the diner and crossed the street.

They hurried to the front of the truck, and when no one was around to see, Ray shimmied through the open window of the cab. Then she unlocked the door to let Pinny in.

"Back here!" Ray moved past a curtain behind the seats into the back of the cab.

"Wow!" Pinny said. "A whole bedroom!" There was a bed sticking out of the wall, a TV hanging from the ceiling, even a tiny coffeemaker.

Ray pulled the curtains closed, then crawled under the bed.

Pinny scooted under, too, but once she was in, she could barely move, and neither could Ray.

"How long do we have to stay down here?" Pinny whispered.

"For as long as it takes to get to New York," Ray said. "Shhh! She's unlocking the door."

Pinny sucked in her breath and pressed her hands against the metal floor. The door opened and Dolly Parton got in. The truck rumbled and growled, and soon it began rocking. Pinny guessed they were driving on the road. She dropped her head onto her backpack and sighed. They were squashed together so tight that she could feel Ray's body rising and falling as she breathed. It wasn't too bad, though. The floor was warm from the truck driving, and she felt sleepy. Still, she had to shake her head every once in a while to keep that awful JT from getting stuck in it. Something else stuck in her head, too. . . . What if Ray disappeared again? The thought made Pinny's stomach sweat. She'd been sure she didn't need the Life Plan, or anyone looking out for her. She'd liked JT so much, and she'd been wrong. She'd been wrong about the money, too. If she was alone, far away from Smokebush, what else would she mess up? If she couldn't find Mama, if Ray left . . . Pinny slammed the door on that thought quick. Nope. Uh-uh. None of that was going to happen. No matter what, Ray would make sure she stayed safe. Ray was a good protector. She just didn't know it yet.

DALYA

It was one week before the wedding, and she didn't have shoes. She'd pushed them out of her mind, focusing instead on the dress she was sewing with the help of Ruth and Mrs. Blumberg. But when Ruth questioned her about her wedding shoes, an ache began in Dalya's heart. There was only one pair of shoes she could imagine wearing to exchange vows with Aaron, one pair of shoes that would carry her across the threshold from girl to woman. Those shoes, and the secret tucked into one heel, were gone forever.

When Aaron heard that she didn't have shoes to wear, he insisted on taking her shopping.

"I'm not letting you use that as an excuse for not marrying me," he said teasingly, and an hour later, they walked into Filer-Machol on Madison Avenue. "I haven't gotten you a wedding present yet. Pick any pair in the store and they're yours."

Dalya smiled and nodded, seeing his wish for her happiness light up his face. It was the way he'd looked on the day he'd proposed, too, always with the same earnest admiration he had a lifetime ago in Germany. He had waited patiently for two years, easing her gently into courtship as she sifted through her uncertainties. Two years where war marked every building with blackout curtains, where it extinguished the glittering lights of Times Square and sprouted victory gardens in every scant patch of dirt available in the five boroughs, where it enticed droves of bright-eyed uniformed young men into the Stage Door Canteen and then sent them sailing across the ocean to die. But Aaron had been right. The war threatened the fringes of Manhattan with U-boats and submarines, but it never swooped in to bloody the streets. Maybe partly because of that, Dalya's courage slowly returned. Instead of annoyance, when Aaron proposed, Dalya felt profound gratitude. Gratitude that there was one person left in the world who had known the Dalya of Before, who was helping her remember that Dalya, helping day by day to get some of her back. That there was a person who understood her nightmares, her heartbreaks, and her sins and, in spite of them, because of them, or regardless of them, wanted her love and wanted to love her.

"Yes," she'd answered. Even though she felt a sharp sadness at the word, she knew, too, that it was right. That she owed it to her family to move through life with someone who could remember them as she did, who could mourn them, celebrate them, and bear witness to the fact that they'd lived, and that they'd been more than the stories she'd told.

Now, as Aaron led her into the shoe department at Filer-

Machol, she looked at him shyly, feeling a fragile eagerness for their future to start. It was elegant, with fashionable settees arranged around the room for fittings, and beautiful shoes shining under satin lights. The shoes were machine-made, though, and the air was perfumed and sterile, without any of the warm pungency of her father's old workshop.

Still, she needed shoes, and she wouldn't—she couldn't—make them herself. So this was where she needed to be. Then she noticed the large wooden cabinet on the floor.

A customer was slipping her foot into a slot at the bottom of the cabinet as a saleswoman prattled, "The fluoroscope takes away the guesswork. If you look through the scope right here, you'll see from the X-ray of your foot that the shoes fit perfectly!"

"Wonderful!" the customer exclaimed. "I'll take them."

Dalya didn't recognize the sound coming from her. The last time she'd made it was years ago. The two women, along with Aaron, turned to stare, and the sound became louder. It was laughter, she realized. Buckling, gulping, breathless laughter that made her eyes water and her stomach shake.

She hurried through the doors, clutching her sides as another wave of laughter broke over her. Only when she was out on the sidewalk, with the traffic zipping past and Aaron looking on, bewildered, was she able to catch her breath.

"A shoe-fitting machine," she gasped. "I've never seen anything so ridiculous in my life!"

"Dalya?" Aaron bent over her, his gaze shifting into concern. "What's this about?"

Dalya shook her head, wiping her eyes. "I can't buy a pair

of shoes from that store," she said. "Machine-made shoes, and gimmicks to tell you they fit."

"All right." Aaron smiled hesitantly. "I'll marry you barefoot."

Dalya laughed again, and then surprised them both by throwing her arms around him and kissing his cheek.

"No," she said. "I'll be wearing shoes. But *I'm* going to make them."

It was Aaron who went back to the Ashburys' for her father's shoemaking bag. He offered to, and she didn't argue. Even with the time that had passed, she couldn't face Henry, not when she was so afraid of what she'd done to him by leaving.

When Aaron came back to the Blumbergs' with her bag of tools, she hugged it to her chest, breathing in its musky, lovely scent. The guilt she'd felt before when she looked at the bag had vanished, and now a sudden keenness pumped through her veins.

"He wasn't there," Aaron said quietly, and she loved him all the more for sensing that she needed to know.

"Thank you," she said.

Aaron's expression turned thoughtful. "There's something I have to ask you," he said finally. "Will I be competing with him forever? Because I'm not sure I'm willing to settle for that. . . ."

She squeezed his hand. "No," she promised. She hoped, for both their sakes, that it was true. Then she smiled and pointed to the door.

"Now you have to go," she said. She nodded at her father's bag as impatience built in her fingertips. "I have work to do."

"Be sure you make those shoes to last for a long time." He kissed her forehead, then turned toward the door. "I want you to wear them again on our fiftieth wedding anniversary."

Even before the door clicked shut, Dalya was on her knees in the living room, the bag in her lap. She opened it with trembling fingers and reached inside to find the tools, where her father had left them, waiting.

So, for the second time in her life, she made her own wedding shoes. But she made this pair differently. Because of the war, the white kid leather she'd hoped to use for the upper couldn't be found. With leather and rubber strictly rationed, materials were hard to come by. Finally, she settled on a wedge heel design that she could make from wood, and she covered the upper with the creamy satin lining from one of Mrs. Blumberg's older skirts. Ruth offered a pair of her rhinestone earrings, and Dalya used them to make a decorative buckle across the top of each shoe. It took a few days for her hands to remember how to grip the tools, how to mold the fabric to the last. Soon, though, they moved on their own, and after hours of work, she looked up in astonishment at what she'd done, not able to recall the process, but delighted with the result. The new shoes were simpler but somehow less girlish, more womanly.

She was happy with them. Still, on the morning of her wedding, when it came time to step into the new shoes, she couldn't do it. A sharp sadness stabbed her again, for the pale pink shoes she'd left in Berlin that night so long ago, and for everything—everyone—she'd lost. It was for a loss so all-encompassing that crying for the shoes alone seemed the only way to contain it.

She sank onto the floor at the back of the synagogue in her stockings, ignoring Ruth's pleas, until Ruth and the Blumbergs went to find Aaron.

It was Aaron who sat down beside her in the puddle of her wedding dress, Aaron who stroked her hair and held her as she sobbed. It was Aaron who knelt before her, slipping her new shoes gently onto her feet, whispering, "It's enough now. It's time."

She desperately wanted him to be right, and so she let him help her up from the floor. Her old shoes had been mourned. She would tuck them away with her other memories, bury them deep, and be done with it. It *was* enough. It *had* to be enough.

As she stood under the chuppah in her new shoes with her new husband, she felt a shift inside her, as if her fractured world were melding together again, piece by painstaking piece.

RAY

Ray's neck was aching and her legs were pinched and asleep. If her disgruntled sighs were any indication, Pinny wasn't faring much better. They'd been on the road for at least three or four hours. From the shifting slants of light in the cab, she guessed it was probably sometime in the afternoon. She stretched the tiniest bit, and an elbow instantly jabbed her in the ribs.

"Don't *do* that!" Pinny whispered in a voice loud enough to carry. "You kicked me!"

"I can't help it," Ray hissed. "And would you shut up before she catches us!" The truck's engine was loud . . . but loud enough to drown them out? Ray wasn't sure.

"I have to pee," Pinny whined.

Ray groaned, dropping her head onto her arms. This wasn't a problem she'd thought about before climbing into the truck. Fabulous. Of course, now *she* had to go, too.

"Try not to think about it," Ray said. As she did, the high-pitched whine of the truck shifted down an octave, and she slid forward on the floor. Was the truck stopping? Her pulse quickened. The engine died, and Ray held her breath, listening for the cab door.

Suddenly, the cab curtain flung open, and brown eyes, caked with mascara crumbs and ghastly purple eye shadow, stared sternly down at them.

"Come on, then," the woman said. "You girls get on outta there before one of you loses feeling to a vital body part permanently."

Ray cursed inwardly. They were trapped. Reluctantly, she untangled herself from their hiding place, with Pinny following.

Pinny blew out a breath and straightened her crooked glasses. "Even my fingernails had charley horses." She smiled at the woman, openly staring. "Wow. Your eye shadow's the color of glitter glue. Luscious Lavender."

"You don't say," the woman said. "What a coincidence."

Her voice wasn't unkind, even if it crackled like gravel. Ray pressed herself against the wall of the cab, her fingers twitching at her sides, her foot cocked in the ready-to-run position. She had no idea what the woman was going to do with them, but she wanted to be prepped for anything.

"How did you know we were back here?" Pinny asked.

The woman rolled her eyes. "Trucks are like husbands, sugar. You always keep one eye on 'em, just in case. I saw you two climb in back in Nashville. But you didn't look too dangerous, so I let you ride a spell." She narrowed her eyes. "*Are* you dangerous?"

"My shoes are," Pinny said proudly, holding up her foot for inspection. "They poked a man's eyeball out this morning. A mean, awful man."

"Chopine!" Ray elbowed Pinny. Great. She could practically hear alarms blaring beneath the woman's shrewd stare. They were screwed.

"Really," the woman said. "So . . . you're fugitives from the law?"

"No," Pinny answered. "Sheriff Wane and Ray go back a long ways. He says she's the reason he stays in business."

"Is that so?" She arched an eyebrow at Ray, then peered at the pale pink shoes on Pinny's feet, whistling long and low. "Those must be *some shoes*. But you've got a dangler there. Can I take a look?" Pinny nodded, handing her the shoe with the broken heel. The woman fiddled with it for a moment, then pulled a wad of gum from her mouth and used it like glue to reattach the heel. "There. It won't hold forever, but it'll do in a pinch." She handed Pinny the shoe, then patted her shoulder. "You best hang tight to them. My boots have a secret weapon, too."

Pinny leaned forward as the woman slid her hand into the top of her boot and pulled out a small handgun.

"I keep this handy when I'm on the road in case Armageddon strikes." She laughed as Pinny's eyes saucered, then whispered, "It's really only a lighter aspiring to greatness. I'm banking on the power of suggestion." She dropped the lighter back into her boot and straightened. "I'm headin' into the Waffle House. They've got an all-you-can-eat lunch buffet that'll grease your guts till kingdom come. You girls comin'?"

Pinny started to nod, then hesitated. "I . . . I don't know. Ray?"

Ray blinked in surprise. Pinny letting *her* make the decision? This was a first. Maybe her close call with JT had put her guard up . . . *finally.* The thought gave Ray a measure of relief, but also a pang of sadness. Somehow, suspicion didn't mesh with Pinny.

Ray weighed their options. If they went inside, they'd be walking into a million questions. Ray didn't know if she could construct enough lies to satisfy this woman. She looked like the type who wouldn't buy into them too easy. No, they should move on before—

The woman made a sound somewhere between growling and spitting. "Here's the short and long of it," she said. "You've been ridin' in my cab without permission. Trespassin' on my property. Now, you can come with me and tell me what you're up to, or I can call the cops. I don't stomach liars or cheats, so you'll have to prove you're neither."

Before the choice got made for them. "We'll come in," Ray said grudgingly.

"Good." The woman extended her hand. "My name's Orpa, and as long as you're honest with me, I'll be glad to know you."

Two hours and six plates later, the girls were stuffed and grateful. But despite Ray nudging Pinny's shins under the table, Pinny had done exactly what she'd hoped she wouldn't. She'd told Orpa everything about her mama and the magic shoes and their quest to get to New York City to find them. Orpa had listened while Ray quailed with visions of her dragging them straight to the nearest police station.

Orpa's smile, though, as Pinny talked, was genuine enough. It wasn't the soppy sort Ray'd seen so many people give Pinny back in Jaynis, the sort that said they were humoring Pinny out of some PC obligation instead of interest. Pinny reveled in it, her face lighting up with satisfaction, and a thought struck Ray. What if that was why Pinny was railing against Horizons Assist? Maybe she knew it meant spending her life surrounded by staff paid to keep her company. God, it would be a shrunken world of forced connections, where some might have meaning, but most wouldn't. Picturing Pinny trapped in it made Ray's throat close. Then she checked herself. *Not my problem, not my problem* . . . the chant began in her head as Pinny went on. Almost as if she could hear it, Orpa lasered her eyes on Ray more than a few times throughout the meal. Ray tried to ignore them, focusing on her food and any escape route from the diner that seemed possible, if it came to that.

After Orpa paid the bill, she folded her arms in a no-nonsense sort of way.

"What a story," she said, with an appreciation that made Pinny beam. "I do hope you find your mama's shoes, too. The right pair of shoes can get you through most anything." She gave her turquoise boots an affectionate tap. "These boots have seen me through two twisters, a night in jail, and a gator bite that could've taken off half my foot, if it hadn't been for these here steel toes." She nodded. "It's all in the shoes." She leaned forward and whispered to Pinny, "And I'll tell you something else. I had a quest of my own once, too, but it wasn't to find something as much as it was to become something."

"You mean like a fairy-tale kind of quest?" Pinny asked.

"Oh, no. This was real life. It would've been a hell of a lot easier if I'd been in some storybook." Orpa snorted. "Then somebody else could've written me brave, or pretty, or smart, no questions asked. But us non-fairy-tale folks? We have to cut our own destinies."

"What was your destiny?" Pinny said, her eyes wide and wondering.

Orpa shrugged. "Well, I spent years helpin' other people with theirs before I knew my own." She took a bite of her apple pie. "Got married when I was seventeen and had four kids by twenty-two. I loved my family and still do, but I lived the first fifty years of my life being everything for everybody else. I never even set foot outside Arkansas. My husband, Hank, told me we'd drive across country soon as we saved enough. Never spent a day apart in thirty-three years." She shook her head. "Well, he took sick, but before he died, he gave me two things. These boots and my rig out there." She gestured toward her truck. "It was his way of tellin' me to take that trip after all. I wouldn't have, except for the boots. They were loud, bright . . . brave. Everything I wanted to be, even without my Hank. I put them on, and they taught me how to become it. Simple as that." She grinned. "Like I said . . . it's all in the shoes."

"No." Pinny shook her head, snapping a photo of Orpa's shoes. "It's all in the people who wear them."

"I'm going to take that as a compliment." Orpa winked, then stood up, turning toward the door. Ray braced herself. This was Orpa's chance to drop them. But instead, Orpa glanced over her shoulder and said, "Well, are you coming to New York or not?"

She didn't have to say it twice. Ray nudged Pinny, who was

gulping her last bite of buttermilk pie, and they were out of their seats a second later.

Ray settled into the front seat while Pinny stretched out in the back to thumb through her stack of shoe photos. Orpa focused on the road, and Ray, relieved to be out from under the microscope of scrutiny, breathed easy for the first time all day. The bumping of the tires on the road, the towns and trees streaking by the window . . . they stirred rhythms in her head, and soon she had her notebook open in her lap, scribbling musical notes to match the beat. Songs pulled her further into herself, obliterating the world around her, and it was only after a neck cramp forced her to raise her eyes that she realized she'd lost hours to her music. Night had swallowed the highway, and stars hissed by the window like silver-tailed comets. Pinny had nodded off in the bunk in the back, and Orpa's eyes steadied on Ray's face for a long moment. *Back into the petri dish,* Ray thought.

"So," Orpa said, "you're bringin' Pinny to New York." She flashed her high beams at a car that was driving without its headlights on. "Then what?"

Ray shifted in her seat. "What do you mean?"

"I mean, you're planning to dump her," Orpa said with finality.

Ray opened her mouth, but discovered that she couldn't deny it. Pinny didn't factor into any of Ray's plans after they reached the city.

"She can go back to Texas," Ray said. "People have made arrangements for her there."

"Sounds cozy," Orpa said drily. "And what do you think of these 'arrangements'?"

Ray shrugged. *Not my problem.* "They're fine," she muttered.

"Fine as a pile of pig manure, I imagine." Orpa shook her head. "So what about her quest? Are you going to help her with it? Or spit her out on the streets of Manhattan to find her mama's shoes alone?"

Ray pressed herself deeper into her seat. "They're not her mama's shoes," she scoffed. "It's some crazy fantasy she has."

Orpa frowned. "What's wrong with that? Everybody needs a decent dose of magical thinking every once in a while. I tell my own kids the same." She stared out at the highway. "Otherwise, life turns tragic too fast."

Orpa winked, and Ray smirked. "And you're speaking from experience, right?"

"There were plenty of times Hank and I didn't have two pennies to rub together, and six mouths to feed on top of it. One year, our oldest, May-Bell, got a Hawaiian vacation stuck in her head. She must have been about eight at the time . . . heard about Hawaii at some state fair at school. Anyway, that was all she wanted for Christmas, this Hawaii trip. Well, we knew she'd be heartbroken if we didn't do something. So Hank and I hit the dollar store in town. Stocked up on plastic pink flamingos, blow-up palm trees, ten-cent leis." She shook her head, remembering. "Course, outside it was colder than a tin toilet on an iceberg. But we even filled our kiddie pool with bathwater in the garage. Strung up some hula-girl lights, and come Christmas morning, May-Bell had herself a regular Hawaiian luau."

Ray snorted. "But she knew it was a crock."

Orpa paused over that. "Maybe so, but if she did, it didn't

bother her any. She spent hours snorkeling in her kiddie pool with her plastic fish and went back to school after break telling everybody she had a tan. She's near forty now, and she still says it was the best Christmas present she ever got, her trip to Hawaii. And she's never been farther west than Santa Fe." She smiled. "I tell you, it can keep you from the brink, magical thinking. When Hank was sick, imagining me drivin' my rig kept us both smiling. After he died, the grief made me buggy enough to give it a try. Probably never would've otherwise." She laughed, but then her face grew serious. "You could use a touch of it yourself. I can see it in your eyes. You've seen your share of hell on earth. Am I right?"

"None of your business," Ray snapped.

Orpa chortled. "Fair enough. But you're going to do something for me. You let Pinny have her magical thinking, and maybe you give in to a little of your own. You give me your word that you'll take Pinny on her quest."

"Or?" Ray challenged.

"Or I'm droppin' you at the next police station I drive by," Orpa said. "And that's a promise." She nodded toward the back of the cab. "That girl doesn't need to join ranks with bitterness. The world could do with more of her kind of optimism." She reached her hand out to Ray. "Is it a deal?"

Maybe it was Orpa's stern gaze, or the fact that Ray was too tired to put up a fight. Regardless, she shook Orpa's hand. "Deal."

Orpa nodded and turned on the radio, sitting back in satisfaction. Ray tucked her knees under her, leaning her head against the seat. When she did, the burden of the promise she'd made pressed her from every side with claustrophobia. Her body told her before her mind could fathom it. Damn. She was going to be true to her word. It didn't make any sense, but then, nothing about her behavior on this trip so far had. Well, this was the last time she was sticking her neck out. No more sorry-ass-puppet-with-a-conscience act for her. Once she took Pinny to the Tree of Lost Soles they'd read about in the newspaper article, and Pinny got the ridiculous shoes, then she'd have to agree to go back to Smokebush without a fight. Ray'd make sure of it.

She closed her eyes, drifting into that heady place between sleep and waking. She thought over what Orpa had said about magical thinking. Of course, Ray had some magical thinking of her own. It had wriggled into her back when she'd had her pink running shoes. She didn't think it had survived her scars, until it came back to life again on the day she met Carter. But she didn't trust it. Not anymore. Magical thinking could do damage if you let it. The night she'd run away, the night of prom, she'd given in to it. It had only been for a few minutes, but that had been enough to break her heart.

She snuck out of Smokebush half an hour into *The Sound of Music* movie night. Curfew wasn't until eleven, and that would give her plenty of time to get to prom and back before Mrs. Danvers checked her room. Even if Nancy or the other girls noticed she was missing, they wouldn't make a fuss. They hated the running commentaries she made when she actually sat through movies. And smarmy ones that OD'd on lederhosen and singing nuns were prime targets. They'd be relieved to be rid of her for a few hours. Of course, she could've told Mrs. Danvers that she wanted to go to prom. Mrs. Danvers would've had fits of rapture to rival the Second Coming just thinking about Ray in a dress. There'd have been teasing about crushes, picture taking, fussing over makeup—a horde of ridiculous rituals. Ray wasn't going to the dance for any of that. No one could know the real reason she was going, so she kept quiet about it.

She remembered how quickly she'd walked through town that night; how she'd had to pin down her smile inside her cheek before it let loose; how her heart had hummed with anticipation. She'd rounded the corner to the school and faltered, nearly turning back when she saw the other kids. The girls were on the arms of their dates, strutting about in their dresses, lip-glossed, life-size cream puffs. The guys squared their shoulders, their hopes for getting lucky pasted in their cocky smiles. There was Careena, giggling with Meg and kissing her boyfriend, Graydon. Travis Ross, scouting out his next conquest.

Ray didn't see Pinny, but she knew she was in the crowd. She'd been gushing about prom for weeks, and she'd even gotten Mrs. Danvers to hand-make a purple sequined dress to match her Keds. Ray seriously hoped she didn't run into her. The last thing she needed was Pinny announcing to everyone at Smokebush that Ray had gone to prom. Ray would never live it down.

Once Careena and the others were safely inside, she headed for the second-floor girls' bathroom, the one farthest from the gym, where she would be least likely to be seen. She smoothed her spiky hair into a girlish pixie style and, in one of the stalls, slipped out of her jeans and faded tee. Then she pulled the dress and shoes from the bag where they'd been hidden, waiting, since the day she'd taken them. The red satin sighed as it glided buttery over her skin. She saved the shoes for last, holding her breath as she stepped into them, bracing for the pain. But just like at the Pennypinch, the shoes melted onto her feet, and suddenly, she was standing in a field of feathers.

She left the bathroom stall and turned toward the mirror, expecting to see a dolled-up freak. A wide-eyed, dark-haired girl stared back, a girl with a delicate cinched waist and slender shoulders. She was completely foreign to Ray, surprising (and not a little frightening) in her prettiness.

Her body was a coil of spring-loaded nerves, but she saw no sign of it in her reflection. *Please don't . . . ,* she pleaded with the mirror. *Don't let it show.* With shaking fingers, she grabbed the CD she'd brought with her off the counter. If she was going to go through with this, it had to be now, before panic changed her mind.

She sucked in her breath and headed down the stairs. When she walked into the gym, it was a moment of raw truth. No one approached her, but heads turned slightly, and there were snorts of laughter. Music blasting from the speakers hummed up from the floor into Ray's feet, giving her the unsteady sensation of walking on a diving board.

"I didn't think she knew what a dress was," someone stage-whispered. It could've been Meg, or maybe Careena, even, as payback for her Queen Careena drawing. She let it go, though. Tonight, nothing mattered except him.

A new song started, and kids spun back to the dance floor, already forgetting.

She hadn't come here to dance anyway, and she certainly

hadn't expected showing up at prom to earn her instant friendships after years as a social pariah. She scanned the room, searching the faces until she saw him. It was only then that she allowed her smile to break free.

Carter stood near the stage at the other end of the gym, half hidden by massive speakers, playing the part of DJ. He had his laptop open, probably mixing music files for the next few dances.

She skirted the dance floor until she stood a few feet from him.

"Didn't you tell me techno was trash?" she yelled over the music.

His head snapped up, but blankness crossed his face, as if he had no idea who she was. Then recognition dawned on him. He grinned, and her heart quivered with the pleasure of knowing it was for her.

"Ray?" He shook his head. "Is that you?"

"In the flesh," she said. "Well, minus the grunge."

"I see that," he said. He took in her dress and hair with an approving nod while her cheeks flamed "Wow, you look good grungeless."

"Thanks," she said. "Don't get your hopes up, though. At midnight I turn back into a rotten pumpkin." She laughed, but he shook his head.

"Don't make it a joke," he said. "You don't always have to blow off compliments. You're worthy."

She gripped the stage to steady herself. This was the moment she'd been waiting for. "So . . . do you think we could go to the music room? There's something I wanted to show you."

Carter tilted his head quizzically, then nodded. "Only for

a sec. I have to man my music, and *you* have some dancing to do. All those guys out there are going to be lining up in a few minutes, you watch." He hit some keys on his laptop, then followed her out of the gym.

She blushed again when he held the door to the music room open for her, then reached behind her to flick on the lights.

"So . . . ," he said expectantly.

Ray held up her CD. "I burned this yesterday. It's my music." She stared at the floor. "I thought maybe you could . . . tell me what you think?"

His eyes widened. "This is legit? Your originals?"

She nodded. "For your listening pain. Just . . . do me a favor and try not to hate it, okay?"

"Hey, remember the first rule of greatness. Even if it's the worst you've ever made, tell the world it's the best. Delusions can be convincing." Then he whisked the CD away to the stereo behind his desk.

"What are you doing?" Ray asked, her stomach plummeting.

"Playing it, of course," he said. "You can't expect me to wait to hear your first solo album. This is history in the making."

"No way." Ray lunged for the stereo, but it was too late. The first notes of "Blue Lightning" echoed through the room.

"The composition's rough, and I haven't got the riff right yet—"

"Shhh!" Carter held up a finger for silence.

Ray shifted on her feet, picking the song apart as it played. This was agony. She should never have made the CD for him.

The music wasn't ready. Not even close. It sounded chintzy and contrived. She reached for the STOP button just as Carter faced her, smiling.

"Your music's got it," he said quietly. "It's the real deal."

"You think so?" Her voice was tinny with doubt.

"I know it." He stepped closer, and she could smell the spiciness of his aftershave and see the green flecks shooting through the blue of his eyes. "You're going to do amazing things, Ray Langston."

His eyes were open, asking. Exuberant certainty coursed through her. This was why he'd come here with her. Why he stood so close that the sleeve of his shirt brushed her bare shoulder. He'd never treated her like a child, or like a student. He'd always treated her like . . . an equal. This was his way of telling her that he knew how she felt, of showing her he was okay with it.

That was when she'd let her magical thinking take over, when she'd tried to let everything she'd dreamt of happening with Carter come true. With her heart pummeling her chest, she closed her eyes and slid her arms around his neck and pulled his face toward hers. She waited for his lips to meet hers. She'd already imagined how their soft warmth would feel against her skin. But he stumbled back, that stricken look she'd forever remember in his eyes. Instead of slipping his hands around her waist, he used them to gently put her arms at her sides.

"No, Ray," he said softly, a puzzled apology on his face. "I'm your friend. You know that, kiddo. This can never happen." He ran a hand through his hair, frowning. "I hope I didn't do anything to confuse you. I never meant to—"

"No." Ray was stumbling out of the room, waving her hands. "No. I was . . . It was stupid." Her laugh was strained. Her insides were parched, her eyes filling against her will. She couldn't look at him; she couldn't be in the same room with him. He'd seen what an idiot she was. Worse, he'd never thought of her as anything but a kid. A sexless, breastless kid with issues, a pity party to gossip about in the teachers' lounge.

"I—I have to go," she stammered, forcing a smile. "Forget it ever happened. We're good. Everything's fine."

She fled down the hallway, vaguely registering him calling her name over the roaring in her ears. She blinked to dam up the tears, but a flood towered behind her eyes, ripe to burst. The only way out of the school was the gym; the main doors were locked by now. The gym. Those people gawking at her crumpling face, their tongues wagging about Freak Show Langston. She wouldn't make it. Gulping air and shaking uncontrollably, she dimly remembered the emergency exit behind the stage at the front of the gym.

She hurtled through the door into the night air, the torrent pouring out of her in drowning sobs. Running, running, running from the horrible thing that had happened. Running until she got to Smokebush. And by the time she got there, she knew she would have to keep running.

Like she was running now, in Orpa's cab, running to New York City. Because no one could know the truth about the horrible thing with Carter, and she could never go back to Jaynis and face him again.

October 1967
New York, New York

DALYA

When the woman walked into the shop on that rain-streaked day in autumn, Dalya knew exactly who she was. She'd seen the wedding announcement in the *Times* last year, and the same porcelain face that looked beautifully out from that photograph was before her now, although this face was more tentative, less poised.

"Excuse me." Her smile carried the same careful measure of grace as her posture. "Are you Dalya Scheller?"

Dalya might not ever have found her voice through her rattled nerves if her little Inge hadn't cried out as she spilled her tin of crayons onto the floor. She scooped her up, kissing her tearful face.

"It's all right," she whispered to Inge, then turned to the woman, adding, "Yes, I am Dalya."

"Oh, I've come to the right place, then." Her face broke into relief. "I'm glad." Her gaze swept around the room, taking in the chaos, and grew doubtful.

"I'm sorry," Dalya said. "My regular clients know that tidiness means nothing when it comes to quality. For first-time visitors, it can be a shock."

"No, it's charming," she said. "Really." As her eyes settled on Inge, she swept a hand across her coat, revealing the telltale belly beneath it. "Your little girl is beautiful."

The comment was intended for Inge, and Inge performed accordingly, grinning and tucking her head coyly under Dalya's chin in five-year-old fashion. "I see you're expecting one of your own?" Dalya made herself ask.

"Yes." She blushed. "It's a boy, or . . . I think it is. I can hardly believe it. We didn't think . . . we weren't sure . . ." Her voice trailed off and she straightened, as if just remembering she was talking to a stranger.

The woman smiled at her rounded figure, and Dalya instinctively pressed Inge closer, remembering her own wonder when Inge had come. She and Aaron had nearly given up, and she'd worried her body wasn't able, after what it had been through so long ago. But then life amazed her with its promise, as it had so many times before, and Inge was born pink and perfect.

"Congratulations," Dalya said now, surprised by the sincerity in her voice.

The woman nodded in thanks, extending her hand. "I'm Christina Ashbury."

Dalya nodded. The name she'd flung about in her head a thousand times, trying to erase. "How can I help you?"

"A friend of mine recommended you," Christina said. "She

said you make the most remarkable shoes of anyone in Manhattan."

"Thank you," Dalya said. It still filled her with disbelief that she had achieved that reputation in such circles. Of course, it had taken her over twenty years. Twenty years that had begun in poverty with Aaron, scraping pennies together each month to save for the shoe shop it took a decade to afford. Most people would have said she'd earned her recent success. There were mornings, though, when she woke chilled and shaking from a memory, when her life seemed, somehow, mistakenly good. But the more time she spent with Aaron and Inge, the more time she spent making shoes, the fewer frightful memories returned.

"So," Christina continued, "I thought if anyone could help, you could...."

"Help?" A fist squeezed her chest. Inge must have felt it, too, pressed against her as she was, because she squirmed until Dalya set her back on the floor.

"My husband, Henry, had polio when he was younger. He walks, but with great pain from his braces." Christina glanced at the floor, her next words cautious, unsure. "I'm afraid it wears on him, and I can't stand to see him unhappy."

"I'm sorry," Dalya said quietly, remembering Henry's bitterness and desperation on the day she'd left him. After Columbia, he'd gone to work for his father and taken over the firm. She'd heard of his success on Wall Street through casual conversations with clients, and she knew, sadly, that he'd become everything he'd feared and hated about himself.

Christina's eyes implored her. "Perhaps ... you could make him a special pair of shoes? Something to make him more comfortable?" She pulled a pair of worn boots and braces from her bag. "I brought these for you to use for measurements." She held them out to her. "Please?"

Dalya stiffened. She couldn't. Suppose Aaron found out who they were for? Aaron was so tenderhearted, so patient with her love—a love that had taken years to flower, starting as deep friendship that, only just before Inge arrived, awoke to a surprising but welcome passion. He'd say he understood, but there would be a wound.

But even as these arguments went through her mind, she heard herself answering, "Of course. I'll try to help him if I can." She took the boots Christina offered, though she knew she didn't need them. Even after these many years, she remembered the shape of Henry's feet, the feel of them in her hands.

After accepting Christina's repeated thanks and saying good-bye, she set every other order aside to work on Henry's boots. She didn't stop, even when Aaron came home from work that night. She excused herself from dinner and locked herself in the shop, working until the street outside grew quiet in the wee hours, then frantic again with a fresh round of rush-hour traffic.

When the boots were finished a few days later, she was prouder of them than of anything else she'd created. They were beautiful leather on the outside, with hidden braces sheathed in shearling on the inside. She had them delivered to the Ashburys' house so that she wouldn't have to see Christina again.

She wondered often, after that, if Henry knew who had made his boots. But then, she reminded herself, it didn't matter. What mattered was that, at last, she'd found a way to help him, by tucking her love for him into a pair of shoes.

RAY

Glorious moments had never been part of her life. In fact, up until now, any moment that had the potential for glory usually ended in a major shitstorm.

But when Ray opened her eyes to a cathedral of sky-scrapers haloed by the sun, the glory of it warmed her to her bones. A sudden sequence of climbing chords streamed through her, and she scrambled to write them down. When she closed her notebook, she noticed Orpa, at the steering wheel, watching her and smiling.

"Makes it hard to lose faith in human beings when you see what they can create when they have a mind to, doesn't it?" she said.

Her skepticism tried to rear its head, but Ray shut it up. The skyline was too fantastic to spoil. She stretched the stiffness from her legs and arms, refusing to take her eyes from the horizon.

They'd been on the road for over a day, stopping every couple of hundred miles for a break. Last night's midnight break had been five hours long, and Ray had spent half of it pacing at the rest stop while Orpa and Pinny slept in the cab.

"Can't drive without sleep," Orpa had explained, but that didn't make the waiting any easier.

Now, finally, here was the city—immense before her, terrifying and enticing. Once it swallowed her up, who would she become? The answer came instantly. Anyone but who she'd been. Anyone . . . who mattered. She crawled into the back of the cab, where Pinny slept on the bed, her shoe photos scattered around her. Ray'd never seen them up close before, and she picked up a few. Pinny'd written descriptions for each one in large, haphazard letters. Under the orange espadrilles, she'd written: **Nina Gonzalez, Joy Full, Bright, Loud.** JT's snakeskin boots: **Slimy, Snake Smile, Poison.** And there were Ray's own safety-pinned Reeboks: **Ray Langston, Spiky, Hurting.** And then in a newer, fresher ink: **Sister.** Ray grimaced. Nothing like a dose of conscience to ruin her mood. It was totally unfair of Pinny, trusting her. It would only make things harder when Ray had to leave.

She pushed the photos into a pile, then shoved them into Pinny's backpack. There. Out of sight, out of mind.

"Pinny," she whispered. "Wake up and look out the window."

"We're crossing the Pulaski Skyway. Then we'll go in through the Holland Tunnel," Orpa said. "We should be in Manhattan in about twenty minutes."

Pinny sat up, rubbing her eyes, then climbed up front and

leaned over Ray's shoulder. "I knew it. It's so beautiful," she said. "Anyplace Mama lives has to be beautiful."

Orpa glanced at Ray, and Ray shifted uncomfortably in her seat, looking away. It was all Pinny had talked about since Nashville, as if the closer they got to New York, the tighter she needed to cling to this fantasy city of her mama's. It might've been nervousness, but Ray wondered if it was really doubt. How would Pinny handle the truth when it came? When no Mama magically appeared?

It was simple. Pinny would have to learn to cope, like everyone else who'd had disappointments. There'd be no way to cushion the blow.

"Well," Orpa said, "I have to unload at South Street downtown." Worry creased her forehead. "The sun will set soon. I wish I could drop you girls off after. I hate to think of you wanderin' around at night in the city. But I'm already behind schedule."

"We'll be fine," Ray said.

Pinny nodded, her downy bangs fluffing with her bobbing head. "Mama's shoes will make everything all right." She grinned.

Orpa's lips thinned. "I'm not going to stand in the way of you girls and your quest." She shook her head. "It's the worried mother in me, but I wish I knew for sure you'd be okay. This running-away business is risky."

"I'm not running away," Pinny said simply. "I'm coming home."

Orpa smiled at Pinny, then handed Ray a slip of paper with a number scrawled across it. "Y'all keep my number in case. Call me if things go topsy-turvy on you."

Ray tucked the paper into her pocket, avoiding Orpa's demanding stare. Its message was crystal clear: Keep Pinny safe. And Ray was going to try, at least until they found the shoes. But then what?

She couldn't call Smokebush herself. Once Mrs. Danvers found out where she was, she'd force her to come back, or get Sheriff Wane to. And maybe Mrs. Danvers would be sick enough of her to give her to juvie this time. No, maybe she could take Pinny to a hospital, or a shelter, somewhere she could leave her without having to give herself away. Or, she could call Orpa. But then Orpa might force her to go back to Smokebush with Pinny.

Ray sighed. Three days ago, when she'd left Smokebush, she'd never banked on these complications. But by tomorrow morning, they'd be over. She'd help Pinny get the silly shoes tonight. She'd find some way to get Pinny back to Texas, and then she'd be free. Free in New York City, with a diamond ring to buy herself a new life.

She turned toward the window again, focusing on that sleek skyline floating over the sparkling Hudson. A place to lose the memory of the toxic version of herself. A place . . . for becoming.

"Only one more block," Ray said as Pinny clenched her teeth through another step. Pinny's hair stuck to her forehead, and she'd stopped talking a half hour ago. The pink shoes had been hurting Pinny's feet since Nashville, and today she'd walked half the length of Manhattan in them. Orpa's gum was holding, but the heel of the right shoe was wobbly and made the going even slower. Still, ever since they'd said goodbye to Orpa on South Street, they'd been making their way uptown, block after block. They'd stopped a few times, once at Union Square, and then to look in the windows of Saks and rest for an hour on a bench in Central Park. But other than that, they'd kept walking, with Pinny as determined as ever to make it to her mama's shoes.

Now Pinny was hobbling. Ray stopped, putting an awkward arm around her. "Lean on me," she said. "Better?"

Pinny nodded, and together they limped the last few steps, until Ray whispered, "Pinny, look up. We're here."

Ninety-Second and Amsterdam, the address they'd found in the article about the Tree of Lost Soles. Ray peered into the darkened shopwindow full of shoes. Luminous in the auburn glow of the streetlight, the shoes in the Art of Heeling had a haunting splendor.

Pinny held up the crumpled newspaper article, studying the photo, then the brownstone in front of them. Her brow furrowed.

"Where's the tree?" She brought the clipping closer to her face. "There's no shoe shop in this picture!" she cried indignantly.

"The tree's here somewhere," Ray said. "We'll find it."

Pinny sank onto the curb, slid off the pink shoes, and winced as she inspected her feet under the streetlight. Angry blisters climbed her heels and toes, her feet two giant red welts.

"Oh man," Ray whispered. Her own feet were throbbing, too, but she was used to the pain. "You should've let me nab somebody's wallet. Then we could've taken a cab, or at least the subway."

"No," Pinny said scoldingly. "You don't do things like that."

"Right." Ray laughed inwardly. She was a saint on a search for magic shoes. Why not?

"Besides," Pinny said. "It was fun seeing the city."

Ray couldn't argue with that. She'd already fallen in love, like she knew she would. Every block they'd walked had its own eccentric melody. The subway pulsed deep under the streets, pumping people out of its tunnels at a frantic pace. The people scurried on the sidewalks, their footsteps and voices swooping and diving over the treble and bass clefs in chaotic notes. Ray wanted nothing more than to sit in the middle of the song to catch each note on her guitar, to make the city's rhythm her own. But she didn't. Not yet.

Instead, she brought Pinny here. It was insanity. She'd traveled fifteen hundred miles with a girl on a quest to rescue a pair of shoes from a tree. Even crazier, she was actually going to help her get them!

Now she stepped back on the sidewalk, looking more carefully at the storefront. Her eyes settled on the iron gate alongside the building.

"Come on," she whispered to Pinny, easing the gate open and stepping into the narrow alleyway between the store and the building next to it. But Pinny hung back.

"I'm scared." Her voice was barely there. "What if . . . nothing happens? What if . . . there is no More?" Every trace of her stubbornness was gone. Her face was open, breakable, waiting for reassurance.

Ray floundered. Everyone lied in moments like this. *It's*

going to be okay. Don't worry. It won't hurt. When you were left, scraping yourself off the ground, bleeding and broken, the lies hurt less than the betrayal of the person who told them. Finally, Ray said the two words that, in this moment, however short-lived, were undeniably true. "I'm here."

Pinny heaved a shaky breath and moved to Ray's side. "I'm ready."

Ray slid through the shadows, feeling the tug on the back of her shirt of Pinny's hand holding tight. The alley ended with trash cans butted up against a high wall, but before that, it opened to the left to reveal a tiny patch of grass, only big enough for two folding chairs. The rest of the space was taken up by a tree. Looking enormous in the shrunken space, the maple tree rose, hearty and rambling, to the third story of the building. Shoes decorated every branch like ornaments, hundreds of them swaying in the breeze in a medley of colors, shapes, and sizes.

"I've never seen so many shoes in my life," Pinny whispered. "They're so beautiful."

But they weren't, at least not from what Ray could see. Some had holey soles peeling back from the toes; others had broken heels bent at awkward angles. Most of them had a dejected look, as if the fact that they weren't on someone's feet was cause for sadness.

"Okay," she said. "Let's find these shoes."

She looked from the photo Pinny was holding to the tree, until finally she saw the silver stilettos dangling from one of the uppermost branches. At the exact same moment, Pinny gave a joyful cry and pointed.

"There they are! They're just how I remember!"

Ray nodded, staring. She had to admit, it was surprising, seeing them outside the newspaper photo. They were real, substantial. Maybe that would be enough for Pinny, even if they weren't actually her mama's. "Of course they'd have to be at the top," she muttered. She dropped her duffel and guitar to the ground. "You keep an eye out to make sure no one comes. I'll get the shoes."

She set one of the lawn chairs under the lowest, sturdiest-looking branch, then stood on it to hoist herself up. She shinnied up the tree trunk and pulled herself to a standing position, climbing the stronger branches like steps on a ladder. The branches were so thick with leaves that it was impossible to see, so she felt her way over the rough bark, giving each branch a shake with her hands before she tried her full weight on it. After ten minutes of weaving through branches, ducking swinging sneakers and pumps, she reached the right branch.

There they were, perched like a glittering, misfit bird atop an umbrella of leaves. Ray flattened her belly against the branch and scooted forward, stretching her fingers toward the shoes. They were still out of reach. She slid out another inch until her fingers touched a cool pleather strap. Her hands closed around the stilettos just as the branch snapped. Then she was falling through the sky clinging to a pair of shoes, absurdly praying they would save her.

DALYA

Dalya sat at her worktable with Kathryn Rosenbak's shoe resting in her lap. She'd tilted her lamp as close as she dared over the shoe, but her eyes were tight and tired from squinting. Her vision wasn't what it used to be, and neither were her hands. The rust of age was niggling its way into her joints. She didn't mind too much. It took her longer to make shoes these days, but she had her steady stream of customers. Better to have lived long enough to rust at all, she always thought.

No matter how brittle her bones became, she'd never give up shoemaking. She'd work until she died in this shop, surrounded by the tools she loved, the shoes she'd poured herself into. She couldn't ask for a better way to go. Besides, she'd already died once on a long-ago night in Berlin. The second time could only be better.

She straightened her back, glancing at the clock on the wall. Half past midnight.

She never stayed up late like this anymore. Not when she woke every day well before dawn. Old age, she mused, liked fiddling with her rest. Or, maybe it was her body, rebelling against sleep because it knew there was an eternity of it coming quickly her way. Either way, if she stayed up much longer, there'd be no point going to bed.

But there was something about tonight, an anticipation vibrating the air and quickening her pulse. A warm, sweet sensation swept through her at intervals, like the feeling she got when she thought of her Aaron, gone five years already. It was the feeling of remembering something lovely. And suddenly, for no logical reason, she knew she wouldn't go to bed, that whatever was coming was much too important to miss for something as ordinary as sleep.

So here she sat, sewing peacock feathers to the ankle strap of Kathryn Rosenbak's shoe as a way to ward off her growing impatience. Kathryn had ordered them for a black-tie fundraiser at the Met, and she'd be picking them up tomorrow afternoon. She bent closer to the vermilion heel, wrestling with the feathers, and then she heard the scream.

June 2013
New York, New York

RAY

The scream tore out of her when she hit the grass, but after that she couldn't make a sound. She had no breath. Pain whipped it away from her, surging from the ground into her skin, wrenching her right arm and hand in a searing heat.

She writhed and choked while Pinny knelt next to her, her hands fretting, afraid to land anywhere.

"Ray," Pinny whimpered. "Are you hurt? Where? Tell me."

But she couldn't, not even when she finally sucked a shallow breath into her lungs. That was when she saw the Payless label across the bottom of the sandals she was holding, and a blinding madness took over. Her arm and hand were broken, lying twisted unnaturally in the grass. Her picking hand . . . her playing hand. The hand that was going to give her a shot at surviving in this city. In the darkness, clutching her howling arm, she had nothing left but rage. Rage at a world that stole her belief in impossible things, and rage at Pinny for still believing. She wanted to rob Pinny, the way she'd been robbed of her winged pink Converse sneakers, the way she'd been robbed of Carter and, now, of her music, too.

"Ray," Pinny was saying, "are you okay? What can I do? What can I do?"

"Get . . . out . . . of . . . my . . . life," Ray spat, throwing the sandals toward Pinny. "Take your cheap shoes and leave me alone."

Pinny shook her head, worry turning to confusion on her face. She whisked up the shoes, hugging them to her heart. "Mama wasn't cheap," she said.

"Your mama," Ray whispered, "is dead. Mrs. Danvers knew it, I knew it, everyone in Jaynis knew it. She's dead! No pair of Payless specials is bringing her back."

She wanted it to splinter Pinny the way she'd been splintered so many times before. No person should be allowed to hope for the magic Pinny hoped for and have it come true. Life sucked, and the sooner Pinny realized that and got back to Jaynis, the better off she'd be.

But when Pinny's face broke into a thousand shards of sadness and tears, Ray had to look away.

Pain settled in a blanket over her, and the world beyond withdrew. She wasn't aware of the shift in the air around her when Pinny's sobs faded. Or of the approaching footsteps. An old woman's face, framed by thick silver hair, floated into her fog.

"What are you doing back here?" the face asked, hovering over her.

Ray's heart rammed her throat. Pinny was gone, and Ray was looking into this woman's ancient, perplexed eyes. "I did a terrible thing," she said, and then, finally, she gave in to the tears.

She didn't want to be here, under the cold, glaring lights in the ER.

"We're wasting time," she said through clenched teeth. "I've got to get out of here."

She had to find Pinny before she got lost among the blaring horns and asphalt, before some ass like JT got hold of her and, this time, didn't let go. She slid off the exam table, then buckled at the fresh eruption of pain.

"Please," the woman said, easing Ray back onto the table, "you'll only hurt yourself more."

"I don't care," Ray said, turning her face to hide her wincing. The woman said her name was Dalya, and she'd insisted on staying with her despite Ray's repeated arguments to be left alone. There was a gentleness to Dalya's face, but her keen eyes didn't miss anything. They stayed on Ray constantly, taking note of every expression crossing Ray's face, every movement she made.

"Are you sure there's no one I can call for you?" she asked *again*. "Your family will be worried—"

"I told you already," Ray snapped. "There's no one. Asking every ten seconds won't change the answer." She was taking a different tack now, hoping if she was obnoxious enough, she'd scare the old lady into giving up and getting out of here.

It didn't work. Dalya looked as unruffled as ever. "I'm sorry," she said. "But girls don't fall from the sky in my backyard every day. And since it was my tree, I can't help feeling a

responsibility to find out what exactly you were doing in it."
She smiled. "Besides, it wouldn't be polite to begrudge an old
woman her curiosity."

"You don't get it!" Ray cried as her panic grew. "Pinny's
out there alone. She's . . . more hurt than I am. I did it to her."
She choked on a sob. "I . . . I lost her."

"Ah." Dalya nodded. "So you weren't alone. Now we're beginning to get somewhere. So maybe next you'll tell me who
Pinny is?"

Suddenly, after years of not being able to see, Ray understood the answer to that question. "Pinny . . . was the only
friend I ever had." She covered her face with her hand, giving
into hot, shame-filled tears.

"Hush now." Dalya offered her a tissue. "Only one friend?"
She shook her head. "Perhaps it's time for another?"

Ray wiped her eyes, blinking in surprise. "You don't even
know me."

"No, but . . . I believe I need to." She said it with such sure-
ness and honesty that Ray wondered if the woman was all
there. She was talking like Pinny, like she knew something secret about the world that Ray didn't. It was craziness, and Ray
didn't want to trust her, but what choice did she have? Dalya
was the only person she knew here, and if Dalya knew the
city, then she might be able to help her find Pinny. That was
enough to make Ray decide to play along, at least for now.

"You see," Dalya went on, "I couldn't sleep tonight. And
strange as it may sound, I think it's because I was waiting
for you."

"Not for me," Ray said flatly. "Pinny maybe. She was the one
who wanted the shoes on your tree. I just helped her take them."

"Which shoes?" Dalya asked.

"A pair of silver high-heeled sandals," Ray said.

Dalya thought for a minute, then nodded. "I know that pair," she said. "I found them in a trash can on Avenue B years ago. But . . . what would she want with them?"

Ray swallowed, staring at the tile floor. "That's Pinny's story. She should be the one to tell it. I don't deserve to. Not when I don't even know where she is."

"We'll find her, then," Dalya said, nodding decisively just as the doctor came in. "Simple as that. And then you'll come home with me, the both of you, to explain everything."

As the doctor wrapped her arm and hand in a cast, Ray told Dalya about Pinny, careful to keep out the details of their trip. Dalya's eyes never once narrowed in judgment, even when Ray told her how she'd screamed at Pinny, how she'd treated her so horribly, so unforgivably. Even more baffling was that, after the doctor left, when Ray explained she couldn't pay for treatment, Dalya simply whipped out a credit card.

"Your story is the only payment I'll accept for now," she said. "I used to tell stories about shoes . . . so many years ago." Her eyes filled. "This will be the first time one's been told to me." She straightened. "Now let's think about where Pinny could be. You mentioned that she used to live in the city. Maybe there's someplace special she knows. . . ."

Ray shook her head. "She was only seven or eight. She'd never remember—" Ray stopped as a memory struck her. A story Pinny had once told her about her red Mary Janes. This time, when she reran the story in her head, she didn't blow it off like she had before. She listened to the words, and she heard Pinny talking about city blocks, about the building she lived in with her mama, about the day her mama bought her the red shoes and got lost. . . .

"Pinny once told me that her mama left her in a building that had a ceiling full of stars," Ray said. "A ceiling that was . . . Tiffany blue?"

Dalya nodded with recognition. "That's Grand Central."

Hope flitted through Ray's heart.

"That's got to be where she is," Ray said, and then she was scrambling out the door, with Dalya beside her.

PINNY

She didn't know how long she'd been sitting on the stairs under the ceiling of stars. Maybe one time through *The Wizard of Oz*. Maybe two. And that movie played for loads of time. The silver sandals sat next to her, cuddled up to her side, waiting with her.

After she'd left Ray under the tree, she'd run. She forgot about her sore feet and how tight the shoes squeezed her toes. She forgot to look where she was going. Honking cars and screeching brakes filled her ears. She bumped into one man, making him drop his briefcase. "Watch where you're going!" he yelled, so close to her face it scared her in a JT way. How many JTs were there in a city so big? The thought made her run faster. Every street looked the same, blinding lights and people rushing by like swarms of bugs.

She was lost. She started to cry, but the heat dried her tears before they ever fell. She tried to shake Ray's words out of her head. They were too awful to belong. But they stuck like glue, making her cry harder. She'd thought she'd run right into Mama, that the silver sandals would lead to her. But when that hadn't happened, she'd slowed down, thinking things over. That's when she knew the place to go.

Of course, she didn't know where the place was. Not anymore. She had to ask a waitress in a diner. The waitress gave her directions, but the second Pinny left the diner, the street names muddied in her mind, and she was as lost as before. After that, she asked a boy on a bike for directions. He had a funny sort of wagon hooked up to the back of his bike. He told her it was for carrying people, and because by then she was limping badly, he offered to give her a ride in it for free.

The boy didn't look snaky in a JT way, but that didn't mean he wasn't hiding his meanness somewhere she couldn't see.

"I sit back here?" she asked, pointing to the wagon. "And you . . . you stay on the bike. Right?"

The boy kept nodding until Pinny agreed to climb in. But she took off one of her shoes and pointed its heel toward the boy, just in case. Luckily, she didn't need to use it.

He dropped her off in front of glass doors tucked under an enormous white building. She walked through the doors and down a long ramp. When the sky opened up over her head, she knew she was in the right place. There were the inside stars and the Tiffany sky, just as pretty as she remembered.

She tried to remember the exact stair she'd sat on with Mama, and she thought she found it. She couldn't be sure. She only hoped.

Then she waited, sure that Mama would come back, from wherever she was, now that Pinny had found her shoes. People walked by. Lots of people. But they were strangers. It was okay that the first few faces weren't Mama's. But the more faces that came, the longer that she waited, the more the Lonelies started. Just like they had the day she'd lost Mama here before. Only there was no one to help her get rid of them.

She didn't know anyone here. She didn't know this place. Not really. The only place in the whole world she really knew was . . . Jaynis. Smokebush. Room 305. She didn't like it. But she wasn't lost when she was there. Not like here.

She ran a finger along one of the sandals, and for the first time, she saw cracks in the straps where the silver was flaking away. There was a spot where a strap was ripped clean through, hanging loose. She frowned.

Magic shoes weren't supposed to break, were they? Unless . . . unless they weren't magic at all.

Then she heard her name being called, and a smile broke across her face. Because her name was being called by someone who loved her.

But when she looked up, it wasn't Mama in front of her, crying, and laughing, and hugging her so tight.

It was Ray.

RAY

Ray found Pinny sitting on a stair in the main terminal of Grand Central, her knees tucked up under her chin, a sad, bewildered expression on her face. For one second, Ray glimpsed what Pinny had looked like years ago, a lost little girl waiting for her mama. Then she blinked, and there was the Pinny she knew again, the Pinny she was so glad to see that she ran down the ramp to get to her.

The words "I'm sorry" poured out of her, along with the breath she'd been holding all the way from the hospital.

Pinny should've slapped her across the face. Or worse. But Ray never gave her the chance, because she grabbed her in a hug before Pinny could move.

"I wasn't sure you'd be here, but I thought maybe . . ." She sucked in air. "I'm so sorry. For everything. And what I said about your mama . . ." The shame of it snagged her words in her throat. "I don't know what's wrong with me. You probably hate me. You *should* hate me."

She peered into Pinny's face, expecting to see anger. But the expression she saw there was even worse. It was the vacant look of someone losing faith, a look she saw in her own reflection in the mirror, but one she'd never seen on Pinny's face. And it was her fault.

Pinny ran her hand over the silver sandals, then whispered, "Mama's not coming back for them, is she?"

Ray hesitated. Before, when she'd told Pinny the truth, she'd wanted to steal her hope, like hers had been stolen by Carter, by Sal and Hugh, by so many people who'd stripped her kindness, her trust. Now, seeing Pinny hugging herself against some invisible bruise, she saw the damage she'd done. She had to make it right, but not with lying.

"I don't think so," she whispered, "but . . . I don't know for sure."

Tears trickled down Pinny's face. She laid her head on Ray's shoulder, and Ray settled into it. It was the first time she ever remembered anyone coming to her for comfort. It was a strange feeling, frightfully full of responsibility, but she didn't pull away.

She gave Pinny's shoulder a squeeze. "Hey. Your mama's not here, but I am. And we're sisters, right? Family."

"We're not really." The bitterness in her voice was unnerving.

"Maybe not by blood," Ray said firmly. "But orphans make their own families. We are whatever we believe we are."

She was hoping Pinny might smile, or nod, or something. Instead, she whispered dully, "I know what I'm going to be. A worker at Fricasweet's. Living at Horizons Assist." She shivered. "I'm going back to Jaynis."

"No," Ray blurted, nearly shouting it. Why hadn't she seen before? Pinny would waste away there. No . . . it could never happen. "Don't say that. You can figure something out—"

"Stop," Pinny said. "I'm no good by myself. I can't do it."

Ray wanted to argue. She wanted to reconstruct the rosy picture Pinny'd had of another life. But it wasn't salvageable. Not when Pinny could see the fake it was.

Pinny tapped the cast on Ray's arm. "Is it broken?"

"In three places," Ray said.

"Good," Pinny snapped.

Ray's cheeks broiled. It was the meanest thing she'd ever heard Pinny say to anyone, and the fact that it was meant for her made it cut deeper. She deserved it, though, and much more.

Pinny sighed. "My feet hurt . . . bad."

"I'll take you to Dalya's," Ray said. "She's the woman who made the Tree of Lost Soles. She wants to meet you. She's outside in a cab, waiting for us." Dalya had reluctantly agreed to wait outside so that if Ray found Pinny, she could talk to her alone.

"But I need your word that you won't disappear," Dalya had said firmly before Ray stepped out of the cab. "That's the only way I'll let you go. Please, don't disappoint me."

Ray found herself promising. Not for herself, but for Pinny. Because she knew that Pinny would want to meet Dalya, the keeper of the Tree of Lost Soles. It was a part of Pinny's fairy tale that Ray could give back to her, and she was planning on it.

Ray smiled at Pinny now, hoping she'd stirred some excitement over Dalya. But her deadened look remained.

Pinny wiped her eyes, turning away. "I want to go."

Ray stood with Pinny, and they made their way slowly out of the terminal.

Pinny stopped once to stare at the constellations sprinkled across the ceiling. "When Mama brought me here, I thought the stars were real. I thought they were magic." Her head drooped. "They're stupid white paint."

"Come on, Pinny." Ray held out her hand. For one excruciating minute, Pinny didn't move. Finally, she slipped her hand into Ray's, letting Ray lead her out the door.

The warmth of Pinny's hand in her own might have been reassuring, if Pinny's fingers hadn't been so rigid, as if they didn't want to be there at all. For the first time, Ray feared for her. Some people weren't built for breaking, and Pinny, she saw now, was one of them.

DALYA

"Here we are." Dalya held her breath as the two girls slunk sheepishly into the shop, wondering if they'd stay or run. Their presence, she sensed, was a delicate thing that could flit away in an instant.

In the hospital, she'd seen right away how Ray carried anger around her like a cloak. Her very eyes glinted with it, so like the way Henry's had. She hadn't been able to save Henry, but maybe she could do something for Ray. She wasn't sure what or how, but before anything else, she knew, Ray would have to stay. Right now, that seemed unlikely.

Ray fidgeted, keeping close to the shop door, glancing at it every few seconds as if she were about to bolt right through. Pinny seemed to be the force holding her here, but for how long wasn't certain.

"Come in, come in." Dalya moved past them to sit down at her worktable. She picked up one of Kathryn Rosenbak's peacock shoes, hoping the shift in attention might encourage them away from the door. Pinny attempted a smile, but it was tremulous and sad. Her green glasses had slipped down to the tip of her nose, and she pushed them up and then gasped as she registered the walls of shoes surrounding her.

"Such pretty shoes," she said. "Mama named me for shoes, you know. I'm really Chopine."

"Is that so?" Dalya said. "Well, anyone named after such a magnificent shoe is certainly welcome in my shop, thief or no."

"Pinny's no thief." Ray's voice lashed out protectively. "We weren't stealing." Ray glanced at Pinny, and her face took on a look of resolve, as if she'd just decided something important. "The shoes were Pinny's mama's. We came to get them back."

Pinny's wilting posture straightened at Ray's words, and she snapped her head up to stare at Ray.

"Your mother's?" Dalya asked Pinny. "Are you sure?"

"I thought they were," Pinny said quietly. "But it wasn't true. . . ."

"Yes." Ray nodded firmly at Pinny. "It *was* true."

Ray's eyes met Pinny's. An understanding seemed to pass between them, and whatever it was brought a spark of life to Pinny's pale face. They both smiled.

"In that case," Dalya said, "the shoes *do* belong to you."

"Thank you." Pinny hugged the silver sandals to her chest, easing into the shop as if she felt safer, now that the shoe question was settled.

For the first time, Dalya noticed her limp, and the wince

Pinny made with each step. "But . . . are you hurt?" She slipped off her stool to move to Pinny's side and, as she did, brushed the rest of Kathryn's peacock feathers off her worktable. They fluttered to the floor in a swirl of iridescence.

"Oh, I'm such a klutz these days." She laughed, bending to pick them up. That's when a flash of pale pink on Pinny's feet caught her eye, and she lost her breath.

She knew them instantly. The fabric, once a true pink, was gray with dirt, but the tiny flowers still blossomed across the toe box, exactly as she'd made them.

A cry escaped her lips, taking with it years of hidden heartache. And overwhelming joy took its place. She sank to her knees, her eyes streaming. "But . . . this is impossible," she cried. "Impossible! It was over seventy years ago."

Pinny knelt, peering worriedly into her face. "What happened? What's wrong?"

"Those shoes." She shook her head at Pinny's feet. "*My* shoes. I left them behind . . . in Berlin. I was sure they were gone."

"You mean . . . those are *your* shoes?" Ray asked in disbelief.

Dalya nodded, hardly able to comprehend it. It was the sweetest dream, so excessive in its happiness she had to place both hands on the floor to stay grounded to the world. "I made them. A lifetime ago." She smiled, wiping her eyes. "They were meant to be my wedding shoes. They were lost, and then I . . . I never spoke about them again. To anyone."

"Why not?" Pinny asked.

"Maybe I was afraid there'd be too much pain in the telling," she said softly.

Pinny smiled and looked knowingly at Ray. "See?" she said. "I told you these shoes needed to come with us." With that, her tepid grayness of before disappeared, leaving a triumphant glow in its place.

Dalya extended a trembling hand, touching the heel of one of the shoes, feeling the curve of it under her skin. Yes, it was real.

"Pinny." She could barely speak. "Could I . . . hold them?"

"Sure. They're too pinchy anyway." Pinny slipped them off her feet. "But the heel's broke. I'm sorry."

Dalya cradled the shoes in her arms, feeling their weight until she was finally convinced that they were here. She turned the right shoe over, examining the dangling heel, which was tacky with the remains of what looked like gum. The tiny hinge in the heel was rusted and worn. She reached inside the hollow of the heel, knowing it would be too much to ask for, but hoping nonetheless. Her finger found the tattered, water-stained slip of paper, but nothing else.

She sighed. "Oh well," she said. "I thought maybe they'd still be there. But that would've been too extraordinary."

"What?" Pinny asked.

"My mother's rings," she said. "I hid them inside the night the Nazis came for us. They've probably been gone for decades now."

"They must've fallen out when the heel broke," Ray said hurriedly, then cleared her throat. "So . . . the message on the paper hidden in the shoe. What does it say?"

"It's a Hebrew prayer," Dalya said. "Translated, it says: 'May it be Your will, God, our God and the God of our fathers, that

You should lead us in peace, and direct our steps in peace, and guide us in peace, and support us in peace, and cause us to reach our destination in life, joy, and peace.'"

Ray's mouth puckered as if she was getting ready to sneer, but then, with some struggle, she checked herself. "Too bad it never happens that way."

"It didn't used to be easy for me to believe, either." Dalya nodded. "Peace was less of a constant in my life, and more of a destination. But I did find it."

"I always thought those shoes had a peaceful look," Pinny said. She peered into Dalya's face. "So we did good? Bringing them to you?"

"Better than good," she whispered, losing her voice to tears. "Much, *much* better." She took a deep breath, letting Pinny help her to her feet. "So, I think we all have stories to tell tonight. And maybe now it's finally time to tell mine." She smiled at Pinny. "I want to hear about your mama's shoes. Shall I tell you my story? And then you can tell me yours."

"I'd love that," Pinny said, and Ray nodded.

Dalya led them through the back of the shop and outside, where they tucked themselves under her Tree of Lost Soles. Then, slowly, holding the shoes that filled her with that same lovely, warm sensation she'd had hours before, when she'd felt something wonderful coming but wasn't sure what, Dalya told their story. There was still sorrow in their tale, but this time in the telling, there was no ending. Only a celebration of their continued journey, from loss into newfound life.

RAY

Ray listened to the words under the city's canopy of night. First Dalya's, and then Pinny's. They fluttered about the tree, swooping in and out of its branches. She imagined them settling on the tips and heels of the shoes, maybe giving them a bit of their own lost stories back. This time when Pinny read the story of the invisible princess, Ray smiled. It was a relief, letting her face do what came naturally, instead of forcing it to harden like she'd always done before. It was a relief, too, that Pinny didn't share details about Smokebush, that she skipped that part of everything, focusing on her mama instead.

Listening to Pinny and Dalya made Ray lonely, though, because she wasn't a part of any of it. Not that she deserved to be. She'd had her chance with Pinny's story, and she'd mocked it. Not out loud . . . no. But she'd tossed it under a "lame" label in her mind. Dalya's interest was so avid, so genuine, that Pinny gained confidence as she talked. Her voice, garbled at first, grew sharper, clearer. Soon, Dalya and Pinny were holding hands, heads bent together, connected by their stories and, even more, by their faith in the magic that had brought them together. A faith that Ray admired from a distance, but couldn't seem to grasp. It was as if Pinny's dependence on her was wavering, and Ray felt herself missing Pinny's company, even as she sat right beside her.

As Pinny reached the end of her story, her voice broke.

"Now I have Mama's shoes back," she said quietly. "And no Mama."

Dalya slipped her arm around Pinny. "And I have *my* shoes," she said. "And no Mama. But . . . we still have their stories to tell, and their love in the words."

Pinny caressed the silver stilettos in her lap.

"Look." She held one up to Dalya. "You can see the fingerprint of her foot. There on the bottom."

Dalya nodded. "The shoes remember her, too."

Pinny smiled at that, and Ray hoped it was a sign she was working through her grief in her own way. Would she ever be able to fully understand what had happened to her mother? Ray didn't know. But maybe it didn't matter. Understanding the world's heartbreaks didn't lessen the pain of them. Ray knew that better than anybody. So why had she worked so hard to kill Pinny's fantasy about her mother?

She'd been jealous. Jealous that Pinny could escape to her own happy make-believes when Ray never could. She'd been wrong . . . so wrong to want to take them from Pinny. She should've been protecting them instead.

Repulsion swept over her. She was sick of herself. Sick of her own cruelty, but maybe—a barb of fear hooked her—she was damned to be trapped in it forever.

Right now Dalya's rings weighed against her thigh, warm in her pocket. She'd had the chance earlier to give them up, but she hadn't. She was still trying to save her sorry self. Without the rings, she'd have nothing. No way to get the money she needed to start over. And of course, she'd have to leave Dalya's. That wasn't even a question.

But she'd be the lowliest kind of scum to take the rings now that she knew who they belonged to, what they meant. *Stop it,* she chided herself. *Don't let it mess with your head. You need them more than she does. Don't feel, don't think. Survive. . . .*

She jumped as a hand touched her shoulder.

"Ray," Dalya said kindly. "We've been telling our stories all night long, but we haven't heard yours yet."

Ray recoiled as their eyes settled on her in expectation. She thought about confessing, returning Dalya's rings. But instead, she shrugged. "My story doesn't matter."

"I want to hear it," Dalya said.

"No you don't," she said. "Not really." She was the intruder here. She stood up, fighting back tears, and looked toward the shop. "I'm sorry. I think I'm just completely wiped."

"Of course." Dalya stood slowly, then leveled her gaze on both of them. "I do have questions. About who you left behind in Texas. I'm sure they'll be worried. We'll need to get in touch with them—"

"No," Pinny blurted, and then her face sagged, the gray pall returning. "I have to go back. I know that. But . . . please. I'm . . . I'm not ready."

315

Pinny's voice was so desperate that Dalya's eyes fogged with concern. "It's all right." She pressed her hand to Pinny's cheek. "You're not going anywhere for now." She studied the sky, lost in thought. "It may be for selfish reasons, but I'm not ready to part with either of you yet. Not after everything that's happened tonight. So I suppose . . . my questions can wait." She smiled. "I'll show you where you can sleep."

"Thank you," Ray said.

Pinny nodded. "Wait. I have to do something." She lifted the red Mary Janes from around her neck and hung them carefully over the lowest branch of the Tree of Lost Soles. She gave them a tender pat. "They like it here," she said. "They want to stay."

Dalya touched their tips gently, setting them rocking on the branch. "I'd like that, too. But you can visit them tomorrow. They'll be here."

Tomorrow. Ray shuddered at the word. She wasn't sure she'd be here then. Best to run before Dalya asked more questions, before she figured out where Ray and Pinny had come from and how to get them back. The only thing keeping her here tonight was her exhaustion, and the fact that she had no idea where to go, or what to do yet. She'd sleep on it, and decide on things in the morning.

Dalya guided them inside and up a set of back stairs to a small apartment above the shop.

"Here you are," she said, leading them into a guest room with twin beds. Then she left to let them get settled.

Pinny gratefully crawled into her bed, for once forgetting her nighttime routine and leaving her bulging backpack on the floor. She was asleep in a matter of seconds. But Ray perched warily on the edge of her bed, her body tense, until a gentle tap on the door made her start.

Dalya peeked her head around the corner, then came to sit next to Ray.

"I thought you might need some help undressing," she said. "It might be difficult with your cast."

Ray glanced at the floor-length nightgown Dalya laid out on the bedspread for her. Better to stay ready to run. "I'm fine sleeping in my clothes," she said. "But . . . I could use some help untying my shoes."

"Of course." Dalya smiled. "What interesting accessorizing." She fingered the safety pins. "I have a client who would love something like this."

Ray winced as Dalya slid the shoes and socks from her feet. As Ray had known she would, the moment Dalya saw her feet, she gasped and pulled back.

"Darling girl," she said, "what happened to your feet?"

Ray shrugged. "It's just part of my story. Not a good part."

Dalya looked at her for a long moment and then, with her weathered hand, smoothed Ray's hair from her forehead. Ray's usual response would've been to cower from the touch, but Dalya's fingers were warm and feathery light against her brow, and she thought that this must be the way mothers touched their children while they slept.

"You know"—Dalya looked out the window at her tree—"ever since the war, I never could stand the sight of abandoned shoes." She nodded toward the window. "That's how the Tree of Lost Soles was born. I was walking down Columbus Avenue with my husband years ago, right after our daughter was born, and I saw this pair of white baby shoes lying in the gutter, drowning in sewer water. It nearly broke my heart that anyone could abandon something so full of memories. I had to bring them home with me." She laughed. "Aaron must've thought I was crazy, but he never said so. I tucked those shoes into our closet, but then I brought home a pair of loafers I found on a boulder in Central Park, and some evening shoes I found on the steps of the Guggenheim. Before I knew it, I didn't have room in the closet for my own clothes and shoes anymore." She shrugged. "That's when I started hanging the lost shoes on the tree. As a testament to the people who walked in them, and their stories."

She patted Ray's knee and stood up, then turned back in the doorway. "So, you found my shoes in that Pennypinch store Pinny mentioned, then you threw them away." Her gaze was curious, unwavering. "Why?"

Ray plucked at the bedspread, thinking over the question before answering. "I hated them for not being able to give me what I wanted."

"What was it you wanted?" Dalya asked, her brown eyes patient and open.

Ray stared out the window at the lightening sky. "To be loved," she whispered.

"Ah." Dalya smiled. "And do you see? You got what you wanted." She nodded toward Pinny, who was snoring lightly in her bed. "Maybe not love from the person you expected, but love, just the same. And isn't it a blessing to have it, in any form?"

She didn't wait for Ray to answer but, instead, whispered good night, closing the door. Ray collapsed on the bed, blowing out her breath. Yes, love was a blessing, but it couldn't feed her or keep her safe. It couldn't erase what had happened with Carter, couldn't stop her from getting sent back to Texas. No, she'd need a lot more than love to survive. She sighed, feeling the pull of sleep. Before she gave in to it, she glanced out the window one last time and saw Pinny's red Mary Janes dancing from their branch in the first, fresh breeze of morning.

RAY

Ray woke up to late-afternoon light pouring through the window, the Tree of Lost Soles casting lacy shadows on the floor. She had the grogginess that comes with sleeping long and hard at the wrong time of day, and it took her a few minutes to orient herself.

Pinny's bed was empty, her backpack gone. The bedrooms were so still Ray guessed she was alone upstairs. Her adrenaline surged. If Pinny and Dalya were down in the shop, this was her chance to leave.

She could sneak out through the back, pawn the rings, and be sitting in some diner blocks away, scouring ads for apartments and jobs, in no time.

The cast made her clumsy with her shoes, and she ended up leaving them untied, but finally, she was tiptoeing down the stairs. Four steps to freedom. Three, two . . .

"Ray?" Pinny's voice came from the shop. "Sleepyhead! You took forever to wake up!" Her bright face appeared around the doorframe. "Come on!"

Ray let Pinny pull her into the shop. Frustration swelled inside her, but so did relief. *Traitor,* she chided herself. *You're an idiot to stay. Just tell them you're leaving.*

But Dalya's smile was too welcoming, Pinny's was too hopeful, and the smell of breakfast too enticing to resist.

"There you are." Dalya handed her a plate overflowing with food. "Pinny and I have been awake for hours. How did you sleep?"

"Um . . . gr—"

"We have a surprise!" Pinny cried before Ray could finish. "Wait till you see!"

Ray looked doubtfully at Dalya, but she only smiled.

"You sit here and wait." Pinny settled her into a chair, then hurried behind the sales counter and came back carrying a large basin of water.

"What's that for?" Ray asked skeptically while she nibbled her food.

Pinny's smile swelled as she put the basin down in front of Ray's chair. "We're making you some shoes."

"Oh, come on. Why waste your time? I won't wear them." Ray sniggered, then regretted it when Pinny's face fell. "Sorry," she tried again, her voice gentler this time. "I just . . . I don't need new shoes."

"*You* may not need them, but your feet do." Dalya squeezed Ray's shoulder, then added softly, "I don't know what's happened to you. But . . . you're safe here. Let us do this for you. Please. It will be all right."

Safe. Ray rolled her eyes. When had she ever felt that way? But there was a hushed reassurance in Dalya's tone—the sort of tone used to keep nightmares from cradles—and some left-over child-part of herself wanted so badly to believe it, and trust it. If Dalya was lying, she supposed it wouldn't hurt any worse than anyone else's lies had.

So, as Pinny slipped off her shoes and socks excitedly, Ray sank into resignation. Didn't she owe Pinny this much, after what she'd put her through? "Fine," she mumbled.

"Yes!" Pinny cried. "You'll love them. You will. You'll see." She pointed to the water. "First, your feet need a bath."

"Right, 'cause I left my Odor-Eaters in Texas," Ray said, trying for lightness. But her heart scuttled as she uncurled her feet from under her. Back in Jaynis, her bare feet had worn out their shock value years ago, and few people ever got close enough to see the scars in all their hideous glory. Here, with unforgiving sunlight pouring through the shopwindows, she felt like Frankenstein reborn. She hurriedly dunked her feet under the suds to hide them.

She'd worried that Dalya might start with prying questions. But for the moment, Dalya was busy showing Pinny the ins and outs of the shop. A crisp peppermint scent wafted from the basin, and the water made Ray's skin tingle refreshingly. She leaned back, her feet cocooned in warmth, letting herself enjoy the sensation.

Relieved not to have to talk, she watched as Dalya gave Pinny a tour of the tools she used. Pinny listened raptly, repeating the names of the tools to commit them to memory. When Dalya handed Pinny a tool called a shave and had her try it on a men's dress shoe, Pinny worked carefully, trimming the excess leather Dalya pointed out.

"That's fine work," Dalya said, inspecting the shoe. "We make a good team."

Pinny nodded. "I like this job. Making shoes. Way better than flipping bug burgers at Fricasweet's."

"Is that where you worked in Texas?" Dalya asked.

Pinny frowned. "I'm going to. When I go back. They're making me. Because it's something I *can* do. But no one asked if I *wanted* to. People always forget to ask."

Dalya's forehead crinkled. "Who's going to make you?"

Pinny shrugged. "Mrs. Danvers. Mr. Sands. The people who take care of me."

"What do *you* want?" Dalya asked.

"I want to take care of myself." Her shoulders sagged as she stared at the floor. "I thought I could. Before. Except I'm . . . I'm not so good at it." She ran her hand over the shoe. "But I'm allowed to want More, though. This is the kind of More I want."

And why not? Ray thought. Pinny deserved a life she liked as much as anybody. What sucked was that nobody ever gave her the chance to get it.

Dalya studied Pinny's face, lost in thought, then she looked at Ray. "Well, Apprentice Pinny, let's get back to our number-one customer, shall we?"

Pinny's shoulders straightened with importance at hearing her new title, and she sat down on a stool in front of Ray with a towel.

"Feet out," she ordered. "Time for your pedicure."

Panic racked Ray's core, and she yanked her feet out of the water, nearly tipping the basin.

"No," she choked, her breath ragged. "No way. I . . . I can't." No one had ever touched her feet . . . not since the doctors, the scars, the pain. . . .

"It's my rule, I'm afraid," Dalya said matter-of-factly, keeping her eyes on some receipts at her counter. "The beauty of a shoe grows from the foot it belongs to. It's time for your foot to remember its beauty."

Ray shivered as the dampness from her feet seeped into her jeans. There was no way . . . But then Pinny met her eyes, her smile encouraging. "Nail polish is easy. It's what sisters do. It won't hurt. I promise."

Maybe it was the certainty in Pinny's voice, or the sweetness she gave to "sisters," or how, ever since she'd arrived here, Ray had longed more and more for the words she'd spoken to Pinny, about family and friendship, to be true. Maybe it was that she wanted to allow herself this one morning of sunshine, peace, and safety before she was alone again for good. Whatever the reason, Ray closed her eyes, sucked in a breath, and settled her trembling feet in Pinny's waiting hands.

Pinny's hands were butterfly wings fluttering over her skin, alighting here and there with peppermint oil, mapping out the welts and ridges with the tenderest touch. Then there were the cool strokes of the polish sweeping her toenails, and the anticipation she felt wondering how it would look. As golden light soaked through her eyelids, Ray gave herself over to being soothed, being helped, being cared for.

It was only when Pinny whispered "Done" that Ray's relaxation jolted into fear again. She reluctantly opened her eyes, but the repulsion she'd expected at the feet she was sure would look pathetic never came.

The polish was a pale pink, the pearly shade of Dalya's wedding shoes, and when she looked at her nails, the scars around them blurred. When they blurred, the outline of her feet became smooth and graceful, a glimpse of how they'd been long, long ago.

"Do you like it?" Pinny asked.

"Not too shabby," Ray said lightly, but she couldn't stop her smile.

Dalya nodded in approval. "Now we'll get your measurements for your shoes. It will take some time to make them. I'll order special cushioning for the sole and the upper, to make them as comfortable as possible. But at least we can make a start, and I can mail them to you after . . ."

Her voice died, and Ray's stomach lurched. *After you leave.* Those were the words she'd been about to say. The anxiety that Ray had almost forgotten about returned, and her face must have shown it, because Dalya sighed.

"I'm sorry," Dalya said. "I didn't mean to bring up the subject of you leaving."

"We can't leave yet," Pinny sputtered. "Not until Ray's shoes are done."

Dalya stared down at the tools in her hands. "Reality can be so rude. I forget about it, sometimes, tucked away in this shop." She sighed. "I'm enjoying having you here, but we can't keep pretending it's not complicated. I can't let you use this as a hiding place forever. Tomorrow, we'll have to let the world in. But I have to admit, I don't want to. It doesn't seem fair."

"Nothing ever is," Ray blurted.

"You're too young to be so angry." Dalya clucked her tongue. "That's the reason I haven't pushed you for answers about why you left Texas. You're so desperate *not* to go back. I don't know what it is you're so frightened of. But I hope, at least, I'm giving you some time away from it."

Ray saw the sincerity in Dalya's face, and suddenly she thought maybe she could find a way to stay, to come clean about Dalya's rings. But if she stayed, what sort of future would she have?

Pinny glanced at Ray, probably waiting to see if Ray'd put up a fight. But Ray reluctantly nodded. "We have to deal with Texas sooner or later. Better tomorrow than today, right?" She'd leave in the morning, before Dalya and Pinny woke up. For now, she had to keep Pinny convinced that they were going to stay together. If Pinny knew what Ray was planning, she'd never let her leave alone.

"Okay," Pinny said gloomily. "Tomorrow."

Dalya smiled. "It's settled, then. . . . Back to shoes."

"Back to shoes," Pinny said, brightening.

But while she and Dalya measured Ray's feet and mulled over designs and colors, laughing and chatting easily, a shadow settled over Ray. Dalya, and even Pinny, might believe they could stall reality for the next few hours, or maybe for the whole day. Not her. *Never* her.

For her, there was only the quiet agony of waiting for the moment when this stolen happiness would be snatched away for good.

PINNY

A yawn snuck up behind Pinny's smile, catching it off guard, but it still stayed stuck right where it was. It had been that kind of sunshiny day. Dalya had called her an apprentice. It sounded important. Like making shoes was important. Like *she* was important. Then they'd gone for a walk in Central Park, and eaten warm pretzels with mustard, and played five rounds of Go Fish. Even Ray had played . . . all five times.

"I beat you two times," she said to Ray as she pulled her backpack onto the bed.

"Don't remind me." Ray's voice sounded grouchy, but she could tell she was faking it. "It's hard to play Go Fish with a broken arm."

Pinny snorted. "Try playing with a broken brain."

"Stop." Ray said it so hard and loud that Pinny jumped.

She stared at Ray. "Why are you mad? I was making a joke."

Ray frowned. "No. Never about that. Your brain is perfect."

Pinny concentrated on unzipping her backpack so her eyes wouldn't go soggy. "It's not," she whispered. "Everyone who looks at me knows it's not."

"Listen to me." Ray took her by the shoulders. "Lots of people's brains are messed up. Their brains are full of ugliness, meanness, lies. Yours isn't full of any of that crap. And I *love* the way you think."

Pinny turned away. Ray was trying to help. But she couldn't . . . not with this. She lined up her treasures on the nightstand—Mama's shoes, then Daddy's watch next to them, cuddling.

"It's why Mama didn't come back for me." She sighed. "I know it is."

Ray shook her head. "Do you know what I think happened? Your mama found her own magic carpet. It flew her higher than the sky, higher than the stars, even. It got so high she couldn't come back. But she's happy . . . up there with the stars."

Pinny shut her eyes, and a picture filled her head, of Mama doing loop-the-loops around the stars, her hair glittery with their light. "You're making up a story."

"Maybe, but we'll never know for sure." She nudged Pinny's shoulder. "Right?"

Pinny couldn't help her smile. It was a lot better to think about it the way Ray told it.

Just then, there was a knock on the bedroom door, and Dalya came in.

"I brought you girls some clean pajamas." She went to lay them on the bed, but stopped in front of the nightstand.

"What's all this?" she asked.

"My treasures," Pinny said. "Mama's shoes, Daddy's watch . . ."

A mixed-up look crossed Dalya's face. "Your daddy's watch?"

Pinny nodded. "You can hold it." She set it in Dalya's hands. "Careful. It's very, very old."

"It reminds me of one I saw before. . . ." Dalya gently turned it over, reading the words on the back, then sucked in her breath. "'Time spent in happiness is never wasted.'" She held it right up to her face. "It looks like the inscription was changed?"

"The words on the back?" Pinny nodded. "It used to say something else. About time and money. Mama had it fixed. She said Daddy had the words all wrong."

"'Time wasted is money lost.' Is that what it used to say?" Dalya gripped the nightstand.

"That's right!" Pinny said. "How did you know that?"

Dalya's face turned egg-white. She cuddled her hands close to her chest. "Pinny . . ." Her voice was barely a breeze. She leaned forward. "Do you know your daddy's name?"

Pinny thought until her lips buttoned with trying to remember. "It was a *K* name," she said slowly. "K . . . K . . ." Yes! She had it! "Kent!"

Dalya gave a soft cry. "Kent Ashbury!" she whispered. Her expression was a jumble of sad and happy, and she couldn't talk for the longest time after that.

"It was your great-grandfather who had the words wrong, not your daddy." She rubbed her hand over the watch so lovingly, like she was rubbing a baby's head. "This watch belonged to your great-grandfather, then your grandfather, and then your daddy. Your grandfather's name was Henry." Her voice hugged his name. "We were great friends, long ago. But then, well, we couldn't be anymore. Henry died a few years ago." She sighed. "Henry must've given this watch to your daddy."

Pinny's heart hopped in her chest. If Dalya knew her grandpa, then did that mean . . . ? "Do you know my daddy? Do you know where he is?"

"I've never met him," Dalya said. "But I'm a great admirer

of his work. He's quite a talented painter. Some of his pieces are on exhibit right now at the Ferenz Gallery in SoHo." She smiled and placed her hand over Pinny's. "Your daddy ... lives right here in this city."

"In this city," Pinny whispered. *Grandfather's watch. Daddy's watch.* The pieces spun inside her head, but they wouldn't come together. She looked at Ray.

Ray smiled. "Pinny, you might be able to meet your daddy."

"Oh!" Her grin stretched so wide her cheeks hurt. Her daddy was real! Alive! Somewhere close by! "Oh, I'd love to meet him!" Then she remembered. "But what if he doesn't know about me?" she whispered, her heart diving to her toes. "What if he doesn't like my ... who I am?"

"No sense dwelling on what-ifs." Dalya gave her hands a squeeze. "We'll just have to hope ... and see."

Pinny nodded. She'd hoped for Mama, and then ... nothing. But she might have enough left ... enough hope for Daddy. She'd find it. She had to.

"We can try contacting him first thing tomorrow." Dalya shook her head, smiling. "I'd like to meet him, too. I always imagined him being the best of his father." Her eyes lit, like she was remembering something too sweet and secret to say. Then she looked back at Pinny. "If it's true, then I have to believe he'll be delighted to know you." She stood. "I'll track down the number for the gallery. We'll start there."

As soon as Dalya said good night and shut the door, Ray said, "I'm tired. I'm going to bed."

"Why?" There was no way Pinny was sleepy, not with excitement fizzing inside her. "We could play more cards. I could paint your fingernails, or—"

"Not tonight," Ray said shortly. "Sorry."

Her heart sank. She'd just heard the best news ever. So why didn't Ray look happy about it? She was quiet in her bed, curled up tight. Maybe it was a bad case of the Lonelies.

Pinny sat down next to her. "If I meet Daddy, he'll be my family. Maybe he can be yours, too. We can share him. Would that make you happy?"

"I *am* happy for you." The corner of Ray's mouth lifted, but Pinny wasn't sure it counted as a smile. "Don't worry about me. I'm fine. And I'm *going* to sleep."

"Sorry," Pinny whispered. She changed into pajamas as fast as she could, checked on her treasures one last time, then turned off the light and climbed into bed.

While she waited on sleep, she bounced a little so her mattress would make its tweeting sigh. She'd noticed before it could do that, when she first sat down. She bounced again. The bed was singing.

She heard Ray sigh from the other side of the room, probably getting mad over the bouncing. She stopped and lay still.

"Pinny?" Ray's voice was small, like it was lost in the dark and afraid.

Pinny shifted onto her side. "Did you have a bad dream?"

"No. I"—her voice turned wavy—"I'm glad you came with me on this trip. I told you I didn't want you to, but I didn't know what I was talking about. I was wrong . . . about so many things."

"*Most* things," Pinny said.

Ray laughed. "Okay. What I mean is . . ." She cleared her throat. "You're the best friend I ever had."

"*And* the best sister," Pinny reminded her.

"Always." Ray's voice was barely there. She sniffed loudly, and Pinny wondered if she might be catching a cold. "Good night."

"Good night." Her eyelids were droopy. But before they closed, she thought of something. Ray's "Good night" had sounded wrong, too sorrowful. Ray's "Good night" had sounded a lot like "Goodbye."

RAY

Ray hadn't slept, and she sat on the edge of her bed in a patch of morning sun, clutching Dalya's rings, steeling herself for what she knew she had to do. She should've gone hours ago. But last night, talking to Pinny, she'd realized it. She didn't want to be one of those ugly minds she'd described to Pinny. She wanted, for once, to be the Ray that Pinny believed in, fairy tale or no. For Pinny's sake, and, she realized with some surprise, her own. So, ignoring the suffocation she felt at sealing her fate, she'd stayed.

She'd heard Dalya leave her room a while ago, and now she heard her voice drifting up through the floorboards. Ray couldn't make out words, only cadences, rising and falling, and the sweet, pleased notes in Dalya's tone. Ray slipped from the bedroom and went downstairs, shaking.

Dalya was just hanging up the phone when Ray stepped into the shop.

"Ray." Dalya smiled. "I have such wonderful news. I put in a call to the Ferenz Gallery this morning, and the owner was able to reach Pinny's father." She clapped her hands in delight, looking surprisingly girlish as she did. "Kent's at his studio in Vermont now, but he's leaving right away to come back. He wants to meet Pinny. All these years, and he never knew about her! Would you like to go wake her? Oh, she'll be thrilled." Dalya chuckled, then stopped, staring at her. "What on earth is wrong, child? You're shivering. . . ."

At first, nothing would come. Her tongue was glued to the base of her mouth. Then, at last, "I'm fine." She waved Dalya's worried hands away, her heart shuddering against her ribs. She closed her eyes, squeezing her fist until the rings dug into her palm.

This was the moment, she knew, when the choice between truth and lies determined her future. The truth about the pink shoes and Dalya's rings, the truth about her own meanness, the kind of meanness Pinny hated. "I—I have something I need to tell you. But"—she heaved a breath—"not without Pinny. She has to hear it, too. I owe her that."

"Hear what?" a voice asked.

Ray turned to see Pinny in the doorway at the back of the shop, her face pale, her eyes bright. Then she glanced at Dalya's kind, unassuming eyes as she sat on her work stool, waiting. "Everything," she whispered.

Pinny stepped to her side, and Ray felt herself growing strong, strong enough for the truth. Pinny was with her, and that made all the difference. She took a breath, clean and full, and slid her hand into Pinny's.

"I told you before what I was afraid of," Ray said to her. "Of not being the person I want to be." She pushed the leaden words out of her throat. "I'm *not* her. Maybe I can never be her. But . . . I'd like to try."

"What do you mean?" Pinny's voice was quiet, scared.

"You don't know who I am, Pinny. Not really." Her voice broke. "I wreck things, like . . . I almost wrecked you. I steal things, too. All the time. Mrs. Danvers's money, the dress I wore to prom, the pink shoes. Those I took from the Penny-pinch. But that's not all." She needed each truth out in the open, away from her. She was vaguely aware of Dalya listening, but she kept her eyes focused on Pinny to make sure she understood who she was, what she'd done.

She stretched her hand toward Dalya, revealing the rings inside. "I . . . I have these for you." She laid them in Dalya's palm.

"My mother's rings," Dalya gasped. Tears spilled down her cheeks as she cupped the rings in her palms, kissing them. Then, through the tears, Dalya's eyes found hers. "You had them all along."

It wasn't an accusation. It was a statement of fact.

Ray nodded as Pinny frowned. "Why would you do that?" Pinny asked. "Dalya helped us."

"I know. I was . . ." She had to keep going. It was the only way through the person she was to the person she wanted to be. "I was going to pawn them. I was going to leave, and I needed the money."

"And what changed?" Dalya asked, running a fingertip lightly, lovingly, over the rings' curves.

She shrugged. "Nothing. Except my mind."

Dalya slid the rings onto her right ring finger, then stood.

"I'm sorry," Ray whispered. "I should never have taken them."

"Thank you." Dalya squeezed Ray's hand. "But they were always safe in your keeping. I believe that."

She shook her head. "I was planning to leave without you knowing. Without saying goodbye." She forced herself to keep looking at Pinny, watching as disappointment crumpled her face. This was her penance. "There was something I was trying to forget." She swallowed. "Lots of things . . . and there was someone, too. Carter." She hadn't said his name out loud, ever. But when she said it now, it didn't bring the pain she'd expected.

Dalya frowned, and a fierce protectiveness lit her eyes. "Oh, sweet girl, he didn't hurt you—"

"No," Ray blurted, shaking her head adamantly. "He would never do anything like that. I tried to get him to, but he didn't want me . . . that way." Her breath caught as she realized what she'd said, and the truth behind it. How had she never seen it before, what he really was? Here she'd been thinking Pinny was her only one, but Carter . . . "He was my . . . friend."

Then the rest of the words spilled out of her. Her story—the one she'd never told anyone—of what had happened with Carter. She thought that it would sound as horrible as it had felt to lose him. When she talked about him, though, she discovered that her memories of him had grown into something new and, somehow, less painful. She pictured him sitting beside her at the lake and saw him clearly, honestly, for the first time. Where she'd thought there'd been desire in his smile, there'd been kinship. His touch on her fingers hadn't been him asking for more, it had been him asking her for trust.

She hadn't understood it or recognized it then in Carter because she'd never seen it before. But she saw it now—the caring—in Dalya and Pinny. This time, she could allow it in without mistaking it for something else. She could finally let it be what it was.

"So much running away," Dalya said when Ray'd finished.

"It wasn't just from Carter," Ray admitted. "It was from Smokebush, too, and Jaynis." Ray stared at the floor. "Everything there is so . . . so small. *I* was nothing."

"Not to me, you weren't!" Pinny blurted. It was the first time Pinny had spoken since Ray had begun, and the hurt in her voice was unbearable. She hated that she'd let her down again, and she gripped Dalya's worktable, her nerves raw knots under her skin.

"You were going to leave. You lied to me." Pinny stared at her. "You stole the shoes. And Dalya's rings."

Ray nodded. "Yes."

"Those were wrong things," Pinny said. She was quiet for a long time, her expression thoughtful. "But . . . you brought me to New York. You helped me find Mama's shoes. You didn't have to be my sister, but you are. And those things . . . were right."

"I didn't want to do any of them," Ray protested. "Don't you see? It's never *in* me to do right. Only, you made it hard to say no."

"Very hard," Pinny said with pride.

"Don't let me off the hook. Not anymore. I don't know what you see when you look at me, but it's not who I really am." Shame burned her cheeks. "So . . . hate me. Go ahead."

Pinny crinkled her brow. "Why do you want me to?"

"Because you should! You're so . . . so good. So much better than I'll ever be. And I'm . . . I'm . . ."

A liar. A thief. A bitch. Words she'd pinned on herself for years, words that built a protective wall around her. Words she hated but that, once she tried them on for size, grew on her and made her what they said she was.

"You're good, too, Ray." Pinny said it firmly, squeezing Ray's hand. "Maybe not good all the time. But . . . good enough. Like I told you before. You're the only one who doesn't know it."

Good enough. The words winged their way into her head, and as soon as they snapped into place, the tears burst out of her. Old tears. Weeks old, months old, even years old. Tears she'd locked away. But now that the well was opened, it was bottomless. There was no controlling the choking sobs as they broke over her, drowning out any other sound in the room. She'd never known until this moment how much Pinny's faith in her meant, but now that she still had it, she realized it was the only thing that mattered. She put her hands to her face and let the flood of relief sweep over her.

She didn't know how long passed before she finally became aware of Pinny's arm around her, but by then her face was swollen and raw. She raised her head slowly, taking the tissue Dalya offered to wipe her eyes.

"Good enough for each other," Dalya said, pressing her hand to Ray's cheek, "is all any of us can be."

Ray stared into Dalya's and Pinny's warm, open faces, and a lightness of being swept over her. She'd done the right thing. Her guilt was gone. So was her chance at New York, but that almost didn't matter. "I'm tired," she whispered. "And . . . I don't want to run anymore." She held Pinny's eyes. "I'll go back to Smokebush if I have to. If *you're* going. I'm with you. No matter what."

Pinny shook her head furiously. "I'm not going," she announced. "Ever. To Horizons Assist. Or Fricasweet's."

"Yes!" Ray cried, hugging her. "It's about time. The old Pinny's back!"

Pinny giggled, then crossed her arms defiantly. "I mean it."

"I believe you do." Dalya gave Pinny's shoulder a squeeze. "We'll talk everything over with your father when he comes. Maybe there's something we can do. . . ."

"Daddy's coming? Here?" Pinny's eyes lit up as Dalya nodded, but then her brow furrowed. "What about Ray?" she asked. "She doesn't want to go back either."

Ray swallowed thickly. "I'll have to, Pinny," she said quietly. "I'm stuck at Smokebush until I'm eighteen. Where else are they going to put a foster kid halfway to juvic?"

Ray's heart clattering seemed to be the only sound in the room for some time. Then Dalya's sweet, soft voice broke the silence.

"What if someone adopted you?" she asked. "What then?"

Ray held her breath. She couldn't wrap her head around it, the idea that they might have real futures before them. But when she raised her eyes to Dalya's, she saw the promise of possibility in them. A newborn yearning, for the kind of life she'd never dared dream of, filled her heart.

"I . . . I don't know." Ray could barely speak. "Nobody's ever wanted me enough to ask."

"I wonder if it's time to find out," Dalya said. "My daughter, Inge, and her husband have a spare room now. Their son's all grown. They've been talking about renting it out, but maybe . . ." She glanced at Ray, her eyes doing the asking.

Ray nodded, barely able to breathe. With trembling fingers, she pulled a slip of paper out of her pocket and handed it to Dalya. "This is Mrs. Danvers's number at Smokebush. She'll want to know where we are. I'm sure she's been looking for us. But"—she glanced at Dalya—"could you make the call? Could you . . . help?"

Dalya took Pinny's hand, then Ray's. "I'd be so glad if you let me," she whispered.

As Dalya picked up the phone, she smiled at them, and for the first time in years, Ray let hopefulness return. For the first time since her apricot chapel, she'd run toward something good. Better, maybe, than anything else she'd ever known.

PART IX

The fairy tale is all about the shoe at the end.

—Amy Adams

PART IX

It was on a windswept autumn day that Ray came back to the city. She dropped her suitcases off at Inge's apartment on Columbus Avenue, but she didn't stay. Inge knew, without Ray having to say it, where Ray wanted to be, and she ushered her out the door with a laughing "Go."

So Ray ran. She ran in the bubble-gum-pink shoes that Pinny and Dalya had made for her. She ran without pain, the breeze in her face and wings in her feet. She ran over the sidewalks with her guitar slung over her shoulder, listening to the song of the great city surrounding her. She ran until she found herself standing under the burgundy awning of the Art of Heeling. She ran home.

She stopped for just a moment to look in the window, and smiled at the two heads bent intently over a pair of shoes at the worktable in the back. Dalya and Pinny. Her friends. Her family.

Dalya was frailer than Ray remembered, but she still held her tools with steady hands as she patiently showed Pinny what to do next. Pinny was beside her, her dandelion hair wisping as she worked, her glasses teetering on the tip of her nose, her face a blend of satisfaction and concentration. She'd become Dalya's apprentice, and when she wasn't spending time with her newfound father, Pinny worked and lived in the shop. Everything about Pinny at this moment said she'd found the More she was looking for. And when the time came that Dalya couldn't run the store any longer, Pinny would have Kent . . . and Ray. Ray would be nearby, somewhere in the city, to help Pinny. She was going to make sure of it.

Ray took the front steps to the shop two at a time, scarcely believing that the long months of waiting were finally over. The inviting smell of leather struck her nose as she stepped through the door.

They looked up together, but Pinny reached her first, jumping off her stool and sending it toppling in her hurry. She launched herself at Ray, and Ray bent backward under the enthusiastic hug, laughing. Dalya moved more slowly, and her hug was feathery and fragile, but her bright eyes showed her delight.

Here, in their arms, was proof of what Ray still had a hard time believing. That she could go from having no one to having so many people who cared. But this happiness wasn't stolen. It was real. And she was going to relish it, soak in it, live in it.

Warmth filled her as she settled into the coziness of the shop. They didn't talk about anything important, but they still talked and laughed, with the easy, open comfort of being together again. Then Pinny asked Ray to play the song she'd composed for her audition. Ray hadn't played it for anyone yet, but she knew that was why she'd brought her guitar with her, because she wanted Dalya and Pinny to be the first to hear it.

Carter was the one who'd sent in her application to Juilliard, along with the CD of music she'd originally made for him. He'd mailed it the day after prom, the day she'd run away. He'd explained it all in the letter that was waiting for her when she'd gone back to Jaynis in June. He'd apologized, too, for "misleading" her, as he called it, saying he hoped someday she'd understand. She'd always be grateful to him for the audition, and she tucked his kind words away in her heart, but she'd already let him go.

Juilliard was a long shot, she knew, especially with her final grades being as poor as they were. Her teachers in Jaynis had agreed to let her take her exams late, and she'd graduated, but only barely. Still, the hope of it had built a nest in her heart. Maybe it was only magical thinking, the feeling she had that Juilliard could happen. But even if magic wasn't actually possible, the belief in the possibility of it was enough to keep people going, to make them create their own.

Ray settled the guitar in her lap, looked into Dalya's and Pinny's smiling faces, and began to play. It was a song about a pair of lost shoes found. About broken hearts mended, scars healed, families discovered, and a love built in footprints, step by step.

The melody rang out clear and strong through the little shop, like it had been created to perfectly suit this moment, this place. The notes washed over the pair of worn pale pink shoes that sat quietly in the corner. And the shoes, full of so many people's secrets and memories, soaked up the music and the peace and the love of the three women laughing in the late-afternoon light.

AUTHOR'S NOTE

Serendipity's Footsteps is a story born from many different hearts. The idea came to me one morning while I was driving and chatting with my sister. I passed a cozy cottage in my town and saw, sitting prettily on a rock in the front yard, a single cherry-red slingback. Mystified and delighted by the sight, I mentioned it to my sister, which immediately spurred a discussion about our random "shoe sightings" through the years: trees dripping with abandoned shoes, sneakers tossed over telephone wires, lonely shoes scattered in the road. Who had been the owners of those shoes? Why had the shoes been left behind or lost?

"You need to write a book about those shoes," my sister told me, and the seed for this story was planted.

But this book isn't just about lost shoes; it's about lost people finding comfort and peace in a rare, extraordinary pair of shoes. It's about these shoes drawing lost people together in friendship and giving them a chance to find love in unlikely connections. Each one of us, whether we've realized it or not, has experienced the magic of serendipity; the connections between those we love and the things they love; the mysterious pull of an old photograph, a tattered baby blanket, a worn shoe. Connections, as Pinny would say, are the More of life.

The characters in this book, their connections and stories, are fictional. However, many of the historical details and events portrayed here are based in truth.

Sachsenhausen Concentration Camp

Some of my dearest friends have shared their families' stories of survival during the Holocaust with me through the years, and their tales of courage and resilience helped to inspire Dalya's story. Sachsenhausen, the concentration camp where Dalya and her family were sent after Kristallnacht (the Night of Shattered Glass), was one of the first concentration camps in Germany. It was built in Oranienburg, only a short distance from Berlin, in 1936. Created as a "model" concentration camp, it was an example of what the Schutzstaffel (also known as the German SS) thought was an ideal camp in design and form.

Between 1936 and 1944, over two hundred thousand people were imprisoned at Sachsenhausen. Following Kristallnacht, on November 9 and 10, 1938, approximately six thousand Jews were arrested and taken to Sachsenhausen. In the next months, some Jewish prisoners were released from the camp if they could provide proof of their intent to leave Germany. Others remained, and the number of Jewish prisoners steadily increased. While the main camp of Sachsenhausen, where Dalya lived in the story, predominantly held Jewish men and male political prisoners, some women and children were imprisoned there as well. Very few women or children would have passed through the main camp during the time of

Dalya's internment. Subcamps were built to house women and children later on in the war, and Ravensbrück was one of the satellite camps where, beginning in 1944, women were kept. By April 1945, near the war's end, there had been a total of almost twelve thousand women imprisoned at Sachsenhausen, primarily in its subcamps. Many of the women who passed through the main camp were only transferred there during the final weeks of the war. Between 1936 and 1945, three thousand children passed through Sachsenhausen and its subcamps. Most of them were boys—Jews, or prisoners brought in from the Soviet Union. There is no record of a girl Dalya's age living at Sachsenhausen or its subcamps until 1942.

The shoe-testing track that Dalya's father marched on was real and can be seen today at the Memorial and Museum Sachsenhausen. The track was made up of nine different materials, including sand, gravel, and broken rocks. Prisoners who marched on the track were part of the Schuhläuferkommando, the shoe-testing unit. Wearing military-style boots made by local shoe factories, they marched on the track for hours at a time to test the durability of the boots. Sometimes they were forced to walk in boots that were too small, carrying heavy sandbags as they marched. There were instances when men fell during the march, and they were left to die or were beaten as a result. I fictionalized the account of men being shot while marching the shoe track. In reality, prisoners who failed in their duties were hanged or shot at guards' discretion as part of larger "killing campaigns." The shoe-testing track was the primary reason I chose Sachsenhausen as the setting for Dalya's imprisonment. Until I began research for this book, I had never heard of the track. When I came across a reference to it in my readings, I knew I had to include it in my story. Shoes played such an important role in Dalya's life and her family history. For Dalya, watching her father march on the shoe track would have been life-altering, and I wanted this moment, painful as it was, to be part of her journey and her struggle.

Because of the poor sanitary conditions at Sachsenhausen, the inhumane treatment of prisoners, and the lack of proper food and clothing, thousands of prisoners died of starvation and disease. Initially, bodies were taken from Sachsenhausen to crematoriums in Berlin, like the one that served as Dalya's escape route in the novel. But in April 1940, a crematorium was built on-site at Sachsenhausen, and in March 1943, a gas chamber was built in an area of the camp called Station Z. It is estimated by the Simon Wiesenthal Center that over thirty thousand people perished at Sachsenhausen during the camp's years of operation.

In writing *Serendipity's Footsteps,* I took liberties with the time frame and living arrangements for Dalya's stay at Sachsenhausen. Although some boys were arrested with their fathers during the pogroms, entire families were not imprisoned at Sachsenhausen following Kristallnacht. Camps interning entire families did not come into existence until later in the war. The women and children passing through Sachsenhausen would have lived primarily in its subcamps, without contact with the male prisoners. I fictionalized the internments of Dalya's and Aaron's families by keeping the families in close proximity within the camp and having the children remain with their parents in the barracks. I chose to have Dalya go to Sachsenhausen before the outbreak of the war so that she could escape Germany in 1940. By 1941, with Europe increasingly engulfed by war, it became nearly impossible for Jews to leave Germany. Prior to the implementation of the Nazis' Final Solution, there was a narrow window of opportunity for those with visas. In some cases, such as Dalya's, the Gestapo could be bribed to honor expired visas. Dalya, at age seventeen, would have been considered an adult, and her odds of getting out of Germany would have been incredibly slim. It may be that I gave Dalya a better chance of survival in the book than she ever would have had in reality, but that, in my mind, is one of the most wonderful gifts fiction gives us—a chance to seize the impossible, to give hope in hopeless situations.

For more information about Sachsenhausen, the following resources are helpful:

Morsch, Günter, and Astrid Ley, eds. *Sachsenhausen Concentration Camp, 1936–1945: Events and Developments.* Berlin: Metropol Verlag, 2008.

"Concentration Camps: Sachsenhausen (Oranienburg)," *Jewish Virtual Library,* American-Israeli Cooperative Enterprise. jewishvirtuallibrary.org/jsource/Holocaust/sachtoc.html.

"The Forgotten Camps," JewishGen: An affiliate of the Museum of Jewish Heritage—A Living Memorial to the Holocaust. jewishgen.org/forgottenCamps/Camps/SachsenhausenEng.html.

Memorial and Museum Sachsenhausen, Brandenburg Memorials Foundation. www.stiftung-bg.de/gums/en/.

"Sachsenhausen Concentration Camp," Center for Holocaust & Genocide Studies, University of Minnesota. chgs.umn.edu/museum/memorials/sachsenhausen/.

"Sachsenhausen: Timeline," *Holocaust Encyclopedia,* United States Holocaust Memorial Museum. ushmm.org/wlc /en/article.php?ModuleId=10007774.

Jewish Refugees in America During World War II

While many individuals advocated relief and aid for Jewish refugees fleeing Nazi persecution, the immigration laws of the United States prior to and during World War II, and complications arising from the Nazi occupation of Europe, made it difficult for refugees to gain safe passage to America. Between 1934 and 1945, one thousand children ranging from sixteen months to sixteen years old came to the United States from Europe to escape Nazi persecution. These children came to America without their parents. They were placed with temporary foster families in hopes of being reunited with their parents later on. Tragically, only a small number of the children ever saw their parents again. A variety of nonprofit refugee and aid organizations, both large and small, helped to orchestrate and fund the children's safe passage from Europe to America and oversee their placement with foster families.

In doing research for this book, I read many first-person accounts of these children's experiences settling into their new homes in America. Many did not speak any English when they arrived, and attended classes with much younger children at school as a result. Siblings were sometimes separated and fostered by different families. Although attempts were made to place children with Jewish families sharing similar religious customs and traditions, many of the children had trouble adjusting to their new lives and homes.

At seventeen, Dalya would have been too old to qualify for the official Jewish refugee programs, which is why she came to America under different circumstances and moved in with the Ashburys, a non-Jewish family. Dalya's friend Ruth was sixteen and therefore qualified for refugee aid, which is why she was placed with a Jewish family, the Blumbergs. It was very rare for older teenagers to obtain the papers needed to leave Germany as the war was getting under way. But there are accounts of people like Leonard Goodman, the fictitious Quaker in the story, helping to bring refugees like Dalya from Germany safely to America.

Throughout the course of the war and after, Americans held fund-raising events for Jewish refugees. One such event was the Night of Stars, which Dalya attends in the book. It was an enormous fund-raiser held annually at Madison Square Garden in New York City. Each year, approximately twenty-thousand people crowded into the arena for the four-hour event, which featured music, speeches, and theatrical performances. Through the years, a number of famous musicians, comedians, and actors performed at the gala, including Glenn

Miller, Guy Lombardo, Danny Kaye, and the Rockettes of Radio City Music Hall. Dalya attended the Night of Stars in 1940, and for the purposes of the story, I took some creative liberties with this scene. Dalya meets famous people who may have attended the event in other years, such as Eleanor Roosevelt, who attended in 1941.

Though the number of child refugees brought to America during the war years was small in comparison to the number who perished in the horror that was the Holocaust, the children who came were able, despite facing numerous challenges, to begin again with hope. For more information about these refugees, visit the website of the organization One Thousand Children at onethousandchildren.org.

The following book also provides inspiring first-person accounts:

Jason, Philip K., and Iris Posner, eds. *Don't Wave Goodbye: The Children's Flight from Nazi Persecution to American Freedom.* Westport, CT: Praeger, 2004.

Down Syndrome

In the story, Chopine "Pinny" Miller has Down syndrome. This condition occurs when a person is born with a full or partial extra copy of the genetic chromosome 21. The physical characteristics of Down syndrome can vary greatly from individual to individual, and the cognitive delays can range from mild to severe. Some people with Down syndrome are nonverbal; some have health complications; some may have autism in addition. Their personalities, talents, and capabilities are as wide-reaching as any individual's. Many people, like Pinny, are capable of taking part in almost all school, social, and recreational activities. They can attend college, have jobs and relationships, and become successful members of society.

While tutoring a wonderful young boy with Down syndrome years ago, I got a privileged glimpse into his life and his challenges. It was amazing to hear recently from his parents about his successes as an adult—his hobbies, his friendships, and his travels and adventures. Pinny is an entirely fictional character. She is not meant to symbolize or represent Down syndrome in any way. She is a shoe lover and a believer in the joy of life and the inherent goodness of human beings, which is something she shares with me and, I hope, with my readers.

For more information, visit the National Down Syndrome Society's website at ndss.org.

Also, the following book is a candid memoir about one father's relationship with his son:

Palmer, Greg. *Adventures in the Mainstream: Coming of Age with Down Syndrome.* 2nd ed. Seattle: Bennett and Hastings, 2012.

Shoes

In my research, I came across some delightful facts about shoes, their history, and the art of shoemaking. The very first pair of shoes was probably crafted nearly forty thousand years ago. Early versions of shoes might have been woven-fiber sandals, followed by cowhide moccasins dating back to BC eras. They helped to protect feet from harsh terrain and keep them warm in cold climates. As time passed, shoes, with their designs and ornamentation, became status symbols to help designate a person's wealth or social standing. Gradually, the purpose of shoes changed. Some shoes were built for comfort, but others were built as art—to make a statement, convey a mood, and enhance a wearer or her outfit.

While most shoes today are machine-made in factories, some people still make custom shoes by hand. Many tools are involved in the process, including lasts, shaves, edge planes, and fudge wheels. Throughout history, different craftsmen contributed to the shoemaking process. A fellmonger got skins and hides ready for the tanning process. A currier softened and thinned tanned leather, making it more flexible and comfortable. A cordwainer, or cobbler, was the shoemaker himself; he crafted the sole and upper of the shoe and melded them together.

Shoes are a fascinating part of human history. In some areas of the ancient world, a father would give his daughter's shoes to her betrothed in the marriage ceremony to show that the groom was taking responsibility for the bride. In some regions of China, a bride's red shoe is thrown onto the roof of her house on her wedding night to symbolize the newlyweds' love for one another. Chopines, for which Pinny was named, were platform shoes rising as high as thirty inches off the ground. They were designed to keep noblewomen and courtesans from dirtying their feet in the mud and muck of Renaissance streets.

In the early 1900s, Mary Janes like Pinny's became a staple children's shoe; though now primarily worn by girls, they were initially for boys. Minnie Pearl's Mary Janes can be found, for the next few years at least, on exhibit at the Grand Ole Opry, just as they appear in Ray and Pinny's visit there. In fact, the curator at the Opry told me that Minnie Pearl's shoes were the very first thing she rescued from the Nashville flood of May 2010. The original pair of ruby slippers worn by Judy Garland in *The Wizard of Oz* is on display at the Smithsonian Institution's National Museum of American History in Washington, D.C.

Heel heights have been raised and lowered throughout history as materials have been rationed or fashion fads have come and gone. Techniques for finding comfortable, well-fitting shoes have also continued to change. From 1920 until the early 1960s, shoe fluoroscopes, like the one Dalya saw in Filer-Machol, were popular in stores nationwide. The boxy wooden cabinets used X-rays to determine whether a shoe fit properly. Eventually, after concerns about exposure to radiation were aired and the effectiveness of the machines was questioned, their use was discontinued.

A colorful parade of shoes has marched through human history and will walk on, but one thing remains certain: There is nothing like the perfect pair of shoes to make you feel comfortable, confident, and magically, mystically extraordinary.

For an informative website that includes a glossary of shoemaking terms and descriptions of the shoemaking process, see Heart & Sole: Boot and Shoe Making in Staffordshire at staffscc.net/shoes1/.

The following book also provides beautiful photographs and a fascinating look at shoes and their history:

Walford, Jonathan. *The Seductive Shoe: Four Centuries of Fashion Footwear.* New York: Stewart, Tabori & Chang, 2007.

ACKNOWLEDGMENTS

If connections are the More of life, then it is my connections to many remarkable people that allowed this story to grow into what it has become. At times, when this story was in its beginnings, I was overwhelmed by the immensity of what I'd taken on. On the morning I began writing the prologue, I asked the higher powers that be for inspiration and guidance. In return, I was blessed with friends, family, and colleagues who encouraged, inspired, and challenged me to persevere. With a heart full of gratitude, I would like to thank everyone who helped me to write *Serendipity's Footsteps.*

Eternal thanks go to my sister, Christy Howe, for asking me to write about "the shoes in the street," and then reminding me (rather relentlessly) to finish it. She has never once laughed at any of my ideas, no matter how ridiculous they sound. And to my parents, who kept me supplied with dozens of journals and diaries throughout my childhood to foster my writing.

My agent, Ammi-Joan Paquette, offered constant encouragement through every draft and gave me the nerve to press on. None of this could have happened without her. I am indebted to her and everyone else at Erin Murphy Literary Agency for the gift of community and fellowship.

My editor, Michelle Frey, deftly stretched my skills where

they needed honing, reinforced when I was hesitant, and taught me to face head-on all the fears that come with revision. It is extraordinary to have an editor who is a mentor and dear friend, and she is both.

My friend Abigail Young moved me by sharing her family's heart-wrenching but remarkable history with me. I have the greatest admiration for how she continues to honor her Jewish faith and culture in her life and the lives of her children.

The Drake family—Suzanne, Scott, Shelby, and Troy—showed infinite patience with me when I was a young and blundering tutor. Tutoring Troy was one of the highlights of my senior year of high school, and Suzanne's candid conversation with me about Down syndrome was incredibly helpful and informative.

There is also a host of scholars I am indebted to for their expertise and astute observations: Dr. Astrid Ley, deputy director of the Memorial and Museum Sachsenhausen, for thoughtfully and patiently answering my questions about Sachsenhausen in email after email; Dr. Verena Buser, research assistant at the German Historical Museum in Berlin, for her wealth of knowledge on the child inmates of Sachsenhausen and its satellite camps; and Dr. Jenna Weissman Joselit, Charles E. Smith professor of Judaic studies and professor of history at George Washington University, for her careful reading of the story and her insights into Jewish culture and life in 1930s and '40s New York City.

Thanks go to Brenda Colladay, museum and photograph curator at the Grand Ole Opry, for rescuing Minnie Pearl's Mary Janes from the floodwaters and then sharing their delightful tale with me. Also, thanks to Dr. David G. Roskies and the University of Nebraska Press for granting me permission to use an excerpt from Abraham Sutzkever's poem "A Load of Shoes." Thanks also go to Janet R. Falkenthal for allowing me to use her charming consignment boutique, Fashion Exchange, as the location for my author photo.

My family is my greatest joy, and their faith in me brings me back to my computer even when I'm faced with that terrifyingly fresh, blank page and blinking cursor. Thanks to my wonderful children—Colin, Aidan, and Madeline—who show no end of patience waiting for me to emerge, drained and glassy-eyed, from my office after hours of writing. And to my husband, Chad, who gave me a "Blue Castle" all my own. Thoughtful, bighearted, and noble, he is my champion and my stronghold.